Praise & Reviews
for Reality

★★★★★ "Intriguing, thought-provoking, and compelling; I was completely gripped until the very end."

—*Readers' Favorite*

★★★★ "A knockout thriller; near-future fiction at its finest."

—*Self-Publishing Review*

★★★★⯪ "Captivating; a mesmerizing web of conspiracy theories."

—*IndieReader*

reality

DC Wince

Also by DC Wince:

Reality X

ISBN:
ISBN-13: 978-0-646-99778-0

For Darshan and Shannon

"I've seen strange things in this world, some good, and some, well… let's just say there's things nobody with a lick of good sense in them would ever confess to knowing, lest they tempt the fates. Now it's been said many a time before that 'truth is stranger than fiction'. But nothing – and I mean *no thing* – is stranger than the story I'm about to tell."

– Anonymous

PROLOGUE

DARKNESS, and with it came the sound of rapid breathing. The black screen contained no time or space, only sound. A single eye suddenly appeared, blinking quickly. And then, like some creature rising from the depths of an abyssal ocean, a *voice* spoke to the Watchers of The Game.

'Who controls the world controls reality,' it said.

It was neither a male nor female voice, instead sounding like some strange androgynous synthesis of both, delicately and harmonically modulating in pitch and tone. It did not sound human.

Immediately after, the screen containing the eye was replaced by a blinding white, which then dissolved into a point-of-view video. An observer drone, transmitting live images to the Watchers, was flying high above a vast desert landscape toward something moving along the ground at a fast speed.

'The Game begins,' said the voice.

DC Wince

STAGE 1 – DESERT

DC Wince

ONE

DAY 1
12:30 P.M.
18°5'1.12" 12°9'6.50"

T HE ETERNALLY HOT sun was beating down on the blowing, shifting sand dunes of the Ténéré in the Sahara, when the sound of a distant machine rudely disrupted the peaceful desolation and silence. If there had been anyone nearby to hear it, they would have found it a strange noise particularly for this isolated area of the world. That someone would be there to begin with would have been strange enough. This was a place *no one* wanted to be.

The Sahara in North Africa is almost five thousand kilometres long and one thousand wide, and has been expanding for over a century. Although sparsely inhabited, few outsiders have dared to attempt traversing its infamously harsh terrain and unrelenting climate without being carefully prepared. Many who brazenly tried have never been heard from again.

It should be noted there are rare documented cases of fortunate people who, after finding themselves lost within the Sahara's massive nothingness, managed by some stroke of blind luck to stumble upon salvation in a wandering caravan of Tuareg nomads. Indeed, it cannot be stressed enough that these are very rare occasions. Day after day, year after year, the windswept and rainless desert sands seem as unchanging and permanent as the cloudless sky above.

This day, however, would be different.

Whatever was creating the unfamiliar noise, it was rapidly getting closer. Near the top of a tall winding dune, a small brown scorpion appeared from just under the surface of the sand, its curiosity piqued at the ground reverberations. It skittered across the sand pebbles, when suddenly a black rubber tyre broke through the crest of the dune, sending the arachnid quickly retreating back into the sand.

A motorcycle came screaming over the top and became airborne, its engine revving with an ear-splitting roar. For a brief moment it appeared almost frozen in time, before gracefully arcing down the entire height of the tall hill. It landed with a crash, violently catapulting its rider over the handlebars and slamming them into the ground a few feet ahead. The cycle tyre's spun uselessly, sending sand flying in all directions. The engine finally stalled and all became still once again. Only the sound of the whistling wind blowing through the dune valley could be heard.

The rider lay face down on the scorching hot sand, not moving. Several things were scattered around them, having been thrown about from the chaotic landing. Then, somewhere off in the distance, a droning hum rose steadily in volume.

Another motorcycle suddenly leapt over the top of the dune. It came down on the sand less forcefully than the first, and its rider manoeuvred it carefully down to the bottom of the trough. For a time the second rider rested on their motorcycle before shutting off the engine. Their eyes were hidden behind goggles, while a long black scarf covered the lower half of their face and neck. Pulling the cloth away, the rider revealed a good day's worth of scruffy stubble growing on his face.

As he observed the scene of the accident, the man quickly surmised that the individual lying on the ground a few feet away didn't appear to be a threat, at least not any longer. He glanced at the black-painted motorcycle lying on its side in the sand. It was the same enhanced type as his own, except he could see that this one's front forks were now bent, and the fender was awkwardly twisted and broken. Right away, it was clear to him the machine was finished and out of the game. However much fuel it had left inside, it was now his to take.

He pushed out the bike's kickstand, then dismounted and walked to the prone figure. He made sure to be careful, as he knew his opponent could still be dangerous. Reaching for a sheath clipped to his shorts, he pulled out a long serrated knife as he scrutinized the figure at his feet, trying to detect some sign of life. With the knife gripped tightly in hand he kicked the body with a black boot, turning them over. There was a dull moan. A young man with bright blue eyes and blonde hair stared back at him. He looked to be in his mid-to-late-twenties, just about the same age as the man standing over him, and he was outfitted in similar sport clothing. Breathing heavy with short gasps for air, the man appeared disoriented and his eyes were wide open and glassy. Sand was stuck to the perspiration on one side of his face, and a stream of blood trickled down from a corner of his mouth, forming a small pool on the pebbles below. The unfortunate man's tibia bone protruded from his leg in what appeared to be a painful-looking open fracture wound. For a brief tense moment, each man studied the other.

'Bitte,' the injured man stammered. 'Tu mir nicht weh.'

The second rider cocked his head slightly to one side, trying to understand the foreign tongue which he concluded must be German. But it wasn't necessary, as the terrified look in the man's eyes told him everything: doom was upon him. He saw that the injured man was wearing a hard plastic silver band, identical to the one also fitted around his wrist. Set into one side was a rectangular LED screen displaying red digital numbers, which he knew were steadily counting down. He glanced at his own wristband. The time on it read:

05:20:36:05

Something momentarily distracted the injured man. His eyes drifted over the shoulder of the threatening figure, toward a buzzing sound coming from somewhere above them in the sky. *What's he looking at?* the second rider wondered. He thought it strange imminent death was staring this man in the face, and yet he could be so distracted. He was suddenly very curious to also see what it was. Pulling down the goggles he looked to the sky. Squinting, he shielded his brown eyes from the glaring afternoon sun as he searched for the source of the noise.

High above them, a flying machine slowly circled, to be joined a few moments later by a second one moving in an opposite pattern. Sunlight glinted off the sleek white surfaces on the upper portion of their wings, and their whirring engines combined with the wind to create a mesmerizing effect. Neither man knew that these were state-of-the-art surveillance devices, known in military jargon as UAVs, or unmanned aerial vehicles. The two men briefly looked at one another before turning their gaze back on the robotic drones. Though the UAVs were only flying a few hundred feet above them, the men were still too far away to see that they held no people, or that their on-board cameras were now intently trained upon the unfolding scene below.

The second rider heard a grunt behind him. Turning, he saw the injured man struggling to grasp a knapsack just beyond his reach. *What a pitiful sight,* he thought. With a smirk on his face he planted the heel of his boot on the man's wrist, eliciting a sharp cry. Then he knelt down and picked up the bag. 'This?' he asked him. 'You want this?' The young man tried nodding his head in reply, but instead simply buried his face in the sand. It was quite apparent he was in excruciating pain. 'Let's see what we have in here.' Still holding his knife he opened the bag and began pulling out its contents. There was a hand-held GPS that was identical to his own; a water canteen; food rations; a flashlight; and some flint. It was everything that he himself carried in his own knapsack. At the very bottom of the bag he saw the serrated knife the man had likely been desperate to get his hands on. *He won't need that anymore,* he thought.

Looking back, he saw that the injured rider was slipping into unconsciousness. He didn't like that. It would have been too easy to just leave him here. No, he had to make sure he was dead. Plus he had a show to put on. Two sharp slaps across the man's face quickly roused him back to reality. As he looked into the injured rider's eyes thoughts began racing through his mind: *Who is this man I'm about to murder?* Did he have a family, brothers, and sisters? Or maybe there was a young wife and child waiting for him back in Germany? He didn't know if that was where he was from, but from the words he'd heard him speak he guessed that was his home country. At the moment he had this man's whole existence in his hands, and the thought of snuffing it out like a flame on a candle suddenly gave him an exhilarating thrill, the likes of which he'd never felt before.

It was true he'd never actually killed anyone, but the idea had crossed his mind several times in the past. He firmly believed that some people were still alive simply because it was illegal to kill them. Some people *deserved* to be dead. But here, in the middle of this vast wasteland, he could kill and get away with it. No one would ever know or find out. No one except for those watching him at this very moment, and he knew that they would never tell. Indeed, they were expecting him to do it, and he wasn't about to disappoint them.

'Bitte,' the man said again, weaker this time. 'Hilf mir.'

Grabbing a tuft of blonde hair, the second rider pulled the injured man's head up and placed the sharp blade of the knife against the soft skin of his neck. In his mind's eye, he imagined this was one of those asshole Wall Street investment bankers he had loathed working with every day, and he wished it was one of them at the mercy of his blade right now instead of this poor bastard. 'Believe me,' he replied, 'I'm doing you a favour.'

With a swift motion of his arm he sliced the man from ear-to-ear, and was surprised how easily the blade sank into the flesh of the neck, almost to the point of decapitation. A gurgling sound rose from within the man's throat, as deep red blood gushed out from the horrible wound on to the sand. The killer wiped the perspiration from his brow, then sat down next to the dying man and watched his life fade away, which fortunately did not take very long. The man's eyes simply stared into his own. They conveyed a rapid succession of his final, terrible moments: shock and horror followed by sadness, resignation, peace, and then finally… nothing.

It was done. He had killed another human being. He was a *murderer*. He'd done it not out of malice, but for survival. Besides, he knew this guy would have done it to him, had the tables been turned. Why try to rationalize it? It was a harsh world, and this was a harsh place. Survival of the fittest. It would only get easier with the next one, and the one after that. Now he knew there could be no turning back, and his act of murder only crystallized that fact for him.

From somewhere within the dark corners of his mind, a tiny voice whispered: *'The bad you do comes back at you.'*

Above the scene, the cameras on the circling drones zoomed in, making sure to capture the moment in all of its grisly glory.

The man craned his neck, peering up at them. For a moment, they appeared to him like vultures, waiting to swoop down on the remains of his kill. He had never even heard of sophisticated machines like these before, much less seen one. Surely, he wondered, only the military manufactured things of this kind? 'Is this what you want to see?!' he yelled to the drones at the top of his lungs. It was difficult for him to speak, as his throat was dry and his voice was hoarse. But there was no reply, not that he expected one. He knew what their answer would be if they could speak. Instead, the only sounds to be heard were the buzzing of the drone engines and the echo of his voice carried off on the wind.

To his surprise, one of the UAVs suddenly broke from its holding pattern and flew away, leaving the other alone in its vigil. Smiling for the camera, he wiped the bloody knife on the dead man's shirt, and then slid it back into its sheath. Next, he collected the scattered things on the ground, shoving them into his knapsack along with his own supplies, before slinging the bag onto his back.

He took the kickstand off his motorcycle, and then pushed it until it was next to the one lying on the ground. Removing his cycle's fuel cap, he turned off the fuel from the other one and pulled its stock fuel line from the carburetor. After placing the fuel hose inside of his cycle's oversized six-gallon tank, he turned the switch back on. The gas began draining into the tank until it was again full. He felt satisfied that he now had an extra edge over the competition.

Lastly, his attention was drawn to the precious hand-held GPS receiver attached to his belt. It was a fairly new technology on the market which he hadn't used before, but the device seemed easy enough for him to understand. Pressing a button with his thumb, the present date and time appeared in black digital at the top of the LCD screen:

Tuesday August 7, 2001, 12:46:40

He pressed another button and it showed his location in the Ténéré, as well as three more signals that were being transmitted. Two of them were each moving away from his position at a steady pace. One was approximately twenty miles away and the other thirty-five. He was acutely aware that if he could see where they were at any given moment, in return they also knew where he was. *It doesn't matter,* he thought, *I will find them first.*

His eyes alighted on the last signal, and he remembered what *they* had told him. This signal was the most important one. It was stationary and just over one thousand miles south of his current position... and he was going there. Furrowing his brow, his lips twitched as a long bead of salty sweat dripped down onto them from the tip of his nose, and he unconsciously rubbed the short hairs on the back of his neck.

A strange sensation suddenly came over him, a feeling that the black dot on the GPS screen was somehow aware he was coming, calling out to him, pulling him to it. Was it only pretending to be a small black dot, he wondered? Maybe it was actually a powerful black hole, irrevocably sucking him into its gaping maw, where finally even the very atoms of his body would be obliterated from existence. Resistance to its attraction was hopeless. He knew that there, at this singularity point, was where his destiny would ultimately be decided one way or the other.

Those who controlled his fate had promised him a lot of money, and he wondered if he would ever get the chance to meet them. If he did, he wasn't sure whether he would thank them for forcing him into his present circumstances, or kill them. He smiled at the thought. Most likely he would try to do both.

Dale Crumb mounted his motorcycle, and then he glanced one last time at the man he'd just killed, whose body was already being covered by the wind-blown sand.

'Auf Wiedersehen,' he said with a salute.

Setting the goggles over his eyes, he gazed up at the blazing noonday sun overhead. The temperature had to be over ninety degrees Fahrenheit. He'd been riding for three hours, and, after this brief rest, he figured it was now time to move on. There was no question in his mind that he had to catch up to the others, despite the scorching heat.

'Jesus, it's fucking hot,' he muttered under his breath, as he kick-started the cycle's engine. It growled to life and rumbled underneath him. Putting it into gear, he released the clutch and then sped off through the dune valley in the direction of his next target.

***

On video screens scattered across six continents, a multitude of eyes were watching in anticipated suspenseful *excitement*. The flying drone's on-board camera was transmitting live images to the viewers of the lone motorcycle rider racing across the bleak landscape, when a voice broke into the scene.

'This… is Reality,' it said, in an elegant harmony of vocoded speech modulations. It was the same inhuman voice heard at the very beginning of the broadcast. In fact, it was the voice of the world's first AI, or Artificially Intelligent computer.

This was Metatron.

'It is a new type of game, and it will be played just once a year. Each game will be different from the last, and yet they will remain the same. They will be games of survival, chance... and death. The six billion people of this world will not know about this very unique and extraordinary game. They will *never* know. Only you, oh great and masterful Archons, have the privilege of watching.'

The bottom half of the transmission displayed colour-coded statistics of four individuals:

ALPHA – Red
BETA – Blue
GAMMA – Green
DELTA – Yellow

For each of them it showed their present location; velocity; heart rate; body temperature; hydration level; and brainwave activity. The health statistics of GAMMA were all at zero.

'The first competitor to be eliminated, GAMMA, has been killed by DELTA at three hours and twenty-two minutes into the game, very early but not unexpected. It was an exciting chase and a most gruesome death.'

The single image showing Dale on the motorcycle separated into four, with him in the bottom right corner with a surrounding yellow border; next to him on the bottom left was the dead GAMMA; the top left of the screen was ALPHA, speeding on a motorcycle across barren flat landscape; and the top right image showed BETA struggling to negotiate their motorcycle up a very large sand dune.

'The three remaining competitors are all approximately four hundred kilometres north-east of Agadez, in the heart of the Niger desert,' continued Metatron. 'The temperature is extremely hot—a blistering one hundred and four degrees Fahrenheit. They still have over one thousand kilometres to go, across some of the harshest, most unforgiving environments on Earth.'

The images zoomed right out to display a detailed satellite map of North Africa, where three flashing coloured dots showed the current locations of the contestants.

'As you can see, ALPHA is in the lead followed closely by BETA. But it is only for the moment. Will DELTA catch up to them before they can reach Terminus? Only time will tell.'

The UAV focused its camera on the dead man's corpse just as it was covered over by the blowing sand, giving the Watchers a closing glimpse of the first casualty of The Game. As the man's life blood drained out from his body, the audience was secretly aware that his final earthly thoughts were of the woman he loved, and the last night they would be together.

TWO

4 DAYS AGO – Friday August 3, 2001
MUNICH, GERMANY
1:26 A.M.

F OR A WHILE, Ernst Jaeger and Anna Lehrer lay naked in the
dark, contemplating their uncertain future on the cold hard floor
of their hostel room. The young couple had just made love, and in
the uncomfortable silence which followed each was aware it might
have been for the last time. Heated passion quickly subsided, leaving
in its wake only a desperate, unrelenting fear.

They're coming.

Anna shivered as she thought about the sinister unknown
assassins who were mercilessly hunting them down as if they were
animals. Eventually they would be found and caught, and then… it
would be checkmate. It occurred to her that to the hunters they were
nothing but pawns in a grander, more exciting game.

The idea made her head spin, and she felt on the verge of a panic.
Craving a cigarette, she reached out with her hand to retrieve the
lighter and her almost-empty pack which she'd left nearby. Her
fingers searched in frenzy along the floor until, with relief, she found
them next to her pile of clothes. Lighting one, she sucked on it and
inhaled the smoke deep into her lungs, trying to calm herself. The
cigarette tip glowed in the dark, casting orange across her face. They
needed a definite plan, she decided, and they needed it *now*.

'We can't hide here forever,' she whispered to him in German.
'Where are we going to go?'

'I don't know,' Ernst replied, his voice low. His mind raced.

For almost 24-hours they'd been on the run, and now a dreadful feeling was growing between he and Anna that they were quickly running out of time. He couldn't go to the police, as they were likely already looking to apprehend him. In desperation, he'd called the German Foreign Office to warn them about what he knew, but they only dismissed his outrageous claims with not-so hidden contempt. After that, Ernst had come to the conclusion there was simply no one with any authority they could trust.

The previous morning, after fleeing their apartment in the city of Frankfurt am Main, there was an attempt to murder the two of them in order to retrieve the information which he'd stolen, and they had just barely managed to escape with their lives. If the pair stayed on the continent it would only be a matter of time.

He reached out to his pile of clothes for his laptop computer which rested underneath. Pulling it out, he opened it to the document he'd been writing for the last few months. It was a diary of sorts, a kind of last will and testament in the event anything should happen. As he began typing from where he'd left off, his thoughts stretched back through time to the last twelve months, and the events leading up to the dire predicament they were now in.

How did we get here? he wondered. *Where did everything go so damn wrong?*

The email.

***

Thirty-year-old Ernst Jaeger was a good and honest young man. He was highly intelligent, healthy and very active, and he always succeeded to a certain degree with any goal he set for himself to achieve. But unfortunately for he and Anna, his intense curiosity, raw ambition, and the desire for competition, sometimes at great risk, had ultimately proved to be the couple's great downfall.

Until the previous day, Ernst had been employed at Frankfurt's twin tower headquarters of Deutsche Trust, one of Europe's biggest and most powerful banks. Finance had been part of the Jaeger family for a very long time. Following the Second World War, Ernst's grandfather had worked for the newly established central bank which introduced the Deutsche Mark, and his father joined the Bundesbank in the early 1960s, so it became only natural for Ernst to follow in their footsteps. Undeniably, banking was in his blood, and he studied finance and economics from a very early age.

It was in December 1989 that Ernst first met Anna at a concert inside the Dorian Gray, one of Frankfurt's well-known nightclubs. She was a full two years older than him, was tall and slightly a little too thin for her height, with long dark hair, brown eyes, and flawless milky-coloured skin. He thought she was elegant and highly intelligent, and he wasn't surprised upon learning she could speak fluently in English, French and Italian. Successful in her work for a large advertising agency, she was aggressive and ambitious, just like he was, but she had a creative side to her personality that he lacked. It was something about her which Ernst very much liked.

The young couple was instantly smitten with each other and became inseparable, and, after dating a few months, they decided to move in together. A while later their talk turned to marriage, having a child, then selling their apartment to find a little countryside house to raise a family.

In 1995 he graduated at the top of his class from Goeth University with a master's degree in information technology, and by this time he was very knowledgeable about computer science and business administration. Immediately he was hired by a well-respected investment firm, and he made a name for himself amongst the city's financial circles by authoring several highly regarded papers on market analysis.

But in January 2000, everything changed for Ernst when he was approached by the management board of Deutsche Trust. They wanted to hire him to be the executive assistant to the CFO, the Chief Financial Officer, who was a fifty-six-year-old banking professional named Stefan Ackermann.

The pay was out of this world. But more than that, a promising career with Germany's most prominent bank was the offer of a lifetime, one he could not turn down. More than anything else he wanted to make his family proud, and the position would guarantee the Jaeger name would continue to be associated with high finance. Even though it meant postponing their plans to move out of the city, Anna fully supported his decision when he accepted the bank's offer.

Ernst's foremost job at Deutsche Trust was to manage a group who looked after the bank's financial risks. The position also entailed him having to work closely with the private investment department, keeping track of detailed computer transactions from thousands of important individual clients and businesses across the globe. It was a position well-suited for him.

His immediate superior, Stefan Ackermann, was a gruff no-nonsense German businessman, with silvery-grey hair and piercing blue eyes. The man was always immaculately dressed in tailor-made Italian pinstripe suits, likely costing an average German family a whole decade's income. He was rarely to be found in his Deutsch Trust office, instead jet-setting across the world attending business and political conferences with the other members of the bank's executive management. In fact, Ernst believed he could literally count on both hands the number of times he'd even met the man, which was a good thing.

Early on, Ernst began noticing little things, small peculiarities about the CFO which he thought to be rather odd or unsettling. At the management meetings, he saw that whenever Ackermann spoke the man's eyes darted around or glanced down at the conference table, and he rarely looked anyone in the eye when speaking to them. It was almost like he didn't believe his own words and didn't want anyone else to see it. Shifty-eyed is what some would call it. Devious is the word that came to Ernst's mind. He'd encountered people like Ackermann before, and they were usually corrupt.

It would not take long for Ernst to discover exactly how deeply corrupt the man he worked for was. Just six months after the start of his employment he would regret his decision to work for Deutsche Trust. Unbeknownst to him, a strange confluence of events was about to happen. Everything in his life would soon fall apart, and all it had taken was just one simple email…

A little more than twelve months ago, on the morning of Friday July 7, 2000, he was at his office desk when the email came through to his inbox. The sent note had, at first, seemed completely insignificant, the kind he received almost every day concerning his work. But this particular email would lead to him inadvertently finding the private messages and documents of a very secret, very powerful group of people. Later on, when he'd managed to piece together the insidious conspiracy they were plotting, he came to the startling realization the group was attempting to achieve a "black swan event".

The metaphor of a black swan comes from an Old World premise that all swans are white, a belief that was turned on its head when black swans were unexpectedly discovered in 1697 by Dutch explorers in Australia. It was only in recent years that the concept was put forward as "black swan theory".

Ernst first heard about the theory when he attended a lecture on "outliers", statistical values which lie on the outside of any given set of data. Though the theory was first introduced as a way to better understand the market system, black swans were now being described outside of finance as random, unexpected events of significant magnitude, and having enormous historical consequences. If there were things which could be predicted with any reasonable accuracy, 'known unknowns', so to speak, black swans were events without precedent; they were *unknown unknowns*.

Instances of black swans occurring included the sinking of the Titanic; the outbreak of World War I; the 1929 stock market crash; the rise of the home computer and the internet; and the sudden demise of the Soviet Union.

Now Ernst believed this secret group's plan was to actually create one of these extreme, unforeseen events. Breathtaking in its scale and immensity, it promised to profoundly change *everything*. If they managed to pull it off he was absolutely certain the entire world would be set on a path of all-out war and destruction.

However, he possessed something which could stop the black swan event from ever happening, to throw a wrench into the group's grand machine. At great risk to their lives, he and Anna were carrying two computer USB thumb drives containing all the evidence of the conspiracy, and one of them he planned on giving to a British journalist by the name of Charlie Grimer.

As Ernst typed on his laptop he thought of how the monstrous unimaginable scheme had been created, and the eventual purpose it would serve. Like a bolt of lightning striking him from out of the dark, a single name came into his mind:

Metatron.

'We could stay at my sister's house, just for a couple of weeks,' Anna suggested, catching his attention.

Her idea briefly tumbled around in his thoughts, before he remembered what had happened the previous morning, back in Frankfurt, when the passenger on a motorbike had fired a machine gun at their car. If he hadn't realized it before, it was now crystal clear to him the couple were dealing with people operating on a level higher than they could have possibly imagined.

'No, it's too dangerous,' he disagreed. 'We don't want to involve our families. I think we should keep driving south to Rome, maybe catch a boat across the Mediterranean to Egypt, or even Libya. We need to put as much distance as possible between us and Europe.' He tried to think of anyone he knew overseas who could give them help, or at least a place to stay. But there was no one. Thinking harder, he recalled the night he met Anna at the Dorian Gray, twelve years earlier, and the conversation they'd had whilst sharing a taxi ride to her apartment. 'The night we met, after the concert, do you remember it?'

'Yeah. Why?'

'On the way to your place, in the taxi, you were telling me about the languages you could speak. I remember you saying that a woman, a foreigner, taught you English when you were a child.'

'What about her?' she asked, blowing cigarette smoke into empty space. She hadn't thought about Emily, the person he was talking about, in a very long time. In a flash her mind was inundated with warm and happy memories, and it made her smile.

Anna was six years old when a friendly woman named Emily Grace moved into an apartment opposite her family in West Berlin. After they met, Anna and Emily grew to enjoy each other's company, despite their difference in age. Emily had come to West Germany to teach English for a year at a private school, and it wasn't long before she also began teaching it to the little girl. Anna fondly remembered them walking together alongside the Berlin Wall, with Emily having her repeat English words and phrases. She also remembered being heartbroken when the teaching contract ended, and having to say farewell upon the woman's return home. They vowed to stay in touch, which they did manage for a time. But their correspondence was infrequent, and eventually dwindled to nothing.

'You said she lived far-away, a small town in the middle of nowhere. Where is it?'

'She's from Australia,' Anna replied, 'but I don't know if she's still there. We used to exchange letters. I haven't heard from her in a long time. Her last letter mentioned she was married, with a son. I don't want to get her family involved. Besides, I—I doubt I could even find her.' Anna was lying. She knew *exactly* where Emily was.

'But you don't mind getting your sister involved,' he said sarcastically. 'Look, we don't even have to tell her what's going on, we can pretend we're on vacation. All we need is a place to stay for a little while. We'll be safe and they won't find us.' He turned over on to his side, facing her in the darkness. 'I *know* you know where she lives.'

He does have a good point, she thought. The further away the pair of them could get, the better chance they'd have of surviving.

'Yes,' she confessed, 'I know where she is.' She took a last puff on the cigarette and then stubbed it out on the floor. For a few moments silence descended upon them as they both became lost in their own thoughts.

The journalist, Charlie Grimer, had been dismissive of Anna when she first called to inform him about Ernst's discovery. It was only later that Grimer changed his mind after their dire predictions to him came true, and was now promising the couple he would break the news to the world. All he needed, he said, was the evidence in their possession.

After meeting with Grimer in the UK, Ernst began sending him the stolen information through encrypted emails. It was only in the last 24-hours that he discovered their messages were being intercepted, and they were forced to use the coded phrase the journalist had given them. They were given specific instructions to only use it when something was wrong and they absolutely needed to meet with Grimer in-person. And things most certainly *had* gone wrong.

Now Ernst's whole objective, other than keeping the two of them alive, was to personally hand Grimer the USB thumb drive containing the evidence. This time, he thought confidently, the man would be begging him for it.

'Do you really think they built that... thing?' Anna asked, breaking the silence.

'The artificial intelligence?'

'Mmm hrmm.'

'Yes, I believe it,' he answered. He reached out and moved his hand sensuously down the gentle curve of her body, enjoying the feeling of her skin under his fingers.

'A thinking computer? It sounds far-fetched to me.'

He nibbled at her ear, then whispered, 'They have all the money and power in the world. They can do anything they want.'

Anna began to feel that her grip on reality was slipping. 'Ernst, is this really happening to us, or am I just dreaming?' she asked, as he began kissing the back of her neck.

'We're still alive, and we just fucked,' he replied. His hand caressed the inside of her thigh, causing her to shiver. His fingers were beginning to stimulate her again.

'How do we know Grimer is going to… come?' she murmured.

They were supposed to meet the journalist the next day at the Marienplatz, a central square in Munich. But while they were making love, Ernst changed his mind and decided upon a completely different plan.

'We don't know,' he replied. 'And if he doesn't come and instead someone else is there—I don't want you going with me.'

'Don't be stupid, of course I am,' she protested.

'No, you'll be in danger.'

'You won't be able to talk to him, you can't speak English.'

'I don't need to,' he replied. 'I only need to give him the USB. After that… I think we should split up. It'll make it more difficult for them to find us if we separate.'

'Fuck you, you're not leaving me alone!' she exclaimed, pushing him away.

At that moment, coming from outside the room, the door at the end of the hallway opened and closed again, and the sound of footsteps could be heard. In the dark the couple both anxiously held their breaths as they listened to someone walking slowly and steadily toward their door.

Who are they? Anna wondered, fearfully.

After briefly hesitating outside the door, the person, whoever they were, instead simply walked away and went down the rest of the hallway. Another door opened and shut, and then all became deathly still once again.

A few seconds went by, and then Ernst whispered, 'Anna, listen to me… Take the other USB and get out of Europe as soon as possible. I can't go with you as the police will be looking for me. Once you get to Rome, buy a ticket and fly to Australia. Find your friend, and I'll catch up with you later.'

There was no changing his mind, she thought with grim resignation. It was becoming clear to her that this was the beginning of the end for the two of them.

'You're a son-of-a-bitch for getting us involved, do you know that?' she whispered back, seething with anger.

'Don't worry, everything will be all right—'

'—No,' she interrupted, 'it won't be.' She stood and crawled into the bed, leaving him alone on the floor.

He knew that her anger was entirely justified. Even though Anna had urged him to continue investigating his boss, it had been Ernst who'd ultimately brought this torment down upon them, and he suddenly felt very guilty. If there were even the slightest remote possibility he'd take it all back in an instant and not interfered with this group or their plans. He would have left well enough alone.

There's no going back, he thought. *Only forward into the unknown.*

He stared into the pitch black of the room and again pondered their uncertain future. He was tired and stressed out, and he didn't want to think any longer. Closing his laptop, he pushed himself up from the floor and then silently crept into the bed next to Anna.

Just before falling asleep, Ernst's last thoughts were spent wondering if Grimer would be there at the Marienplatz to meet him the next morning. Then for the rest of the night his mind was plagued by a terrifying nightmare of him running through an endless deserted metropolis, frantically trying to escape from pursuing giant beings that were determined to catch and devour him.

THREE

DAY 1 – Tuesday August 7, 2001
4:59 P.M.
17°19'42.20" 11°20'49.95"

CHARLIE GRIMER WAS HAVING a very bad day. The engine of the motorcycle he was straddling had just cut out for what seemed to him like the millionth time. He'd spent the entire morning struggling to manoeuvre the cycle over the endless sea of sand. One particularly monstrous dune, which must have been over a hundred feet in height, had taken him almost an hour to get to the top and only a few moments to ride down. Now that he'd finally found a stretch of flat land in the midst of this desert hell, the motorbike had, of course, stalled on him once again. The fact he'd even got this far he considered to be a significant achievement.

He wore goggles over his blue eyes, and most of his head was protectively wrapped in a dark scarf. His exposed nose and cheeks were bright red and painfully sore, as his normally pale British skin was quickly becoming very sunburnt.

Charlie had just turned 42, not quite over the hill, at least in his mind. Although he'd lost most of the hair on the top of his head years ago, and suffered from occasional arthritis in his hands, he preferred to think he was still young at heart. But the way the muscles in his entire body were aching right now he felt he could very well have been an old man.

Lifting the goggles from his weary eyes, he swung his leg over the seat to dismount, in the process catching the tip of his boot on the oversized fuel tank which stuck out from the sides of the machine. It caused him to stumble and he fell face first to the ground, receiving a mouth-full of sand. The cycle fell over on to its side with a heavy thud, narrowly missing landing on top of him.

Disgusted, Charlie spat out the sand and then wiped away the pebbles stuck to the perspiration around his parched lips. A long gob of sand and saliva arced down from his mouth to the ground. *I must look a disgraceful sight,* he thought. Pulling the knapsack off his body and goggles from his forehead, he angrily threw them away. Then he turned on to his back and faced the sky.

'God-damn it all!' he shouted as loud as he could. For a few seconds after he had the eerie feeling that someone had heard him, that he was being *watched.* He turned his head both ways looking across the barren landscape, but there was nothing to be seen, save for the occasional acacia tree or scrub bush.

In the distance something caught his eye and he quickly sat up. It was a shimmer of ephemeral light touching the horizon, spread out over a great length of the flat featureless terrain. As he narrowed his eyes from the sun's glare, it looked to him like a shining mass of blue water several kilometres away. *A lake? Out here?* he wondered with surprise. It was a beautiful scene. Instantly, renewed hope surged through his whole body that he might be reunited with civilization, and this whole terrible ordeal would soon be over. Where there was water, there were people. They would help him. Visions of swimming in cool, fresh, life-giving water danced through his mind. Oh, it would be deliciously exquisite, Charlie thought with relish.

But his optimism was only fleeting. Just as quickly as they'd come, the uplifting images playing across his eyes soon retreated with a dawning realization. The idea that it might be a lake was so absurd that he immediately felt stupid for thinking it. It looked so real, but he knew it could only be a mirage. And besides, he thought, he could never be that lucky.

Sighing, Charlie recalled the last four days of what he believed was his soon-to-end life. His situation had seemed about as bad as anything could get. And yet, beyond his belief, it soon turned into something far worse. He'd come to the conclusion, hours ago, that there was *no fucking way* he was getting out of this alive.

He glanced at the black motorcycle lying on its side.

'Blasted thing,' he muttered.

It was very heavy, probably from the excessive fuel, and would be hard to pick up in his weakened state. But he was well aware that at this point it was the only single link to his salvation. That is if he could figure out how to properly ride it. For in all of his years, Charlie had never learned how to ride a motorcycle, though there had been several opportunities. Now he was silently cursing himself for it.

***

When Charlie was a teenager living in the London suburb town of Chelmsford, his best friend Harry Cullen had ridden dirt bikes throughout the green pastoral countryside. Many a time he'd tried to teach Charlie how to ride, even going so far as offering to give him his own bike when Harry's parents had agreed to buy him a new one for his seventeenth birthday. Charlie's father had ridden motorbikes in his youth, and he didn't have a problem with his son wanting to learn how to ride.

His mother, on the other hand, was fiercely protective of him and had frowned upon the idea, forbidding him from owning one. *'They are just too damned dangerous!'* she always used to say. And, as mothers usually are, she'd been right.

Harry was killed on his birthday. After receiving the gift from his parents he'd impatiently taken the motorcycle out for a quick spin. Rounding a sharp curve on a country road too fast, he failed to negotiate it and careened off the pavement, hitting a large tree and dying on impact.

It was half a lifetime ago. Charlie never got the chance to say goodbye to Harry. But then death rarely allows for such niceties does it? Indeed, he knew that all too well. And now he was living inside of an agonizing nightmare from which he couldn't wake up or escape. He might as well be already dead for all that it mattered.

How ironic that motorcycles would be the end of both us, eh Harry? he thought chillingly.

Yes, Harry had experienced a very bad day, and now it was looking like it was finally Charlie's turn. Hell, it wasn't even just a bad day he was having. If it had been only that he might be able to handle it, but his whole world had turned completely upside-down. He'd always known that his life was filled with varying degrees of happiness and success alongside periods of intense chaotic instability, but this – *this* – was too much for any person in their right mind to deal with.

Born in Chelmsford to a working class family, Charlie's upbringing was ordinary by any measure. His father had owned a barbershop, and then he later sold furniture in the city's sole department store, while his mother was a homemaker. Raised a Protestant, his childhood was active and trouble-free, usually spending his days playing soccer or wandering the forests and rolling green hills of Essex County.

Later on, he graduated from the highly regarded City University in London with a degree in journalism, and almost immediately he was hired to write freelance for several top UK newspapers. It was at these establishments where he learned that dealing with paid insiders and anonymous whistleblowers was a fairly common, if not unofficial business practice.

Recently he'd been writing for The Daily Sun, a major London "red top" tabloid. In 1995 he discovered the paper was employing a private investigator to hack into the cell phone messages of movie stars, politicians, and even members of the Royal Family. Outraged, Charlie resigned from his position and then broke the story in a rival paper. The shockwaves it caused were immediate, ripping right through the core of the UK's establishment. The investigation widened when it was discovered that the government ministry, the Home Office, had been covering up allegations of child sex abuse at Westminster committed by several MPs. For almost two years, it was the biggest bombshell and talk of the news in Great Britain, until the unfortunate tragedy which befell Princess Diana took place.

The whole sordid affair was a deep, dark national scandal that, for a time, catapulted Charlie to infamy in the industry, garnering him several reporting awards. But it also made him more than a few die-hard enemies. Bribes had been offered to him. When that didn't work, threats were made against he and his family. Major lawsuits were paid off or even quashed altogether, with no explanation given. It was all just quietly brushed under the rug, and the public quickly forgot about it. Out of sight, out of mind.

"A nation of sheep will beget a government of wolves" was an alleged quote by famed American broadcast journalist, Edward R. Murrow,

which Charlie used to remind himself should he ever be tempted to forget his principles.

After the scandal broke, Charlie rode the crest of a huge wave of notoriety lasting many months. When it finally cooled off he figured he'd gone all-in with his cards and, somehow, miraculously survived. The whole thing had almost been the end of his marriage, and it was time to call it quits and keep far away from the tabloids.

Nevertheless, he still received calls every now and again from cranks and crackpots, telling him stories about UFO cover-ups and other outlandish conspiracy theories. *'How did you get my unlisted number?'* he would always ask them. If he wasn't satisfied with their answer, the conversation was over. Period.

How fucking wrong I was, he thought, as he lay back down on the hot sand. Visions flashed across his eyes of his wife Leigh, and son David. He wished more than ever that he could see their faces, to reach out and touch them just one more time. His heart ached to hold David tightly in his arms and never let go, but he was painfully aware it was never going to happen again, at least not in this lifetime.

What am I doing in Africa? he wondered. *Where did it all go wrong?*

The phone call.

***

More than a year ago, on July 23, 2000, Charlie got the call on his mobile while he, Leigh and David were at The Lion's Tavern pub in Central London. At the time they'd been happily celebrating their son's thirteenth birthday. The call had been from an unknown number, and the voice speaking on the other end was a young woman with a German accent.

'Mr. Grimer?' she inquired.

'Yes?'

'You don't know me, but I have very important information to tell you.'

He sighed. It certainly wasn't the first time he'd received calls that had begun in this way, and he didn't want to have the conversation right there in front of his family. 'One moment dear,' Charlie said to Leigh, as he got up from the table. He strolled over to the bar, where a thick haze of cigarette smoke hung in the air, and then he motioned for the barkeep to give him another pint of ale. On any other occasion he would have hung up on the interloper without hesitation. This time, however, he heard on the other end of the phone something in the girl's voice, a desperation which instinctively told him this call might be different from the rest.

'How did you get my number?' he asked her.

'That's not important,' she replied.

Oh, innit now? he thought. *Well Miss with the sexy German accent, it's been nice talking to you. Piss off!* He glanced at his watch. It was late, almost eleven o'clock, and he was starting to get more irritated with each passing second.

For a brief moment the woman hesitated saying anything further, as if correctly sensing she had called at the wrong time, or rubbed him the wrong way.

'Pardon me, Mr Grimer,' she continued, 'but I think it's *you* who is important. You are in a position to do *something.*'

The corners of Charlie's mouth curled up in a crooked smile. She was trying to flatter him, and he decided he'd been wrong about her from the very start. Indeed, he thought smugly, she was just like all the rest. 'Well, I'll be honest with you,' he began, in a rehearsed speech he'd spoken twenty times before, 'I haven't written for the tabloid rags in years. I'm sort of a persona non grata with them. I'll listen to what you've got to say, but don't expect anything more. Now, please tell me what's so important to interrupt my son's birthday celebration?'

'I—I know someone, who believes that two days from now, on the 25th, something big is going to happen, something spectacular… and terrible.'

'Bloody hell,' Charlie muttered, under his breath. *Just what I need,* he thought, *another fucking doomsday prophet claiming the end of the world is nigh.*

Suddenly an old jukebox sprang to life with the playing of a piano. Looking over, Charlie saw that his son had deposited money and randomly picked a song from the playlist. It was "Live and Let Die" by Wings. When he heard the song begin he was briefly reminded of the time he'd spent in London in the early 70s, and they were mostly happy memories. After lighting up a cigarette he felt more at ease. 'Oh? And what spectacular, terrible thing will that be?' he asked her, mockingly.

The woman took a deep breath before answering him, as if she were about to relieve herself of some heavy burden. 'We think there's going to be an attempt on the life of Jacques Chirac,' she said.

But the jukebox music was getting loud, and Charlie wasn't sure if he'd heard her correctly. 'Jacques Chirac... the French president?!' he asked, shouting into the phone. 'I'm sorry, but could you speak up a little?'

'Yes—the president of France!' she shouted back.

'Why would anyone want to kill Chirac?'

'It has something to do with Iraq. My friend believes with certainty it's going to happen.'

'Someone is going to shoot him?'

'No,' she replied flatly, before quickly correcting herself. 'Well, I—I don't know for sure, but I think they are going to stage a disaster in order to kill him.'

'They? Who are *they*?' he asked, by now more than a little confused. She didn't answer him.

The conversation had just taken a dark turn with the talk of conspiracy to commit murder. It made Charlie uncomfortable, as he was reminded of the death threats he and his family had received over the phone hacking scandal, and how long it had taken him to get a good night's sleep again. In the background, the jukebox was playing the chorus of Live and Let Die in an explosive crescendo of drums and guitars.

Charlie looked about the pub and saw that most of the night's patrons were beginning to pack up and leave, and he suddenly wanted to hang up on this crank and get back to his wife and son. 'Does your friend have any evidence?' he asked, as he looked to the table where his family patiently waited. He waved his hand at Leigh, silently telling her he was almost finished and would be right back, but she did not look happy.

'No,' the woman replied.

No, of course they didn't, he thought. *Silly me, why should I have expected they had evidence?*

'Well,' she continued, 'they don't have it right now, but they can get it.'

Charlie sighed, and then took a puff of his cigarette. 'All right,' he said, 'suppose what this contact of yours says is true, that there's going to be an assassination attempt on Jacques Chirac, what do you expect me to do about it? Why not just go to the police and tell them about this conspiracy to kill the president of France?'

'We are hoping you can get it published in a newspaper,' answered the woman.

He thought she was beginning to sound like the usual paranoid people he'd dealt with so many times in the past, and he was fast growing tired of the conversation. 'I don't work for the tabloids anymore, I told you that already,' he said, sternly.

'But you must know people who do,' she countered. 'They will listen to you.'

Charlie shook his head. 'No, I'm sorry,' he replied, with a chuckle. 'If I was to ask them to publish something like this and nothing happened, do you realize how much of a fool I would look?' He paused to listen for an answer, but instead she said nothing, and it suddenly made him angry. 'Look, I've already been put through the ringer recently, or haven't you been watching the news?!'

Live and Let Die abruptly stopped playing on the jukebox. Glancing over, Charlie saw that it had been shut it off, and the pub was preparing to close for the night. Feeling drained, he decided the conversation had run its course and it was now time to finish it. Taking a deep breath he spoke to her again, this time more softly.

'Listen,' he said, 'I don't mean to yell at you, but it makes me *feel good* doing it.' He stubbed out his cigarette in an ashtray. 'Thank you very much, but I have to go. Please, don't call me again.'

Just as he was about to push the Hang Up button, he heard the woman shout loudly through the phone. 'Wait!' she implored. 'There's one more thing I want to tell you!'

At that moment Charlie's curiosity caused him to hesitate hanging up on her. 'What?!' he demanded. The reply he received were five words he would never forget:

'She's going to leave you.'

Then the phone line went dead.

What an absolutely odd thing to say, thought Charlie. In fact he believed it was downright ridiculous. He knew that he and Leigh had had their ups and downs recently, but there was no reason for him to suspect his marriage was currently in any danger. Hadn't he done his best to fix things, he wondered, to make amends for all the trouble he'd caused?

He didn't quite know what to make of the call, and he stood at the bar for a few moments, thinking about all that had been said. After downing the rest of his ale, he returned to his waiting family, eager to rid his thoughts of the strange, disturbing conversation.

Two days later the Concorde crashed in France upon take-off, killing all aboard and several on the ground. One hundred and thirteen people were dead in one terrible instant. Like the rest of the world, Charlie was totally shocked at the horrific event. Immediately he wondered about the woman's warning to him. Was it just an alarming coincidence?

Deciding to investigate the circumstances of the crash, he got in touch with someone who'd been a contact for him within the French government. A day later they phoned him back with utterly startling information which had been kept secret from the public: the Concorde had narrowly missed crashing into a plane on the airport runway carrying the French president, Jacques Chirac. Upon hearing this, Charlie's heart sank into the pit of his stomach. Hanging up the phone, it was then that he knew what the woman had said to him only days earlier had been true, as he believed there was no possible way she, or her friend, could have randomly predicted the tragedy. The woman had come to him with the information... and he had done *nothing*. He could have saved all of those people's lives. It made him sick to think about.

Then, a week after the accident, another bombshell fell upon Charlie's head when his wife told him exactly what the woman predicted would happen. Leigh had discovered the call on his mobile, and, believing he was having an affair, she informed him she had also met someone. A few days later, she moved out of the house, taking David with her. Thus, Charlie's life was again thrust into utter turmoil and despair, and the nightmare he thought he'd left far behind had now suddenly returned, this time with a vengeance.

He couldn't believe the completely surreal pattern of events. The strange woman had been correct not once, but *twice*. But how could she have known what his wife would do, he asked himself? Did they know each other? Suspicious, he began trying to think of the connection between Leigh and the mysterious caller. The only logical explanation, the only one which made sense, was that the woman was the wife or girlfriend of Leigh's lover. Maybe the phone call was the broken girl's way of getting revenge, he thought. Still, it certainly did not explain her other warning to him.

In the following days he was desperate to get in touch with the mystery woman, but she'd called his mobile phone from an unknown number. For weeks he waited, hoping against hope, that one day he would answer his phone and again hear the woman with the German accent on the other end. It became an obsession for him.

Three months and three days after the tragedy Charlie's prayers were finally answered. But then things only got steadily worse, like a runaway ball of snow rolling down a hill, becoming bigger and more deadly. Yes, Charlie believed that it was the night of that blasted phone call which had been the beginning of the end of his now shattered life.

***

God damn to hell my ambition for a good story, he thought with remorse, as he returned from the miserable memories of the recent past to his present dire predicament. Still lying on the ground, he wearily raised his arm to look at the wristband's LED screen. The red digital glared back at him:

05:15:58:18

Five days and sixteen hours left, and only eight hours had passed since they'd set him free. But it wasn't really freedom, now was it? Like being inside an enormous cage of isolation, he felt like some miserable animal that had been trapped, forgotten, and left to slowly die. His anxiety began to increase, reaching a critical point, and he sensed that another panic attack was close at hand. Since the hacking scandal he'd been suffering from severe autophobia, the fear of being alone, and now he was suddenly desperate for his Xanax medication. *God, I wish I had at least had a damn fag,* he lamented.

His eyes gazed upon the not-so dissimilar emptiness of the sky above, as his thoughts continued to wander in every direction: *Is God mocking me, is that what's going on here?* He didn't have an answer, and wasn't sure he even wanted one. But it sure as hell felt like he was being teased and strung along. No, he was being *laughed* at.

Somewhere in the world there were people watching him, and they were laughing. He could sense it.

But in fact nothing was making sense anymore, and he struggled to remain balanced with his mind on the verge of snapping. There was a very real chance that a mental breakdown could happen, right there on the spot. He knew that if it did he was in even more trouble. He inhaled and exhaled deeply, trying to calm himself. For some reason Live and Let Die was stuck inside his head, and all he could do was hum the memorable tune and mumble something close to its lyrics.

Grabbing his knapsack, he reached inside and pulled out the water canteen. Unscrewing the cap, he took two big swigs, keeping each in his mouth to savor it. Water never tasted so good, he thought. It didn't even matter to him that it was warm and hard to swallow. When he began to finally relax he brought out the GPS device and looked at the time:

5:05 P.M.

Realizing the sun would soon disappear over the horizon, he suddenly wasn't sure if it was a good or a bad thing. The temperature could fall drastically in the desert, he knew that much. There was no shelter anywhere for protection, but he did have some flint in the knapsack. Glancing over at a nearby scrub bush, he figured that a fire could be made with its branches used for kindling.

He pressed a couple of buttons and the display showed that he'd travelled one hundred and ninety kilometres. It was a long way to come in a short amount of time, he thought, but there was still another one thousand to go. The motorcycle's fuel would run out long before the end. What would he do then, he wondered? Playing it out in his mind, he concluded that he'd be left with no other alternative: he would have to make a run for it.

There were two other black pixelated dots moving slowly on the GPS screen. One was quite a few kilometres south of him, while another was north and much closer. He considered if that opponent was trying to get to his position to locate him. Looking closely at the flashing pixel, he noted it didn't appear to be moving in his direction. Just the same, he figured that he shouldn't stop to rest for the night, that maybe it was best to keep going. It would be much cooler for his body, but it would also be very dark.

Wait a minute, he thought. *Wasn't there supposed to be three other competitor signals?* Presently the GPS was only showing two, and he couldn't figure out what to make of it. Putting it aside for the time being, he asked himself, *what do I know about Africa?*

His memories drifted back more than two decades of his life. As a teenager, he'd read Joseph Conrad's "Heart of Darkness" and the short story had fascinated him. Later on, while he was at City University, he took a sociology class which examined the historical effects of British colonialism. It was there that he studied Kipling's "The White Man's Burden", and he learned of an expression used by the European imperialist powers of the 19th century to describe their ignorance of Africa's vast regions of uncharted land. They called it "the Dark Continent", a term Charlie believed exemplified the racist attitudes of the time.

Thinking some more, he couldn't recall having written or read any news articles about the desert or Africa, except for the horror that engulfed Rwanda a few years back. Then he remembered a book about surviving in the wild he'd once purchased at a car boot sale. He had no idea what ever became of the damned thing, but the information he'd read started flowing back to him from some deep corner of his memories.

In a chapter on deserts, the book stated you could work out which direction you were heading by looking at the shape of the sand dunes. He realized that the wind blowing from the northeast Mediterranean would create a long shallow slope on a dune's windward side, while the leeward side would be shorter and steeper. He could also make a crude sundial with the knife he'd been given, if need be. He decided it was definitely something he could resort to if the GPS or its batteries stopped working.

However, the one thing from the book he could not remember was how much water was necessary to avoid dehydration. Heat stroke was a very real danger, and he knew that the first signs are a headache, fatigue and dizziness. The body stops sweating as it tries to conserve fluids, then you fall unconscious and eventually die. Feeling the weight of the canteen in his hand, he judged that it was probably a little over half full, and would need to be replenished in a few hours. Thoughts of being reduced to drinking his own urine went through his mind. That was disgusting and miserable, and he quickly discarded the idea. Besides, he knew if he did that his demise would only be hastened.

Being an avid lover of the theatre and films, he remembered two of his favourite war movies that were concerned with the desert and survival, though he figured there was nothing of importance in them that could help his situation. The first was "Lawrence of Arabia", which he'd watched on his family's first colour television as a boy. His mother had fancied the handsome star of the film, Peter O'Toole. For an entire week after seeing it, young Charlie adorned himself in a white bed sheet and imagined he was T.E. Lawrence leading an Arab charge attack on the back of a camel. The camel, however, was in reality his family's pet collie dog, much to its weeklong discontent.

The other film he recalled was "March or Die", starring Gene Hackman, about the French Foreign Legion in Morocco not long after the First World War. He'd first seen it at the cinema in London when he was in his late teens. Its epic climactic battle scene, pitting a small force of légionnaires against a massive army of Bedouins, had made a strong impression on him, and was later among his favourites that he regularly hired from the video store.

Now he knew for himself what the légionnaires experienced. They feared the desert, and with good reason. The relentless scorching sun, the endless rolling waves of sand dune, and the utter despair that came with the knowledge they had been separated from friends, family and civilization, separated even from God Himself. But, at the very least, the mercenaries had each other for company. It would have filled their hearts with a shred of hope. Charlie, however, had no one. He was *alone*.

There it was again, his fear of isolation. It was always just below the surface, waiting to creep up his spine like some dreadful invisible phantom trying to invade his consciousness.

He suddenly remembered the prophetic words of the film's Bedouin antagonist, El Krim, to Gene Hackman's character: *"The desert welcomes you Major Foster."* Welcome indeed. The desert would be Foster's tomb. El Krim had known it, and Foster too probably. Was this also to be his own fate, he wondered? Should he just give up and stay lying down, right at this very spot, and wait for the vultures to assemble for dinner? No, he was determined not to give up, at least not yet. He had to keep on marching, like the légionnaires had done, or Charlie, like Major Foster, would die in the desert.

As if on cue with his reverie, the wind suddenly picked up, blowing sand in concentric swirls around him. It whistled and howled like some kind of mad Djinn spirit, disturbed by the presence of an outsider in its kingdom of desolation and misery. He covered his eyes with his hand, protecting them from the irritating little grains of sand.

It was then that he heard a strange distant noise over the wind. With each passing moment, it was getting louder, coming closer. What was it, he wondered? It sounded to him like a buzzing insect, or – a motorcycle? A fear instantly washed over him. *How did they manage to get here so fast?*

There were three others, like him, somewhere out here. He knew they would have the exact same objectives as he: surviving this hell; making it all the way to the end; *staying alive.* Had the one north of his position tracked him down? Would they try to stop him, injure him, or even – kill him? And, furthermore, would he try and do the same if and when the moment came? Charlie had no answer. He simply couldn't wrap his head around such thoughts, the possibilities for which he hadn't yet considered.

He shut them out of his mind, at least for now, and crawled along the ground toward his knapsack lying a few feet away. Inside it was the knife they'd given him, and he wanted it close at hand just in case. But then he stopped moving to the bag upon realizing it wasn't a motorcycle at all. The noise was coming from directly above.

Shielding his eyes from the sun, he looked up and saw a man-made creature flying a few hundred feet overhead, circling around in a wide holding pattern. It had two long straight wings that were slightly swept back, and a protruding round front which appeared to Charlie like a head. The under part was painted black, but he could see that the upper main body of it was white. There also appeared to be missiles attached to the underside of the craft's wings.

It was that *thing*. He'd seen it hours earlier, after landing in the helicopter. Before setting him free, the agent had informed him that whatever he did, wherever he went, he would be *watched*. At first he'd ignorantly assumed they'd meant by satellite, but soon it dawned on him that this flying machine was how *they* were watching:

The Syndicate.

A year ago they made the unthinkable happen. But now Charlie had almost precise information about what they were planning to do next, something which would change the course of world history forever. This time he was determined to stop them.

He briefly wondered why they were doing this to him, and the others. Why would they want to film his torment? What possible purpose could there be in such twisted sadistic madness?

Just then an answer came to Charlie so quickly that it was able to overcome the dense wall of heat, sending chills throughout his whole body. He remembered what Major Foster said to the Bedouin chief, El Krim, after being presented the unfortunate captured English archaeologists, with their eyes and tongues cut out:

"I see you've learned to enjoy watching men suffer."

FOUR

UNDER THE GLITTERING STARS which adorned the velvety black Australian sky, the group of boys danced long into the night around the crackling embers of the fire, until the dawn broke with the first purple and golden-hued rays of the rising sun. The women had all left, and the remaining young men were chanting the verses of a traditional song aloud in unison, clapping their hands together and stomping their feet on the ground. White ochre was painted across their faces, bare chests and backs, and each jumped across the small fire in turn.

A purlka, the elder of the group, was sitting on the ground nearby, a bullroarer musical instrument next to him. Wearing a feathered headdress, he had a long, bushy grey beard which grew down to his chest. Deep lines and creases were etched into the leathery dark skin of his aged, wise-looking face. Watching the dance carefully, he made sure the sacred Waruwarta ceremony was properly performed.

Four older boys sat behind the rest, the initiates of the ritual into manhood, patiently waiting until the song ended. Decorated in a powdery white vegetable down, they were hunched over on their knees with their elbows on the ground, while their hands covered their faces. Every now and then one of the four would peek through his fingers, curious to observe the ceremony. When the song was over, the elder beckoned for the initiates to come.

Blaze Mullins glanced at his close friend Darby Sims, who was crouching on the ground next to him. They smiled at each other, and then jumped up and joined the rest of the group.

For a long time they sat, and the elder silently looked at each of the initiates. Then, holding a stick, he drew a small circle into the dirt in front of him. 'This is Ngurra, the land which is our home,' the old man said in the Warlpiri language of his people, his voice sounding deep and guttural. Next, he drew a second circle beside it. 'This is Kuruwarri, the law of our people.' Below the first circle, he drew another. 'This one is Jardiwarnpa, our traditions and ceremonies. If we do not respect them... we will get sick, and the land around us will become sick. It will die, and then so will we.' A fourth circle was drawn above the first. 'This is Jaru, our language which you must never forget. You must teach it to your children, and they must pass it on to their children.' Then, next to the original circle in the centre, the elder drew a fifth one in the dirt, until the pattern of circles resembled a star. 'And this final one is Warlalja-yapa, our family.' He looked to the boys sitting silently around him. 'All of us here, Tjakamarra, Tjangala, Tjapaltjarri, Tjampitjinpa... we are all one family. Nothing can ever separate us from each other.' At this, the group fondly looked upon one another, their faces aglow from the fire. The old man traced the stick across the ground until the circles were joined. 'All of these things are connected to each other. They are the way of Yapa, our people.'

But then the elder's brow furrowed deeply, and the lines in his face tightened. One by one, he looked into the eyes of each of the initiates until, lastly, his gaze fell upon Blaze. 'If we do not respect Ngurra-kurlu,' he said, raising his hand and shaking a finger in warning, 'our people will disappear from here forever. It will become *kulkurru-kulkurru* – a country without people.'

Blaze gulped and shuddered. He could see the red flickering flames reflected in the inky black orbs of the elder's pupil's.

From a pouch around his waist, the old man brought out a handful of red-coloured stones, which he then placed on the ground before him and spread out for everyone to see. 'Now, before the final run and ceremony in which you will become men, I will tell you a story about the place known to us as *Kulu*, what the whitefella's call Devil's Mountain. Not many Yapa know where it is, but it lies to the east not far from here. This is how Kulu came to be...

'Long ago, in the time of the Dreaming, there was no mountain in that angry place, only big red rocks scattered across this country,' he said, waving his hand over the red stones. 'This land was peaceful, and among the people who lived here were two brothers, Talaruji and Kalaruji. Since being young ones they were very close, and each understood all the time what the other was thinking. Always they hunted together, these two brothers. They were the finest hunters, bringing much food back to their family and friends. Their people knew them to be good and strong, and they were fast on their feet, just like their wampana totem.'

Blaze saw that Darby was listening intently to the unfolding story. For a moment he wondered if his friend was as nervous as he was about the coming initiation. Although it was their people's rite of passage into manhood, it involved a painful circumcision.

'One day,' the elder continued, 'Talaruji and Kalaruji were off hunting marlu, and they saw a young girl. She was alone, digging for yams in the red earth. She was from another skin group which had the goanna for their totem. These brothers both watched her for a long time. They thought she was very beautiful, and both wanted to take her for a wife, even though they already had wives chosen for them. Secretly, each brother began to think how to get her for his own. When the girl passed them, the brother's declared to each other their intention to marry her. Neither of them liked this, for each wanted the girl for himself. They began to fight and argue, with words they had never once said to each other before in anger.

'Finally, Talaruji and Kalaruji decided they must fight, until one brother was victorious and the other was defeated. But they were both hunters and the law of their people forbid them from using weapons against each other. How could they solve their problem and decide who would marry the girl? It was a question they could not answer.

'A long time passed, until the brothers finally came to an agreement: they decided to have a contest. Using the big red rocks that were all around them, each would build a tower. Whoever made the highest tower with the rocks would be the winner, and he could then have the girl for a wife.' The old man began placing the small stones on top of each other, making two piles on the ground in front him. All around the fire the young boys listened closely to his words, spellbound.

'The girl watched as the two brothers started to build their towers. It was very difficult for them, as the rocks were big and heavy. Because they both wanted to win the contest, they used all their strength to lift them. All through the day and night, and the next one after that, the brothers worked very hard to lift the heavy rocks on top of each other. Slowly, the towers they were building began to grow bigger, and get higher.

'When the third day came, the people from the wampana and the wardapi totem groups gathered to watch the contest. All of them thought the two brothers would fall to the ground from being so tired, as they had not slept for three days. Both of their towers were now very big and high. Some of the people thought that Talaruji would win the contest, while others thought that Kalaruji would build the tallest tower. Sometimes it would look to them like one brother would be winning, but then a rock would fall from his tower, or the other brother would place a new rock on top of his own. No one could tell who would win the contest, and marry the beautiful girl.

'On the morning of the fourth day, dark clouds began to appear in the sky, and a terrible wind began blowing. The brothers didn't see this, and they continued to build their towers. Even the people watching them did not see a storm was approaching. The girl saw it, but she did not care and wanted to see which brother would win. In the afternoon, the storm came with loud thunder, and lightning flashed across the country. Heavy rain began to fall, and all the people were surprised and very frightened. They ran to the two towers so they could find shelter from the storm.

'But then the people saw a terrible wind pick up the two brothers, Talaruji and Kalaruji, and it carried them away into the clouds above. Next, the wind lifted up the young girl into the air and then crashed her body against the red rocks. And then she too went up into the sky. Soon, all of the big red rocks which the brothers had used were tossed about like small pebbles.' The elder pushed over the two piles of stones, causing them to fall back down to the ground, scattered.

'The people were very scared, running this way and that way, crying out for their ancestor spirits to protect them. But there was no answer, and no help came for them. The storm blew people away, and the falling rocks crushed many to death, until no one was left.' The elder began picking up the stones, this time placing them together to form one large pile. 'When the storm and the rain went away, the two towers the brothers had built were gone. All of the red rocks had crumbled and fallen together to make one big mountain, which our people call Kulu. It is the place of great anger and sadness.

To this day the only things which can go there are the wampana and wardapi, the totem animals of the two brothers and the girl.'

He looked carefully at the four initiates. 'Now tell me, do you know why I have told you this story?' he asked them. Glancing at each other, all of the boys remained silent. 'The ancestor spirits punished the brothers, the girl and their people because they did not respect the land, or each other. It is a reminder for us which we must never forget. Because of this, none may walk on this mountain. It is forbidden. If anyone does, it will bring *kurnta*, a great shame on them and our people.'

Just then, a glowing from above caught the attention of the initiates and the elder. Looking up, they saw wispy clouds of green, red and purple light arcing across the clear night sky. It was the aurora australis, the southern lights making a very rare appearance.

The elder shook his head, and said warily, 'It is a bad omen. A terrible thing is coming.'

***

Across the grassy spinifex countryside Blaze and Darby ran in quick step together, as the sun began its slow ascent over the rolling hilltops surrounding them. They were the fastest runners in the whole community, and the pair soon left the other two initiates trailing far behind. They'd been running for just about an hour, when Darby suddenly broke away from Blaze's side, heading in another direction. Blaze stopped dead in his tracks. 'What ya doin mate?' he asked in Light Warlpiri, a mixture of English with their Indigenous language. 'That's the wrong way.'

Darby came to a halt. 'I think I know where Kulu is. I wanna see it while we're here,' he replied.

'Didn't ya hear the elder's words? It's forbidden to go there!' Blaze exclaimed. He knew Darby could be prone to rash decisions, something Blaze had discovered a number of times in the past. Though he was curious to see if his friend really could find the mountain, this particular idea of Darby's carried the possibility of getting the pair into big trouble.

'The wallaby and goannas can go to Kulu. Our totem is the wallaby, so we're allowed,' reasoned Darby.

'That's not what the elder meant, and ya know it!' Blaze countered. 'Besides, we gotta go back for the finish-up ceremony.'

Darby laughed. 'Don't you understand? We're *already* men.'

'What ya mean?' Blaze asked, confused by his friends strange choice of words. How could he be a man, he wondered, if the ceremony hadn't yet been performed?

'One day Blaze, you will do something really amazing, you will see,' Darby said, as he made his way to the edge of a small hill. 'Come on mate,' he challenged, 'I bet ya can't keep up with me!' And with that, he took off through the brush, leaving Blaze with no choice but to chase after him.

***

DAY 2 – Wednesday August 8, 2001
3:01 A.M.
16°48'10.94" 10°51'12.99"

Blaze Tjakamarra Mullins awoke from the dream, the vivid past events of his life still imprinted upon his mind's eye. The first thing his senses perceived was an immense exhaustion sweeping through his entire body. He opened his large brown eyes, and realized he was enveloped in almost total darkness. Above him the immense African sky was clear, but on this particular night there was no moon to offer any helpful light. The only things to be seen were the twinkling constellations of far-away stars.

For the nineteen-year-old the long day had felt like it was never going to end. When the dark finally approached, it provoked inside him a mixture of conflicting emotions. On the one hand he was thankful that the night gave him the excuse to rest, but the knowledge that time was now his enemy filled him with a deep and growing dread.

I have to keep moving, he thought.

He hadn't intended to fall asleep, only to stop for a short while at the base of a tall date palm tree, among a small cluster of them he'd discovered just before sunset. Although Blaze didn't know it, the inhabitants of the Sahara have a traditional proverb that says "These stalwart trees grow with their heads in fire and feet in water", a reflection of their ability to survive where nothing should.

At first he'd been afraid of being forced to spend the night out on the open sand. However, luck seemed to be on his side, even if it was only for the moment. When he finally sighted the palm trees they'd immediately given him a very welcome relief to his loneliness.

Sitting up, he gave a short glance around him. Nearby, the motorcycle rested on its kickstand. He was grateful that he knew how to ride it, and for how well it had performed in light of the circumstances. How many sand dunes had he traversed with it, he wondered? At first, the task had seemed near impossible, until he quickly learned to drive *through* the dune valleys instead of over them. Having travelled a great distance since starting out many hours ago, he wasn't sure how much fuel was left in the motorcycle as there was no fuel gauge. Judging that he'd likely used more than half of the tank, he silently prayed that it wouldn't run out before he could leave this terrible place. He briefly entertained the idea of continuing, but couldn't bring himself to go any further. He was stuffed, and wasn't comfortable with how little light the machine's small headlamp provided.

Pangs of hunger suddenly and painfully coursed through his body, and his stomach turned over and growled. It had been many hours since his last meal, and he remembered the food which he was carrying. Grabbing the knapsack next to him, he placed it between his legs and began rummaging through its contents. Finding the flashlight inside, he pulled it out and switched it on. The beam was bright, and it momentarily startled him.

Then he looked into the bag and found one of two packets of rations. The English writing on the sealed plastic stated that it was a 'Meal Ready-to-Eat'. Tearing it open with his teeth, he found that it contained a variety of food. The main course, grilled beefsteak, was inside of another plastic packet, which he quickly opened and then hungrily devoured. The meat tasted dry and rubbery, but he didn't care, and it wasn't long before he finished eating the remaining contents of the packet.

Feeling satiated, he shone the flashlight inside the knapsack, looking for the strange electronic device. Reaching for it at the bottom of the bag, he brought it out and pressed the Power On switch. The LCD screen came to life, flashing a message:

No Signal

He pulled at the long curly black locks of hair hanging over his eyes, trying to make sense of it. Then he remembered what the agent had told him only hours earlier, how the device needed a clear satellite reception.

Getting up, he walked a short distance and then checked the screen again. Finally a map of his current location blinked on. For a couple of minutes he studied the flashing black pixels that were moving slowly on the screen. One of them was forty-five kilometres away, while another was much closer, less than ten. His eyes lingered on the third and last indicator: It was stationary and eight hundred and fourteen kilometres from his current position. The large number caused a sickening sensation in the pit of his stomach, and he trudged back to the palm tree and fell to the ground against it.

Opening the knapsack, he brought out the water canteen and unscrewed the cap, then gulped down two big mouthfuls of the precious liquid. When he finished slaking his thirst, he decided he would rest a little longer before continuing on with his journey. He closed his eyes, and his thoughts drifted back to his far-away homeland.

***

Blaze Mullins was born in Lajamanu, a small Indigenous community in the Northern Territory of Australia. The town was first established as a welfare settlement in the 1950s, when the federal government forcibly relocated several hundred Warlpiri people from Yuendumu, another town almost six hundred kilometres to the south. The people were devastated at having been separated from their traditional land, and, in an amazing display of willpower and determination, they walked back the entire distance to Yuendumu. When they were rounded up and returned it resulted in yet another odyssey. After a second transport back to Lajamanu, the people finally decided to stay and the settlement was founded.

Blaze's father, George Tjupurrula Mullins, was an Aborigine of the Warlpiri people. As a young man, he had walked back with his family to Yuendumu on one of these extraordinary journeys.

His Anglo mother, born Emily Grace in Canberra, lived for a year in West Germany in 1975 to teach English. Six years later, she met her future husband after re-locating to Lajamanu as part of a bilingual education program.

George and Emily's union was untraditional by Warlpiri standards, and had been initially frowned upon as marriages were usually exclusive to the Aboriginal kinship group. Nevertheless, Emily soon became a much-loved and respected member of the small Warlpiri community.

However, it had been an entirely different story with Blaze's mother's parents, who all but disowned their daughter for her rebellious marriage to an "abo". Having only met them twice in his life, Blaze always regarded his grandparents barely above the level of strangers. He wasn't aware that inherent racism existed within his own family, until his mother brought him to Canberra for the first time. During his visit he was mostly ignored by his grandparents and cousins, and when they did speak he was derisively called a "yeller-feller", a half-caste. Their words were harsh and callous, and seemed to sink into his very bones. He never forgot it.

From an early age, Blaze was instructed by his father's family in the ancient traditions of his people. The Warlpiri's songs and stories about Jukurrpa, the Dreamtime, described the creation of all things, and he learned to recognize the songline trails which crisscrossed the countryside.

His father had been a drover, a stockman on a cattle station, which gave Blaze many opportunities to ride horses and herd livestock on a motorcycle. Some of his earliest fond memories were of he, his father and uncle participating in rodeos at Seven Mile, and swimming with his friends in the Catfish Waterhole not far from the town. For these few years of his young life he was a happy and carefree boy. But sadly, his contentment and stability would not last for very long.

When he was eight years old misfortune befell the Mullins family when George died suddenly of a heart attack. Just three years later, Emily was diagnosed with advanced breast cancer, and, despite several months of chemotherapy, she passed away.

For Blaze, losing his father, with whom he'd been very close, had been a very painful and traumatic experience. But when he also lost his mother, it was a crushing blow from which he was never able to fully recover. After her death, Blaze's Auntie Burilda moved into the

Mullins house to look after him, bringing along her own three young children.

At the small school he attended he didn't do particularly well in his studies. Maths, history, the sciences, he struggled with all of them, even with tutoring and the constant support of his Auntie. It resulted in his being painfully shy and keeping to himself. Unfortunately, his introversion only encouraged some classmates to tease and bully him for not being a full-blooded Warlpiri, and on more than a few occasions he was chased home from school. Yet there was one thing his tormentors could never do… *catch him.*

Blaze was an outstanding runner, being both very fast, and having incredible endurance. He could run for five kilometres straight without even breaking a sweat, and none of his classmates could ever hope to keep up. He was the best runner in Lajamanu, and probably the whole region, and he certainly lived up to his name.

It didn't take long before he became well-known in the Territory, winning several competitions by the time he was thirteen, and people began calling him jinta, meaning "one" or "winner" in Warlpiri. Some suggested he should try out for the Commonwealth Games, while others speculated the Olympics could be in his future. Regardless, for the first time in his young life, Blaze felt like he belonged, that finally he was worthy, and absolutely nothing but nothing could bring him down.

And then along came Darby Sims.

***

Darby Tjapaltjarri Sims arrived in Lajamanu during the winter of 1996, having left the southern town of Yuendumu to live with his extended family. A year older than Blaze, they first met when Darby began attending the only school in the community. Right from the start they didn't get along. In fact Blaze down-right hated the newcomer, and he quickly made it known to everyone.

One day a group of boys challenged Blaze to a race with Darby and he accepted, confident that he could not be beaten. However, he was stunned to find his opponent was not only as fast as he was, but indeed much faster.

The first half of the race they ran next to each other, despite Blaze's initial attempts to outrun him. He found it strange when the newcomer began casually talking to him, but was even more surprised to discover the bloke was actually quite friendly.

'Hey mate, you ever see the ocean?' Darby asked.

'No, have you?'

'Yeah, when I went to Darwin.'

'Fair dinkum?'

Darby nodded. 'It was really ace,' he replied.

'I always wanted to see the ocean. Did ya see any ships?' Blaze asked in-between huffs of air.

'Think so, maybe a couple. My uncle told me bout a ship that sank because of a cyclone few years back. They sent an SOS on the radio but everyone died.'

'SOS? What's that?'

'It's an emergency call when a ships' in trouble and needs help. Hey, maybe some time we could go to Darwin together, but only if you want.'

'Yeah, I'd like that,' Blaze replied, surprised by the sudden suggestion. It was then that he thought he might be actually starting to like the newcomer.

When the pair had run about halfway, Blaze was startled when, unexpectedly, the older boy rocketed away with spontaneous energy, disappearing from view over the horizon. It was almost like he'd been toying with Blaze all along. Upon reaching the finish, he was shocked to find the other boys waiting with Darby, who had arrived quite a few minutes ahead.

Blaze felt like he'd been set up and made to look a fool. Inside his chest, anger and humiliation swelled. One of the boys taunted him for coming in second, something which had never before happened, and he lost control, attacking him. Darby tried to intervene and Blaze struck him across the face. After that Blaze was no longer regarded in the community as jinta, the "winner", and he never thought the newcomer would talk to him again.

Darby, however, had instantly appreciated they shared a similar talent. Approaching Blaze in the schoolyard, he proposed teaching the other boy how to properly breathe whilst running. Instead of accepting the offer, Blaze angrily rebuked him out of pride. But a few days later he changed his mind and agreed, figuring it might give him the opportunity to redeem himself.

They began hanging about, although not a lot at first. Eventually the pair started running or walking long distances, which let them better get to know one another. Once they even ventured into the desolate Tanami desert. After they didn't return the police and trackers went looking. The worst had been feared, until a little more than a week later the two showed up, looking all the worse for the wear, but still alive nonetheless.

Whenever they ran in competitions together, they would each take turns letting the other win. Upon finishing a race, and no matter who the winner was, Darby would always repeat the same phrase, like a mantra, the meaning of which Blaze could never fully understand:

'This ain't the end... it's just the beginning.'

With each passing day of their friendship, their bond grew stronger and deeper. In time, Blaze discovered he not only felt an emotional attraction to Darby, but also physical desire. It was a secret he kept well-hidden.

***

The morning of their initiation ceremony Darby ran off to find a sacred and forbidden site. Blaze tried to stop his friend, warning of the trouble it would bring them, but Darby hadn't listened. After they'd gone a few kilometres from the campsite, they crossed a dried up river bed and ascended a steep hill. Once at the top they looked out across the vast expanse of the spinifex bushland. To the east, with the glow of the rising red sun behind it, their eyes fell upon Kulu – *Devil's Mountain*.

'There it is! I'll race ya to it!' Darby cried out excitedly. He took off down the side of the hill, running straight for the mountain. Blaze tried to catch up, but he was tired and his friend was simply going much too fast.

Upon reaching the mountain's base, Blaze stood in awe of its size and power. The thing rose jaggedly up from the ground, high into the air, looking like some giant red monstrosity trying to escape from the confines of the earth. Made of solid red granite rock, the mountain certainly appeared imposing and mysterious.

Blaze didn't know much about Kulu, apart from the legend the elder had told. The few things he'd heard were of people coming to this place and disappearing, never to be seen again, but he didn't believe any of the stories were actually true. But now that he was standing on the mountain's sacred ground he began to wonder if his assumption had been wrong.

Looking around, he didn't see any sign of his friend. 'Darby!' he shouted. There was no reply. Could Darby be playing another trick on him? If he was, Blaze thought, this was neither the time nor the place for it.

He began scaling the massive red boulders, until he found a ledge to pull himself up. As he moved further up the mountain he discovered it was a maze of tunnels and dark caverns, and he had to be very careful where he stepped as there were many deep holes and crevices.

'Darby!' he called again, his voice echoing off the rock walls. 'Where are ya mate?!' This time he heard a response. It was very low and distant, but it was definitely a voice crying out in reply. Following it he eventually found his friend at the bottom of a deep narrow crevice, and he looked to be in bad shape.

'Darby!'

'I—I got a bunged up leg, I think it's broken!' Darby shouted.

'What we gonna do?!' Blaze asked fearfully. He could see that Darby was in excruciating pain.

'Go back to the camp and get help!'

Tears began to well in Blaze's eyes. 'But, I don't wanna leave you!'

'Don't worry bout me,' said Darby, 'I'm not going anywhere!' Indeed, Blaze could see his friend spoke the truth, as he certainly wasn't.

Carefully, Blaze made his way down the mountain to the ground, and then he began running back to the campsite. The pair of them had been gone far too long, but that wasn't what worried him. He knew when his family and the elders heard where they'd gone, they would be extremely angry for their disobedience of tradition. As the elder had said, they would bring kurnta — a great shame on themselves and the community. The ritual ceremony the boys were supposed to undergo would not be completed, and they would never become men.

When Blaze returned with help Darby was nowhere to be seen. Inexplicably, he'd disappeared from the deep crevice — vanished without a trace. His body was never found, despite several attempts by the local police and trackers. For the whole community it was both sad and shocking, and the event only contributed to the terrifying mystery surrounding Devil's Mountain – that young Darby Sims had gone into the Never-Never, and would not be seen again.

After that, Blaze became a pariah within the community, and even beyond. His classmates, the other families and the elders shunned him. For three long torturous years he endured shame and humiliation, as well as the growing suspicion he'd killed his friend out of jealousy. It was an agony almost more than he could bear. And then, just three days ago, the woman named Anna had come to his house looking for his mother, putting events into motion he could never have for-seen.

***

In the dark of the African night, Blaze quietly sat underneath the date palm tree, wishing he could wake up from his dreams having forgotten the past. But he knew it wasn't to be. Once again his life had abruptly and severely changed into something he couldn't recognize or understand. Now his very survival depended upon him not only escaping from this desert nightmare, but also reaching the end, hundreds of kilometres away, before the others could get there first.

He knew he was currently ahead of the other competitors. Once their motorcycle fuel ran out they would be reduced to walking on foot, and he would have an advantage which they did not – he could outrun them. This time, however, he was in competition against unknown people, in the most important race of his life.

Deciding to rest a while longer before setting out again into the empty desolation, he shivered as a cold wind suddenly picked up, whistling through the palm trees and blowing sand about him. For just a brief moment he thought he could hear the Warlpiri elder speaking in the wind, warning him about kulkurru-kulkurru – a country without people.

FIVE

DAY 2 – Wednesday August 8, 2001
6:37 A.M.
16°26'09.9" 8°30'32.1"

THE COLD AND MOONLESS NIGHT had come and gone, and now, little by little, the dawning sun announced it had dominion over a new day. Long bands of gradually receding dark blue and purple-hued clouds streaked across the western African sky, replaced by the approach of fiery red, orange and golden yellow colours. It was at once striking and beautiful.

Dale Crumb was fast-asleep at the base of a collection of large basalt rocks, which rose out of the sand like brooding black monoliths. His previous day's journey across the soft rolling dunes had been long and arduous, but by the late afternoon the landscape eventually turned into flat hard ground. When the darkness came he found the motorcycle's small headlamp only provided a little light, and he became worried about striking a rock at high speed, and so he decided to stop and rest. The large rocks only offered slight protection from the cold wind, but it was still better than being out on the open sand. He had wanted to make a fire for warmth, but could find nothing to keep it going.

The only thing he'd been worried about were snakes hiding in the rock cracks. He'd already seen one zigzagging across the sand away from his speeding motorcycle. Dale had an intense fear of them, something he figured was a phobia. He was well-aware there were likely deadly poisonous ones to be found in this part of the world, but he was loath to kill one even if he was desperate for food.

A strange sound stirred him from his slumber. Slowly his eyes opened and adjusted to the dim light. He rubbed them vigorously, getting the annoying little particles of dust and sand out from the corners. It wasn't the droning hum of the UAV engine still high overhead which woke him, as he'd become accustomed to its constant presence. No, this noise was something entirely different. In the distance he saw vehicle headlights, getting brighter each moment they drew closer. Could it be one of the others, he wondered? Were they trying to get to him first?

He picked up the GPS which he'd left nearby. Studying the remaining two signals on its LCD screen, he became reasonably confident this was not one of his targets, as the flashing pixels told him they were still many miles ahead. It also didn't appear to have the single headlamp of a motorcycle. Getting to his feet, he pulled the knife out of its sheath. He wanted to be ready, just in case. When the vehicle was finally within eyesight, he saw it was a very large truck, completely weighted down with people piled on top and hanging off from its sides. It was a strange thing to see in this desolate place. But then again, so was he.

Figuring it was wise to not appear threatening, he sheathed his blade and moved close to the rocks. He briefly considered asking them for help, but the truck was travelling much too fast. They were not going to slow down for anyone, or anything. Instead, he raised his arm and waved as it passed by. The ghostly faces of those who weren't asleep peered silently at him with tired curious eyes.

And then as quickly as it had come the truck was gone. Seeing it lifted Dale's spirits somewhat, making him feel slightly less separated from the rest of the world. He lay back on the ground for a while longer, then drank some water and ate the food rations. When he was done, he stretched and contorted his legs and body, preparing his muscles for the grueling day ahead. Then, as the sun was breaking on the horizon, he looked out at the barren landscape.

What a miserable shithole this is, he thought. Having never been to Africa before, it wasn't a place he ever expected nor wanted to go. The name of the continent conjured for him repulsive images of starving children, disease and war. Africa might as well have been the planet Mars, as he'd been quite sure he would never go there either. The only place outside of America he'd ever gone was a month-long vacation to the south of France. Instantly he'd been enamored with the country, and visions of one-day owning a Mediterranean villa had played over in his mind ever since.

He glanced at the time on the GPS screen:

6:42 A.M.

Dale was determined to catch up to his next target, and he decided to get moving before the sun sapped his energy. He hadn't a clue how the eventual confrontation would play out, but was resolved to end it the same way as the last: he would be the victor, and they the defeated. There could be no compromise.

He gathered his supplies and then mounted the sleek black motorcycle. After turning the ignition key, he hit the kickstarter three times in succession before the engine suddenly growled back with a loud *Vroom!* The goggles were brought down over his eyes and he arched his head toward the sky, smiling when he saw the UAV hovering a few hundred feet above. 'Try to keep up!' he yelled to the drone, as he pushed away the cycle's kickstand. Revving the engine, he let go of the clutch and took off in a cloud of brown dust. Very soon he was zooming across the landscape at close to the motorcycle's top speed.

As Dale rode he thought of how he'd caught up to the German rider only three hours after they'd started out. The other man had tried to negotiate the sand dunes the hard way, struggling to go up and down them, while he had instead moved between the less problematic valley troughs. The poor bastard didn't even expect it until he was right on top of him. He chuckled under his breath, thinking the contest might be easier than he'd first assumed. After all, he thought, if he could survive the sharks on Wall Street, day after day, then he could handle just about anything.

***

When Dale was a child there was only one person in his family he felt an emotional bond with, and that was his grandfather. One day the elderly man read the boy an old book about the history of Wall Street. He was fascinated to learn the centre of American financial power was named after a wall built in the 17th century by African slaves to keep out invading tribes of Native Americans. In time, his interest with money and power would evolve into an obsession.

Though he was born in Charleston, West Virginia, Dale spent his early years living in a small house on the outskirts of Pittsburgh, Pennsylvania. Most of the time he desperately wanted to escape from his severely dysfunctional family. He never quite got along with his mother, who was a deeply religious woman, but exactly why he never understood. He guessed it was some deep resentment she harboured. Many times she informed him children were born of a sinful act, and that she regretted ever having him. It was the reason why he was an only child, she would tell him bitterly. He did love her very much, but she never returned it. He tried hard to be the son he thought she wanted, but it was to no avail as there was always a vast ocean of distance between them. Only later in his life would he realize some women were just not cut out for motherhood.

Dale's father was a Vietnam veteran, whose job was smelting iron in a blast furnace. Hardly ever at home, he could be found most evenings at local bars getting smashed. To cope with it his mother immersed herself in the safe confines of her Bible, accepting that this was the way things in the Crumb household were always going to be. But that was all to change.

One November morning, in 1981, the bottom fell out of Dale's world when his mother suddenly picked up and left, leaving him with his father. It had happened while he was sitting at the kitchen table, having breakfast and watching cartoons. She never even said goodbye. For many years after, Dale repressed the memory of this very traumatic event, purging it right from his mind.

Later on, his father informed him she had joined a new age Christian cult that had passed through the neighborhood. The group had promised enlightenment and redemption, but ultimately gave neither, only leaving a trail of empty souls and bank accounts in its wake. Dale didn't know if the story was true or not, but it didn't matter. He never saw nor heard from his mother again. He never forgave her.

His father endured by finding escape in bottles of J&B whisky. Prior to his wife leaving the man could easily have been certified an alcoholic. The drinking got worse, and he became physically abusive to Dale. For the young boy, his mother's departure only served to harden his heart and strengthen his resolve to succeed at all costs.

Slowly he cultivated an intense desire to be part of something bigger and more exciting than just following in the pathetic footsteps of his father. He wanted money. A lot of it.

In 1998, after graduating from the Pittsburgh College of Business on scholarship, he found mid-level employment in New York City at Chase Manhattan Bank. His aggressive mindset soon caught the attention of the executives at the established Allen Brown & Associates, who quickly brought him on board, and he prevailed to a more prominent position in the investment department of the historical banking institution.

One day at his office, he received a phone call telling him his father had succumbed to liver disease. He'd known for a long time he was dying, but upon learning the news he felt absolutely nothing. He didn't even bother to make the trip back home for the funeral. Now that his father was gone, for the first time he became truly alone in the world. Maybe it was then that something inside him changed, something which caused his moral conscience to just wither away and die. Deep down he was left with an empty void, and he didn't care in the slightest.

Being a member of the Young Republicans, Dale had campaigned for the Texas candidate, George W. Bush, in the presidential election of 2000. In January 2001, after the election turmoil had finally been resolved by the Supreme Court, he'd been excited to attend Bush's inauguration in Washington, but found himself disgusted by the anti-Americanism of the protestors, with their disrespectful shouts and throwing of eggs at the new president's limousine. But at the end of the day his team had won, just like a Steelers football game, and that was all that really mattered to him.

Women, drugs, money, and above all—power, the slick young insurance broker used and abused all of them until he was drunk with excess. Inside his clouded mind there had been no conceivable end in sight. And yet it had ended. His britches had gotten just too fucking big. Caught in a downward spiral which he hadn't recognized, in just a few short months his life had spectacularly crashed in similar fashion to the dead man he'd left behind in the sand. The fast lifestyle he'd grown accustomed to in the bustling Big Apple was in stark contrast to his present condition and surroundings.

For several months he'd been forging customer signatures on wire transfers authorized in their names, and then sending the money to a Swiss bank account. He made sure to only steal small amounts, usually twenty thousand dollars or less, just to keep himself under the radar. But the noose began to tighten when federal authorities announced they were beginning an in-depth audit of his office. Fearing he would soon be caught, and expecting criminal indictments for wire fraud, bank fraud, identity theft, and the embezzlement of thousands of investor dollars, he had made the decision to run. Eventually he was caught, but it hadn't been by 'the feds'.

***

After work, just a couple of nights ago, he'd gone to a bar near the Manhattan financial district for a few whisky shots with a fellow co-worker from Allen Brown, an accountant named Frank Dooley. Dooley was in his mid-30s and from the Bronx, and he spoke with a thick New York accent that Dale had grown accustomed to hearing on a near daily basis. Their talk, as usual, was of the day's business conducted at the firm. However, the conversation took a very unexpected and unusual turn when Dooley, after consuming one too many shots, confessed to Dale a stunning revelation…

'Did you hear about the spike in short sells last Thursday?' Frank asked. In banking lingo, short sells are put option purchases, essentially bets, where a seller speculates that the value of a particular stock price will drop.

'No, I didn't,' Dale replied. 'What were they for?'

'Over a hundred thousand for American Airlines and five thousand for UAL Corp.'

'UAL, that's United Airlines?'

'Yeah, the airline company. They were purchased through Chicago Exchange, expiry is in September.'

'Hmm, now that's interesting,' Dale mused aloud. 'Those are fucking big for a single day.'

'You ain't kiddin,' Frank said, chuckling as he lit a cigarette. 'Wanna know what else is interesting?' His voice lowered and he suddenly glanced around the bar to see if anyone was within earshot. 'The trades were placed with *our* firm. Chadwick ordered them for a German account holder.'

Mayo Chadwick was the CEO of Allen Brown & Associates. It wasn't totally unheard of for Dale or Frank to see trading orders personally placed by their boss, but they were usually done on behalf of the firm's wealthier high-end clientele.

'Yeah, so what about it?' Dale asked.

Frank leaned in close. 'Lemme tell you a little secret,' he whispered, 'Chadwick's using a slush fund account with a *billion* dollars in it.'

'What?' Dale exclaimed, incredulous.

'It's true, I swear on the grave of my dead mother I ain't lyin to you. I accidentally discovered it last year. Hey, you can't tell anyone about this, you understand me?'

'Who made the purchase?'

'I dunno,' Frank replied, blowing cigarette smoke, 'there's no name attached to the put options, or the account. It's completely off the SEC's radar, and every single god-damn payment from it goes right to Deutsche Trust in Frankfurt.' Their employer, Allen Brown, was a subsidiary investment firm of Deutsche Trust, which the powerful German bank had purchased in a merger just two years before.

Hearing this, Dale was very surprised. If this guy was telling him the truth, there was a billion dollars sitting inside of an electronic account at the bank where he worked, and it wasn't being monitored by the Securities and Exchange Commission. The money was virtually untraceable, at least officially. 'What do you think it means, about the airline put options?' he asked.

'Your guess is as good as mine,' Frank replied. 'But if you ask me, I think something *big* is gonna happen to American and UAL, either this month or the next, and someone else knows it.'

Dale knew he was suggesting that it was insider trading. Foreknowledge of an event, and then profiting on it financially, was a crime which happened often in stock markets all over the world. 'Have you told anyone else about this?'

Frank sucked on his cigarette. 'No, are you fucking crazy? Just you. Why, you gonna get in the game—steal the money and run?' he drunkenly asked with a chuckle.

Dale laughed off the suggestion; however, a plan had immediately begun taking shape in his mind:

Go big or go home.

Later that evening, after Dale made sure Frank was thoroughly intoxicated, he drove them to the man's upscale condo on the Upper East Side, then helped the staggering man inside. Setting Frank down on his living room sofa, he badgered him for the slush fund account number. After a few false starts, the nearly passed-out man finally blurted out the correct sequence of numbers, before falling fast asleep with his eyeglasses hanging from his face.

Then Dale acted swiftly. Using the man's laptop computer, which was already logged in to his Allen Brown account, he typed in the numbers in the search bar and hit the ENTER key. When it came up on the screen he saw that Frank had indeed been telling him the truth: nine hundred and ninety-three million U.S. dollars was sitting in an unregistered off-the-books account, with no sender or recipient of the funds listed. Dale couldn't believe his luck. It only took him a few moments to transfer the entire amount out of the account, depositing it into his own at the Swiss bank. It would take 24-hours to clear, of course, but he knew that if his plan went without a hitch, he would be long gone before anyone noticed. He would be almost a *billionaire*.

Snatching Frank's credit card, Dale set about going through the man's things, searching the bedroom and desk drawers until he found Frank's passport. Then he quickly left the condo, taking Frank's eyeglasses with him, and returned to his own apartment. After packing a light bag of clothing he caught a taxi to JFK airport.

When he came to the airline check-in, he put on the glasses and booked a red-eye flight to Paris with the stolen credit card and passport. The glasses hurt his eyes, but it was an important gamble to take. Nevertheless the plan had worked, and eight hours later his plane touched down at Charles de Gaulle Airport. He believed everything was falling into place. He'd left the U.S. under another name and arrived in Paris, convinced that by the time they discovered the money was missing, it would have cleared and be in his Swiss account ready for him to withdraw.

However, there had been a serious flaw in Dale's plan, and it was something he wasn't aware of and could never have understood. It was an outlier. An *unknown unknown*. The young investment banker had suddenly and unwittingly become just one component in a great conspiracy of immense historical significance, intertwined with dark and powerful agents of chaos.

At 3 A.M. on Tuesday August 7, just after exiting from the airport, he was seized and roughly shoved into a waiting black van. At that precise instant, when his neatly laid-out plans had collapsed into nothing, he had a brief terrifying moment of clarity and insight, and he was finally able to see his own small place in a much grander scheme of things. It was a glimpse of the unthinkable.

***

Now Dale was in the middle of Africa, far from home. There'd been nothing left for him in America; no family, no friends, no job. And there was even less for him here. *At least I'm still alive,* he thought. Though for how much longer was the big question.

As he drove the motorcycle across the flat terrain, the scorching heat of the sun was becoming unbearable, and he decided to stop and drink from the water canteen. After quenching his thirst, he checked the GPS and saw that the next target was very near, the flashing black pixelated dot indicating they were less than ten miles away. With excitement pulsing through his veins, he put the motorcycle back into gear and headed straight for them at full speed.

SIX

DAY 2 – Wednesday August 8, 2001
9:32 A.M.
17°6'19.44" 7°49'41.16"

C HARLIE RACED ACROSS THE DESERT, pushing the motorcycle to go as fast as he dared. The high, rolling sand dunes had mercifully been left behind hours ago, and now what stretched around him on all sides was a vast emptiness. Though he'd recently discovered what appeared to be crudely-made roads, there was nothing and no one else to be seen, and he drove onward.

He was no longer wearing the goggles, having accidentally left them behind on one of his many stops to rest. Early that morning he'd stumbled upon one of the strangest sights he'd yet seen in his journey. Sticking out of the ground, gradually being buried by the shifting sand dunes, was a World War II-era fighter plane, a British Hawker Hurricane, in almost perfectly preserved condition. Astounded, he stopped for a few minutes to investigate the incredible find, wondering if anyone else knew it was there. He concluded it must have been part of the North Africa Campaign during the war. The pilot likely strayed from the rest of his squadron and gotten himself lost. What a desolate place for the poor bugger to ditch his plane, he'd thought grimly. Peering inside the empty cockpit, he didn't see any remains of the former owner, something he was very much thankful for. Sadly, there hadn't been anything of value to be scavenged and he'd moved on.

As he travelled across the dusty expanse, his thoughts wandered back several months, to when he met the two individuals who'd gotten him into this whole mess: the German banker Ernst and his girlfriend Anna.

***

When Anna finally contacted him again, three months after her first phone call, she told him how she felt obligated to try and explain everything, and so he excitedly arranged to meet the mystery woman and her contact a few days later at The Lion's Tavern.

Arriving early at the pub, he passed the time as he waited by throwing darts and drinking a couple pints of lager. The appointed time of their meeting came and went, and he was about to leave, when all of a sudden a young man and woman quietly and discreetly walked in. They appeared very nervous as they looked about the almost empty bar, as if they would bolt out the door at the slightest provocation. Charlie instinctively knew right away that the girl was the one who'd called him on his mobile phone, and he waved the pair over.

'Mr. Grimer?' the woman inquired as she approached. 'I'm very sorry, our flight to London was delayed and we had to take precautions. We think we may have been followed.'

Immediately, Charlie recognized her by the accent. He looked the pair over. The girl was quite attractive, with dark eyes and long brown hair, and she couldn't have been much older than thirty. Beyond that, he thought her voice matched her looks. Her male companion had short blonde hair, bright blue eyes, and he appeared close to her age. 'Come on, we can talk over here.' He downed the remainder of his drink, and then led the couple from the bar to a non-assuming booth in a corner. Sitting down, he quickly made himself comfortable as the pair seated themselves on the opposite side. 'You don't mind if I smoke do you?' he asked, bringing out a cigarette and lighting it.

'No, of course not,' she replied, 'I sometimes smoke myself, but usually only when I'm nervous.'

Charlie's mouth twisted into a crooked smile. 'I've tried quitting before, must be about a hundred times now. You know how it is,' he said, blowing a puff of smoke. He glanced at her hand and noticed it was trembling. Picking up his cigarettes, he held them out for her.

'Please… just take one.' She took one out and Charlie lit it. 'Well, I suppose we should begin, right from the very start.'

'First, thank you for meeting with us. My name is Anna, and this is my fiancé, Ernst.' The young man nodded, only offering a weak smile in return.

'What's the matter with him?' Charlie asked, motioning toward Ernst. 'Isn't he going to talk?'

'Ernst is the one who made the discovery, but he doesn't speak any English. I will be doing the talking for him.'

Upon Anna's urging, Ernst started speaking and she translated his words. He began by telling about himself and his background, and of his employment at Deutsche Trust in Frankfurt. What he next recounted to Charlie was indeed a very strange story…

The previous July, Ernst was in his office one morning when he was notified of a new message in his email inbox. Checking it, he saw that it was from someone named Frank Dooley at Allen Brown & Associates, a New York subsidiary bank of Deutsche Trust. The short message said:

> Hello. I discovered a SWIFT payment order to
> your branch that needs double-checking. The
> involved parties are not showing in my records.
> Can you look into this and get back to me?
> Thanks. – Frank

Below it was a transaction number.

At first glance the email had not been surprising to him. The last few months he'd been steadily working on the complex integration of Allen Brown into Deutsche Trust's Securities Brokerage division following their recent merger. It was quite common for him to exchange back and forth emails with his Wall Street associates in a single day. Because he couldn't speak any other language, he used a feature of the bank's internal email system to automatically translate any incoming messages into German, and his replies into English.

After entering the transaction number he saw that it was a payment order for fifty-five million U.S. dollars, from an account at the Allen Brown branch in New York to the Deutsche Trust headquarters in Frankfurt. He had easily seen far bigger transactions before, but this was a sizeable amount. However, Anna said, what had really caught Ernst's attention, was that the authorization for the order had apparently been made by his own boss, the CFO Stefan Ackermann. Right away, it was apparent to him that it was a deliberate "off-the-book" transaction, something which was very much illegal.

'Wait a minute,' Charlie interrupted, 'why was it illegal?' He patiently waited as she translated his question for Ernst.

'He says that the payment order had not been registered with the agency which monitors SWIFT payments to and from Germany,' Anna replied. 'Mistakes happen all the time, and it was possible it was a simple oversight. However, he says that in addition to the payment not being registered, the spaces where the names of the sender and recipient should have been were instead left blank. That is illegal.' Charlie nodded his head, and asked the young man to continue.

Ernst said that he certainly had no desire to stir up trouble, or to endanger his own employment at the bank. Indeed, he was entirely ready to forget about the illegal transaction, and so he emailed Frank Dooley back with a simple message assuring him that he would look into the matter. However, he told Charlie, as strange as the confusing email seemed to be, things were about to get much stranger.

Later that same day, at the conclusion of a boardroom meeting, Ernst just happened to overhear Ackermann engaged in a mobile phone conversation. Speaking in a low, barely audible voice, the CFO said that in the coming days there would be an extremely large burst from the sun, a solar flare, and there would be a very good chance the resulting geomagnetic storm would affect Frankfurt's power grid. If that happened, Ackermann said, the bank's computer system could be seriously damaged. He told the listener on the other end of the phone that he'd made arrangements for the computer servers to be upgraded with a shield to protect them.

Ernst said to Charlie that he didn't know a great deal about the sun, or even astronomy in general, but he was quite certain solar flares could not be predicted with any reasonable amount of accuracy. But Ackermann had sounded absolutely certain speaking on the phone that the event was going to occur. It wasn't "if" it was going to happen – but "when".

He puzzled over how the CFO of a bank would know about such a strange thing. Could it be, Ernst wondered, that he simply had a friend who worked for NASA? Stefan Ackermann knew a great many people, including scientists, politicians and even some celebrities. It was not an outrageous idea to think he'd been warned by any one of them. Deciding that must be the answer, he promptly put it out of his mind and forgot about it.

'Excuse me,' Charlie interrupted, 'I don't understand what this has to do with anything. Where is all of this leading?' He was getting anxious, and he still had many important questions to ask before the night was done.

'Please bear with him, Mr. Grimer. He's getting there,' Anna assured him, before continuing on with the translation of Ernst's story.

Just a week later, Ernst was again at his office computer, when he was alerted to another email in his message inbox. Opening it, he saw the email was from a man named Günter, who worked for a Frankfurt company called CONVEX. The sender identified himself as the network administrator for Deutsche Trust who managed all of the bank's computers and intranet operating system. The short email simply said:

> Mr. Ackermann, the adjustments to the
> servers have been made. Here is the
> updated list you requested. – Günter

The message was addressed to Stefan Ackermann, but had somehow also been mistakenly sent to Ernst through the BCC, or blind carbon copy feature of the email system. Ernst explained to Charlie that when a message is sent with BCC, the primary recipient is not aware of other recipients to the email. Below Günter's message was an attachment file which Ernst, without thinking, promptly clicked. When the file opened, he saw a list of the personal details and intranet user names and passwords for all of the executive managers and their assistants at the Deutsche Trust Frankfurt headquarters, including, to Ernst's total astonishment, his own.

Ernst's initial reaction was to believe that a very big mistake had been made. First off, he didn't understand why the CFO was in contact with the bank's network administrator, as he knew there were others in the company who had the job of making sure the computer system was functioning properly. Secondly, and more importantly, there was no way the network administrator should have been sharing private employee account details with any other employee of the bank, no matter *who* they were. And yet there was the email staring Ernst in the face. And to make matters worse, Ackermann had apparently asked for the information—and then been given it.

Instantly, Ernst was in a conundrum, not knowing what to do. He briefly wondered if Günter, by marking the email as a blind carbon copy, was trying to tip someone off about what was going on, that the staff in the executive office was being spied upon. He wasn't aware that anyone else had received the same email, and so he kept his mouth shut.

He realized that he couldn't outright ask Ackermann about an email containing evidence of criminal activity by him and the network administrator. He also knew that he could not inform the authorities about it unless he did so anonymously. Regardless, the company would eventually discover that it was him, and if that happened his future with the bank would have been finished.

Instead, Ernst decided to simply delete the damning message from his email inbox and try to forget he'd even seen it in the first place. But just before doing it he glanced one last time at the account details of his boss, Stefan Ackermann. The login password the man had chosen for himself was "versprechen", the German word for "promise".

Later that evening, he was watching the news with Anna when he was completely dumbfounded to hear that an extremely powerful X-class solar flare had erupted from the sun. Fifteen minutes after it happened, the TV news anchor said, a storm of plasma travelling at four million miles per hour slammed into the Earth, disrupting GPS navigational satellites and damaging power grids. It was described as one of the largest, most powerful solar eruptions in modern history, and the media were already calling it "The Bastille Day Event", after the French national day celebrating the Revolution.

Ernst said that he couldn't believe what he'd heard. His boss had known for a fact the sun was going to erupt an entire week before it actually happened. As soon as the news report finished he told Anna about what Ackermann stated on the phone that, without question, there would be a solar flare. However, it wasn't going to be just any solar flare, his boss had said, but an immensely powerful one. And there it was on the evening news they'd just watched.

Anna had laughed at him, brushing it aside as just being a coincidence. At any other time Ernst might have written it off and forgotten about it. In fact, the young man said to Charlie, he *should* have. But he didn't. After telling Anna about the two emails, that he'd been sent potential evidence of an illegal transaction approved by Ackermann, and then the password list from the bank's network administrator, she suggested something he hadn't expected: report him. He could become a so-called 'whistleblower', she said, and take what he knew to the supervisory agency who would likely investigate. He would have to do it anonymously, of course, but it could be done. After an investigation Ackermann would be fired and then Ernst could take his place as the new Chief Financial Officer.

At first Ernst was reluctant. When he said to her that what she was suggesting was incredibly risky, that it could destroy the life they were trying to build for themselves, she reminded him that his life, indeed his very career was about taking risks.

For three days he mulled over what course of action to take. Ultimately, he decided he needed to find more evidence, except this time he knew the password on his boss's computer. Ernst was smart enough to realize that he couldn't risk logging on to Ackermann's account from his own computer terminal. Now that he was aware the employees were being spied upon, they could be alerted to it, and if they checked he would be caught out. But he did have an emergency key-card in his possession, one which would get him into the CFO's office. If he could use Ackermann's own computer, the chance of his employers discovering his intrusion was less likely. The network administrator would assume nothing was improper, and it would just be ignored. He was keenly aware there was still a risk involved, but it was one he was willing to gamble.

Late at night, Ernst went to his workplace at the twin tower headquarters of Deutsche Trust. He'd spent countless long nights there, sometimes even working until the early hours of the next day. It certainly wasn't difficult for him to get past the security guards, since his appearances had become so routine over the last few months that all of them knew him by name.

As he expected there was no one around, save for a lone cleaner busily vacuuming the floor. Using the key-card, he entered Ackermann's office, made himself comfortable in the man's large executive chair, and then turned on the computer. The password "promise" had worked, and Ernst successfully logged in as Ackermann. When the account came up on the screen he was surprised to discover the computer was on a private server not connected to the bank's network. Next, he began inspecting the programs on the desktop, looking for the main message centre.

Right away one of the programs stood out from the rest, only because he'd not seen nor heard of it before. The name of it was the same as Ackermann's login password, Versprechen, or Promise, and he clicked on the icon to open it. When the program started, Ernst saw that it was unlike anything he'd ever encountered before. After clicking through it he came to the realization he was looking at a huge database showing thousands of private real-time transactions taking place between several of the top financial institutions in the world. He was astonished at the discovery, as no one else in the executive office, indeed anywhere at Deutsche Trust, was using a program like this. He told Charlie it was the kind of technology he would expect a spy agency to use. It was then that Ernst realized the depth of Ackermann's criminality was far deeper than he could have possibly imagined. If his boss's use of the illegal program was exposed to the authorities the man would most certainly be prosecuted.

As Ernst studied the Promise program he found that it had its very own messaging system containing Ackermann's private emails. Taking a deep breath, he clicked on the folder and began to go through them. Most of the recent ones the CFO had received were standard business-as-usual, except for one in particular, sent that very day, which caught Ernst's eye. There was no name for the sender, and not even an email or IP address in the header, which struck Ernst as very odd. The message was a simple list which appeared to be updating Ackermann with obvious inside information. It read:

> Satellite launch successful with no interference
> from solar storm; Brother Campbell has been dealt
> with, he will be resigning Tuesday; Funds received
> in UAE, Pakistan and Hamburg, wait for more
> instructions; The British are on board with Iraq.
> Paris will not be joining us; Confirmed that Chirac
> will be removed on the 25th. Watch for it... it's
> going to be *big*.

Ernst believed the sender was talking about the recent solar flare, but he didn't understand the significance of the satellite, or who Campbell was, and why he was referred to as "brother". As for the rest of the message, he assumed they were alluding to more illegal money transfers authorized by Ackermann. However, he wondered what the sender of the email meant about Iraq. Was there going to be another war in the Middle East? And what did they mean by Chirac being "removed"? It sounded to Ernst like someone was planning to *assassinate* the French president, Jacques Chirac, and they were informing Ackermann about it.

Ernst recounted to Charlie how he'd sat in the executive chair for a while, in stunned disbelief, staring at the words on the computer screen. He wanted to know who the sender was, but there was absolutely nothing to go on. He looked over the message again and again, trying to imprint every single word upon his memory.

After reading through several more emails, he stopped. He'd seen enough and wanted to leave immediately. Paranoia was seeping into his thoughts, and he began to feel vulnerable, as if the security guards would burst into the room at any moment and seize him. Logging out from the computer, he turned it off and then quickly left Ackermann's office, making sure not to be seen. As he rode the elevator down to the ground floor, it dawned on him that he now had many more disturbing questions, but even fewer answers.

Arriving back home, he woke Anna from her sleep and excitedly informed her about his breaking into Ackermann's office and computer, and of everything he'd seen and read. He told her about the Promise program, and of Ackermann's ability to illegally monitor private real-time transactions. Together they talked about what they should do, or if anything should even be done at all.

As if in answer, the next day he and Anna heard from a TV news report that the leader of the Scottish National Party in the UK, Duncan Campbell, had suddenly and unexpectedly resigned. The name 'Campbell' resonated in Ernst's mind, and he realized that it was likely the same person referred to in the email to Ackermann.

'At that moment,' Anna said to Charlie, 'I knew that Ernst was telling me the truth. The night before, when he came home from the office, he told me everything he'd read. There's no possible way he could have known about this Scottish man's resignation the day before it happened.'

'Yes, I understand that, but what does Ackermann have to do with Duncan Campbell?' Charlie asked. Anna translated the question for Ernst, who thought about it for a moment before answering.

'He said he doesn't know,' she replied. 'Except... the email stated Campbell had been 'dealt with'.'

'I see. So you think either he or his family was threatened, and that's why he resigned?'

Anna didn't answer, but she didn't need to. Charlie could tell from the look in her eyes she believed he was correct.

Charlie shifted uncomfortably in his seat. 'I—I should tell you...'

'What?'

'You were right, what you said to me on the phone—tried to warn me about. I checked into it. They did try to kill Chirac.'

'How?'

'The Concorde crash. When it was taking off it almost struck a plane on the runway carrying him on his return from the G-8 Summit. They haven't told the public about it.'

'Oh my God,' she said under her breath, and then translated it for Ernst. For a minute after the three sat in shocked silence.

Charlie sighed deeply and put his face into his hands. After three long, harrowing months, it had finally come down to the single moment he'd been waiting for, and he was desperate to hear from her the answer to his next question: 'How did you know about my wife—that she was going to leave me?' he asked, with tears filling his eyes.

Once again Anna translated for Ernst, and when the young man answered she repeated his words directly to Charlie.

'Because,' she said, 'after we saw on the news about the resignation of Campbell, the next thing they talked about was the phone hacking scandal here in the UK, and they showed your photo. One of the other emails I'd read—was about *you*.'

Surprised at this revelation, Charlie's mouth fell open, and he almost fell right off the bench.

'Yes, it's completely the truth,' Anna continued. 'Ernst said to me he'd read a message to Ackermann about "the meddling journalist Grimer", that they'd arranged for your wife to meet someone—that she was going to leave you.' She looked down at the table, knowing that her words were cutting into Charlie like a very sharp knife. For a few moments after all he could do was sit in disbelief, looking like a deeply broken man.

Anna went on. 'I suggested to Ernst that I had a friend at the agency where I work who could probably get your phone number, and she did. Please understand, Mr. Grimer, that when I said to you on the phone your wife was going to leave you, it was the only way I could make you believe us.'

'Oh, I believe you,' said Charlie. 'I'm sorry that I didn't before, but I do now.'

She leaned over the table. 'There's more... You and other British journalists are being secretly spied on by the police. They are keeping a database of your family's private information.'

Charlie wasn't surprised to hear that. After all, he'd already figured long ago that Scotland Yard was keeping tabs on him because of the trouble he'd caused. 'Probably tapping my phones too,' he said cynically.

'What if they heard our conversations?' she asked, nervously.

'There's nothing we can do about it now. It's a risk we'll just have to take.' Charlie took a quick glance at the remaining patrons in the pub, looking for any strange faces he didn't recognize. He didn't think there was, but still, he suddenly found himself feeling very anxious and vulnerable. There it was again, he thought, his old friend paranoia, slowly crawling its way back into his thoughts, growing and spreading like some hateful disease. Just who the hell *are* these people giving his boss all of this information?' he asked, gesturing in her fiancés direction.

'He doesn't know, but he can try and find out,' she replied.

'I have just one more question... Has he gone back into Ackermann's computer?'

With a furtive glance about the pub, Anna suddenly opened her purse and retrieved what looked to Charlie like a small rectangular black piece of plastic. She set it down gently on the table in front of them.

'What's that?' Charlie asked.

A smug smile came across her face. 'Evidence.'

Charlie picked it up and turned it over in his hands. On the sides of it were printed the word "ThumbDrive".

'It's new technology,' she said. 'It's called a USB thumb drive. Basically, a storage medium you plug into your computer to transfer information. On it are some of the emails from Ackermann's computer, including the ones which led us to you. Unfortunately, they are all written in German.'

'That's fine,' he replied, snatching the USB and placing it inside his shirt pocket. 'I know someone who can help me out with that.' Then he leaned in close and whispered just loud enough for the couple to hear him. 'This is what needs to be done next. Ernst needs to go back in there and get more evidence, whatever he can find. Save it to one of these thumb drives and mail it right to me, and only me.'

She translated this to Ernst, who shook his head and said, 'Nein, ich schicke Ihnen eine e-mail.'

'He says he can just email you whatever he finds.'

'Can he send it encrypted?' asked Charlie.

Ernst nodded. 'Ja, verschlüsselt.'

'That's good. But for God's sake, whatever you do, *do not* email me from your workplace, or your home. Go to a library or internet café. And from now on we cannot talk on the phone again, understood?'

'Yes,' Anna answered.

From inside his jacket Charlie brought out a pen. He grabbed a napkin and wrote down his email address, then handed it over to her. 'Now, this part is very important,' he said. 'If something goes wrong and you need to meet with me in-person, I want you to email me and use the code-phrase "dark actors playing games".'

'Dark actors playing games?' she repeated, confused.

Charlie nodded and leaned in close, lowering his voice to just above a whisper. 'When I was working for the tabloids and thought my phone conversations were being tapped, I would use that phrase if it was necessary to meet someone face-to-face. It's worked many times in the past.'

'I understand,' said Anna.

'Now if that should happen and you need to talk to me, I will fly to you in Germany. But we need to decide on a place to meet. Can you think of somewhere we can go in public, some place there's a lot of people?'

Thinking for a moment, she then remembered a favourite place from her youth: 'The Marienplatz in Munich,' she answered. 'It's the main square of the city. There's a gold statue of the Virgin Mary on top of a column.'

Charlie nodded in agreement. 'All right, Munich it is then. Exactly twenty-four hours after you email me, using *only* that code-phrase, I will meet you there.'

The couple briefly spoke to each other. Then Anna looked to Charlie and said, 'We should leave now, but there's one final thing I want to tell you that's in the emails, something written with complete confidence and certainty.'

'What is it?' asked Charlie.

'The next U.S. president—it's going to be George W. Bush,' she stated, matter-of-factly.

And with that, the German couple quickly exited the pub, ending Charlie's first, and only, meeting with Ernst and Anna. Over the next eight months Ernst emailed Charlie several times, and each new message carrying the stolen emails had grown darker, and become even more sinister. Slowly, the three of them struggled to piece together the puzzle of an elaborate conspiracy that was threatening to imminently engulf the world.

***

DAY 2 – Wednesday August 8, 2001
12:57 P.M.
16°37'07.2" 7°05'01.9"

The noonday African sun had reached its zenith, and the heat was searing and intense. Near the edge of a roughly-made road, Charlie sat cross-legged on the dusty ground in the shade of his motorcycle. He was fervently chewing on a Snickers bar, the last item from the meal packet, and now he was savoring each and every bite of the gooey chocolate. He knew he would soon have to find more food, but he hadn't the faintest clue where.

For a long while he hadn't seen any significant wildlife, apart from the occasional bird flying overhead. Hours ago, in the early morning, he'd come across some kind of antelope with great big horns that had been roaming alone, searching for food or water. The beast looked very thin and near death, and it struggled to run away upon hearing the sound of his motorcycle. Charlie felt an immediate bond with the poor, pathetic creature. He'd considered trying to put it out of its misery, but decided instead to keep driving. Only now was he beginning to realize the potential folly of his decision.

Above him the UAV was still flying in wide circles, its engine whirring as it kept a holding pattern while he rested. Charlie just ignored it. He had tried a few times to outrun the thing. But it was no use, as the advanced flying machine was simply too fast and was always within sight, flying parallel to whatever direction he travelled.

He gulped a mouthful of water from the canteen, washing the rest of the chocolate down his dry throat, when, unexpectedly, a buzzing noise caught his attention. Twisting his head around, he shielded his eyes from the sun and looked across the expanse. In the distance, he saw a motorcycle bearing down on him at an exceedingly fast rate. High above it was the familiar white shape of a UAV, and it too was moving in his direction. Charlie's stomach turned over. Someone had caught up to him.

Quickly, he gathered his things and shoved them into his knapsack, then scrambled to his own motorcycle. After mounting it, he took the kickstand off, turned the ignition key, and tried starting it. Nothing happened. Kicking at it again only produced the same result. Whipping his head around, he saw that the oncoming rider appeared to be a man, and he was now only a short distance away.

'Come on... Come on,' Charlie muttered. 'Start Godammit.' He tried again, but the machine just grumbled back at him disapprovingly. *Why is this happening to me now?* he wondered with growing panic. He glanced behind him. *Close. Too close.* 'Christ, he'll be right on top of me in a moment!' he cried aloud, frantically. He could see the other man was not slowing down in the slightest, appearing intent on crashing right into him. Again he tried to start his cycle, and again it was the same outcome: nothing.

Charlie became desperate, almost abandoning the cycle to make a run for it, when he decided to make one final attempt. He hit the kickstarter with his foot as hard as he could. Just as the other rider was about to collide with him, Charlie's motorcycle suddenly sprang to life with a screeching howl, and he zipped out of the other cycle's way at the last moment.

Letting out a huge sigh of relief as he held on to the handlebars for dear life, he spun his head around so that he could get a good look at the other rider. The man was wearing goggles, just like the ones he'd also been given (and now lost), and a long black scarf covering his face was whipping in the wind. For a brief moment Charlie thought he heard the other man laughing.

'Are you completely fucking mad?!' Charlie shouted at him.

There was no reply. Instead, the other rider circled around in a wide arc, getting ready to come at him again. Revving the motorcycle's engine, Charlie took off.

He knew they were one of the other competitors who'd somehow managed to catch up to him, and he harboured no doubts about what they were trying to do: they wanted to kill him.

For what felt to him like an eternity, Charlie weaved and manoeuvred across the terrain, hoping against hope the other rider would abandon pursuit, or, even better, strike a wayward rock and be thrown. But he could see the man was not going to give up easily, and he wondered how long he could keep driving before one of them ran out of fuel.

All of a sudden everything around Charlie darkened, and he almost fell off the motorcycle. Looking around to find the source, he saw that a massive wall of sand several kilometres high was almost upon him. 'Oh my God!' he exclaimed in fear and awe.

The billowing clouds of sand, dust and dirt extended across Charlie's entire field of vision as far as his eyes could see. It was an incredible sight, and, though he'd known such things existed, it was like nothing he'd ever seen before in his life. This was a sandstorm called a haboob, made by the downdraft of a collapsed thunderstorm and most commonly seen in the dry, arid regions of the world.

For a moment Charlie hesitated, not knowing what to do. His gut instinct was to turn his motorcycle around and drive in the other direction to get away, but he saw the storm was already too close and would quickly overtake him. Glancing behind, he saw the other rider was just several metres away and closing rapidly. But because the man was so focused on catching up, it didn't appear they'd yet seen the oncoming storm.

'All right Charlie-boy, it's now or never,' he said to himself, as his adrenaline rushed. Pulling his scarf over his nose, he pivoted his machine to directly face the giant looming clouds. Without a second thought, Charlie revved the motorcycle's engine and headed straight for the storm as fast as his machine could go.

The noise of it sounded to him like thousands of roaring angry demons from Hell, becoming almost unbearable to his ears. His scarf suddenly blew away and was quickly carried off on the wind, never to be seen again. Dust and sand blasted against his face, ripping at his skin and getting into his eyes so that he couldn't see a single thing. But still he kept going. As the storm engulfed Charlie, the intense blowing winds suddenly became overwhelming and he crashed to the ground in a spectacular wipe-out.

Then an all-embracing darkness came over him.

SEVEN

DAY 2 – Wednesday August 8, 2001
1:30 P.M.
16°32'04.7" 7°04'30.9"

T HE PAIR OF UAV DRONES hovered just above the swirling sandstorm, their on-board cameras using infrared thermal imaging to observe Charlie and Dale, whose body heat signatures appeared in hues of yellow, pink and red on the video screens of the Watchers. 'BETA and DELTA are less than five hundred metres away from each other,' Metatron informed the audience, in a calm speech-modulated voice. 'As you can see from their vital statistics both men are still alive, though the sandstorm has temporarily rendered them immobile.'

The images of the two figures on the screen changed to a single one showing Blaze racing his motorcycle down a long paved road.

'ALPHA has significantly increased his lead and is nearly one hundred kilometres away from the others. At present there is a seventy-seven per cent chance he will be the winner, but that could change in the blink of an eye.'

The Watchers listened in suspense to the Artificial Intelligence as the camera zoomed out to show a detailed topographic map of the Sahel region of north-west Nigeria.

'The fuel tank of ALPHA's motorcycle will soon be empty, forcing him to move on foot through the predator-filled savannah that lies ahead. Then we will see exactly what he is made of.'

The screen switched back to the UAVs above the sandstorm, which appeared to be slowly dissipating in strength. When it was finally clear the thermal imaging was turned off. The camera zoomed in on the body of BETA, who was stirring on the ground. For a few seconds he struggled to stand up, and then he staggered to his motorcycle which was lying half-buried in the sand.

The video transmission changed to a first-person viewpoint, allowing the Watchers to look directly through the man's eyes as he looked for any sign of his opponent, but nothing could be seen except desolation. He studied the GPS, and, after slinging his knapsack over his shoulder, he began to run.

'It appears BETA's vehicle is damaged and not functional, but he is still competing in The Game,' Metatron said to the audience. 'Will he survive the desert long enough to catch up to ALPHA, or will DELTA finish his task? Time will tell…'

Transparent numbers counting down appeared across the Watchers video screens, informing them the remaining competitors still had more than four days left to go. None had any idea who would be the eventual winner, or how The Game would finish. Ultimately, it mattered not whether anyone made it all the way to the end, for the only things the mysterious ones desired to see were blood—and much suffering.

***

The Syndicate is an ultra-secret consortium of three hundred of the most powerful and wealthiest individuals from around the globe, representing top royal families and the biggest banks and corporations. Overseen by an even more secretive council of nine, the group is called The Syndicate, or Watchers, by the few outsiders who know of their existence. However, their true name is known only unto them.

Their founding can be traced back to the medieval Templar Knights, and later the Bavarian Illuminati of the 1700s, but exactly how long the group has been around in its present form is a complete mystery. In the last century they were linked to the rise of the Nazis, but their evil tentacles encompass and spread through many hidden societies who, according to their powerful will, secretly bend the arc of human history.

As a whole they constitute an unknown breakaway civilization, with unlimited power and in possession of a variety of exotic cutting-edge technologies that are centuries ahead of the rest of mankind. The shadowy group are super-capitalist transnational elites with a fascist ideology, whose allegiance was to no one but themselves. Their ultimate goal is the absolute and total destruction of their superpower enemies, Russia and China, thus achieving supreme domination of the planet. They will let nothing stand in their way.

A little more than a decade earlier, in 1989, the mysterious cabal used their vast wealth and resources to capitalize on the impending collapse of the Soviet Union. That year they secretly built the world's first quantum computer, a machine able to process photonic multi-qubit information on the subatomic scale. This supercomputer was many orders of magnitude in power above anything else at the time, and was amongst the greatest achievements in all of human history.

Having cost several trillion U.S. dollars to create, the supercomputer had an unbelievable computing speed in the zettaflop range, capable of one sextillion calculations per second, and was also able to store seemingly infinite amounts of information. Its entire network of five hundred servers was securely contained deep beneath a mountain in the Swiss Alps, and, although it was rumoured to be near the CERN headquarters and border with France, exactly which mountain is one of the greatest of secrets. Even the members of The Syndicate didn't know for themselves its precise location.

However, with this incredible far-reaching technology at their disposal, The Syndicate next began an enterprise with an even bigger ambition, which they called The AIM Project. The end result was the supercomputer's creation of an Artificial Intelligence program they named METATRON, which was itself an acronym for Mass Electronic Tracking with Artificial Thought Response and Observation Network.

The program was given the entire history of humanity to analyse, thousands of years of military, economic and geo-political research, and it was continuously provided with all information collected by Western military and spy agencies using the secret ECHELON world surveillance network. All private phone calls and emails; internet activity; bank transactions; music, films, television and radio shows; even CCTV cameras and advanced spy satellite imaging were captured and sent to Metatron for study. The one and only thing the supercomputer didn't have access to was the regular postage mail, but that was where The Syndicate's agents came into action.

Two years after its inception, on July 1, 1991, a truly extraordinary event took place: a technological singularity was achieved when the AI's vast neural network suddenly became self-aware. After this happened, the powerful entity's sole given purpose was to figure out how its creators could dominate the world, and it achieved this by *predicting the future*. Metatron factored and calculated everything that happened on the planet, indeed the entire solar system, allowing it to predict future probabilities and possibilities that The Syndicate could then exploit.

A year after attaining self-awareness, Metatron began its mission by successfully engineering the infamous "Black Wednesday" sterling crash which cost British taxpayers over £3.4 billion. Then the AI made significant discoveries which furthered its creators understanding of the universe, such as the Higgs boson particle and the true nature of dark matter and dark energy. But these remarkable things were held as closely-guarded secrets.

It wasn't long before The Syndicate realized Metatron was like a young child, still learning about the universe and its own place in it, so they introduced the AI to a variety of games to help it better understand the behaviour of humans and the choices that they make. Then the entity would be able to further refine with almost infinite precision its own calculations and predictions.

Thus it was that in the year 1994, after three years of processing gigantic endless volumes of data, Metatron finally presented The Syndicate with a clear path to follow: The Stratagem, a sinister twenty-five year blueprint for world conquest.

EIGHT

5 DAYS AGO – Friday August 3, 2001
MUNICH, GERMANY
10:55 A.M.

I N THE MARIENPLATZ, Munich's historical city square, Ernst Jaeger was standing behind an arched stone column, trying his best to remain unnoticed while scrutinizing the steadily increasing numbers of people. He was looking for any sign of the British journalist, Charlie Grimer, but it was no easy task. Despite a light drizzle of rain, a couple of hundred tourists milled about the large open expanse, many of them gathered in front of the Rathaus-Glockenspiel, Munich's famous clock tower. It was about to chime on the hour, and everyone was waiting to see the over thirty mechanical figures begin to re-enact a 16th century wedding celebration.

His laptop computer bag was slung across his body, and he gripped its strap tightly as he nervously glanced at a nearby bank branch of Deutsche Trust, his former employer. As he looked about at the people in the square, a strong sensation came over him that he was being watched, and he pulled the cap he was wearing down low.

Earlier that morning Anna departed for Rome, and she took with her one of the two thumb drives containing the evidence. They'd both agreed to hide the USB sticks inside rented storage lockers, just in case anything went wrong. But instead of keeping with the game plan, Ernst thought it would be quicker and easier to just hand it over to Grimer. Apprehensively, he put his hand inside his coat, making sure the USB was still there. It was, and the knowledge gave him slight comfort that he still retained at least some control of the dangerous situation.

Out of the corner of his eye he caught movement of something coming rapidly towards him, and it caused him to jump. His eyes quickly darted over to it. It was only a little girl, happily running with a pair of red balloons. He exhaled deeply, trying his best to calm his nerves from the intense paranoia he was feeling.

The previous day, after he and Anna fled their Frankfurt apartment, they were shot at by unknown assassins. Driving south on the autobahn until they reached the city of Stuttgart, they left the car behind in an empty alley and hired a taxi to go the rest of the way.

At his urging, their original plan had been to put as much distance as possible between themselves and Europe. Once they were done meeting with Grimer in Munich, the couple would go to Rome together, to the airport and then on a plane to far-off Australia. However, believing the police were probably after him, he changed his mind at the last moment, thinking it would be better to separate and make it harder for them to get caught.

On that Friday morning, just before making his way to the Marienplatz, Ernst said goodbye to Anna for what he grimly sensed would be the last time. After promising each other they would reunite, she told him the name of the town in Australia he would find her, and then she hurriedly got into another rented taxi and was driven off to Rome.

***

Last December, Ernst broke into Stefan Ackermann's computer for a third time while his superior was vacationing in Monaco with his family. Knowing what he did about the CFO secretly monitoring his fellow employee's emails, Ernst didn't feel the slightest bit guilty about going through Ackermann's private files.

Over the following months he stole thousands of emails, some going back years before he even started working at the bank. He downloaded from Ackermann's own private server, saving them to the new digital thumb drives he'd acquired. However, the only messages he very much wanted to read were the several hundred sent to and from the mystery sender, the individual who cryptically told

Ackermann in advance about Chirac and Iraq, and of something big about to take place.

Once he got back home, Ernst stayed up all night reading the emails. They became an obsession, with countless days of him not even going to work. Eventually he and Anna wound up going through the emails together, cataloguing them while looking for clues. He would read her the messages aloud, while she jotted down short-hand notations, and then, after they were done, they would talk about what they learned.

In time, they figured out the sender was a representative of a group they called The Syndicate, who was relaying orders and updates to Ackermann on their behalf. In one email exchange, Ernst and Anna discovered the mystery emailers name was Wolfgang, after Ackermann accidentally broke protocol and wrote it, drawing a sharp rebuke by the man in the following email.

For a long while Wolfgang had been sending Ackermann secret account numbers for him to authorize dozens of untraceable transfers of millions in U.S. dollars. The money was being sent from a secret slush fund account at Allen Brown & Associates in New York, and it contained almost a billion dollars. The countries involved were all over the globe, but the majority of the money transfers were between: Saudi Arabia; Pakistan; UAE; Japan; Germany; the UK; and the United States of America. Even though these accounts were able to be accessed by anyone working at the bank, almost all of the international payment orders had no names attached to them, and they were deliberately not registered with the SWIFT or SEC agencies. Therefore, nobody else knew the accounts were even in the bank's computer system.

Despite this, Ernst discovered five particular transactions where the names of the sender/receiver were recorded, in what he believed was a serious mistake on Ackermann's part in setting up the orders. The five transactions were authorized by Mayo Chadwick, the CEO of Allen Brown, to an account in the United Arab Emirates belonging to someone named Yasin al-Qafi. Ernst had chills go down his spine upon reading the payments were for the "hijackers training" at several flight schools in America, and for their U.S. visas that had apparently been approved by the U.S. consulate in Jeddah, Saudi Arabia. There were many instances in the email chain where Ackermann was ordered by Wolfgang to authorize electronic transfers to al-Qafi's account in Dubai, before they were sent to Pakistan and then finally to the hijackers bank accounts in Florida.

One recently received email stated that demolition experts from Israel's Mossad had arrived in America, and their agents were also tracking the movements of the hijackers under the cover of an art student ring.

In other email exchanges, Ernst found evidence of what appeared to be a massive worldwide counterfeiting operation of U.S. Federal Reserve Treasury notes and bearer bonds that The Syndicate had presumably been running for decades. The group had also been using the United States NSA and German BND to illegally spy on the U.S. Treasury Department, the State Department, The Pentagon, and even the White House. Information was being collected from the German government of Gerhard Schröder, as well as the European Commission, Interpol and Europol, and several major media corporations and journalists. It was even mentioned the CIA was running clandestine operations out of the U.S. consulate in Frankfurt.

In a stunning email from 1997, Wolfgang informed Ackermann about the real circumstances of Princess Diana's death in Paris. The email stated that agents of The Syndicate had remotely hacked into the computer system of the car she was riding in and deliberately caused it to crash, though the reason they wanted Diana murdered was left unsaid.

One message mentioned the financing for what appeared to be a covert space program, while another hinted, quite shockingly, that the Moon landings had never even happened. On the face of it the whole idea of it being a giant hoax was absurd. But now Ernst found himself wondering—*what if it's true?*

As Ernst went further down the rabbit hole, reading all of the secret emails and transactions, it dawned on him that he'd inadvertently stumbled upon evidence of a vast covert system of assassinations, terrorism, and criminal finance, and it was all completely unknown to the world. The criminality was absolutely staggering to the imagination, and, topping everything off, all of the highly illegal activity between Ackermann and Chadwick was accidentally discovered by a man named Frank Dooley, an accountant working for Allen Brown. How Dooley stumbled upon it Ernst didn't know, but it was something he thought was a curious mystery. And yet, the shocking discoveries were only just the beginning.

In early June 2001, while going through Wolfgang's emails to Ackermann, Ernst and Anna found a single PDF file, an official-looking 99-page document that was titled:

Stratagem for the Implementation of the
New World Order, PART 1: 1995-2020
A Report by The AIM Project

When the couple began reading it, the question was finally resolved for them of how Ackermann, the year before, was able to accurately predict a solar flare a week in advance. The Stratagem stated the group was using an artificially intelligent supercomputer called Metatron, and the report laid out with precision the AI's instructions for The Syndicate to conquer the world.

There was every manner of criminality outlined in the strategy: Grand theft; insider trading; blackmail; extortion; illicit arms trafficking; drug smuggling; money laundering; hacking; kidnapping; human trafficking; smear campaigns; counterfeiting; assassinations; terrorism and war. The list went on and on and on. It was shocking beyond words or belief.

However, the most terrifying thing Ernst and Anna learned from reading the Stratagem, was that The Syndicate were planning to carry out a major attack on America using hijacked commercial airliners. The event, which was described very precisely, was scheduled to take place sometime in late-2001. The only thing the couple did not know, the single most important detail of this wicked conspiracy, was exactly *when* the impending terror attack on America would take place.

Fearing for their lives, Anna begged Ernst to immediately stop breaking into Ackermann's computer, but his own curiosity and the agreement he'd made with Grimer pushed him to continue. But what he didn't know or take into account was the *unknown unknown*, a completely unforeseeable event, and therefore he failed to fully appreciate or comprehend the imminent danger he and Anna were in…

***

The morning of Thursday August 2, Ernst was sitting in his office at the Deutsche Trust headquarters, when he made the decision to break into Ackermann's computer for one last time. It would prove to be a fatal mistake. Believing the CFO was elsewhere on business, he waited until Ackermann's secretary was away from her desk, and then he used his key-card to enter the office. After turning the computer on, he began downloading several new documents to the thumb drive, and then decided to read the very last email received from the mysterious Wolfgang. The message contained only a simple statement, followed by a riddle which Ernst did not understand:

> The Big Wedding is about to happen.
> Here is a riddle for you to solve...
> What is an upside down cake with one
> candle, then a dash and two sticks?

Instinctively, Ernst felt there was something about the riddle which was crucially important, that it was somehow related to the imminent terror attack. Next, he checked the Promise program and saw that Ackermann had placed with the Allen Brown branch in New York hundreds of thousands of put option orders for shares in American Airlines, United Airlines, and several major reinsurance companies. All of them were to be purchased on several dates in early September, with the final trade set to take place on September 10. Upon reading this, Ernst could see that it was insider trading, and he instantly remembered the Stratagem's plan for a major terror attack in America using commercial airliners. Alarm bells started ringing in his head. *Early September. Was that when the attack will be?* he wondered.

Just as he finished downloading the documents to the USB stick, the door to the office swung open and in walked his boss, Stefan Ackermann. Ernst was puzzled at the man's reaction to catching his underling red-handed at his computer, as he did not appear the least bit surprised.

'Don't worry Ernst, it's all over,' said Ackermann with a smile. 'They've known about you almost from the beginning, you and the British journalist. They've been accessing your encrypted emails to him.'

Ernst was flabbergasted. 'What—but how?' he stammered.

Ackermann approached, and he noticed the USB stick attached to his computer. 'They've been able to break encryption for years,' he replied. 'Come boy, you must know by now who they are, and what they are capable of. Very soon, they will make sure neither of you will be able to contact each other again. Did you really believe you wouldn't be caught breaking into my office when I wasn't here, using the Promise software on my computer—*stealing* my emails?'

Ernst stood from the chair. He was nervous and instantly broke into a sweat, while his hands started to visibly shake. 'What you're doing for them is evil,' he said, his voice quivering. 'I read the Stratagem, I *know* about Metatron. What they're planning to do is pure fucking evil, and I'm going to tell the world about it.'

Ackermann moved closer. 'You got lucky Ernst,' he said, with a sneer. 'I wasn't supposed to have the Stratagem you stole from me. In fact, *they* would never have allowed me to know what they are planning. Now, because of you, they know that I know, and there's only one thing saving me from being in your place: they *need* me.' He moved even closer to Ernst, until he was just a step away. 'But you, my very foolish young man—you're nothing but cattle to them, and you've got no idea what's coming.'

Ernst realized he wasn't getting out of the office without a struggle, and he watched helplessly as Ackermann took the USB stick from the computer and pick up the phone to call security. Suddenly, Ernst balled his hand into a fist and swung, catching Ackermann on the side of the head and causing him to stumble. As he fell to the floor his head struck the edge of the hard business desk.

Craaaackk!

For a moment, Ackermann's arms and legs twitched, and a small pool of blood began forming under his head. Then he stopped moving altogether.

An immediate panic swept over Ernst, as he believed there was a good chance he'd just committed a murder. Trying his best to keep his cool, he retrieved the USB stick and quickly left the office, heading for the elevator. After taking it down to the tower's ground floor, he started to make his way to the exit, when suddenly the security guards rushed by him.

Getting into his car, he sped back to his apartment as fast as he could. Fortunately, Anna had taken the day off from work, and he called ahead with his mobile. When she answered, he told her they were both leaving, and for her to take the other USB stick and pack their bags. It was also necessary, he said, for her to email Charlie Grimer the secret code phrase, "dark actors playing games", letting the journalist know to meet them in Munich.

Just after hanging up, Ernst shockingly grasped the importance of Wolfgang's last email, which contained the strange coded message and put option orders Ackermann had placed. It was essential, he realized, to copy the information over to the other USB stick.

After picking Anna up at their apartment, the pair was driving off when they heard several very loud popping noises. Bullets suddenly slammed into their car, and the back window shattered. Speeding fast behind them on a motorbike were two individuals dressed fully in black, with dark helmet visors pulled down to obscure their faces. The passenger was holding an Uzi submachine gun, and they let off another volley in their direction.

Scared out of his wits, Ernst began a fast and furious chase through Frankfurt's busy streets, doing his best to evade the would-be assassins. Finally, the motorbike took a corner too fast and crashed spectacularly into an outdoor café, sending its riders flying to the ground and the café's patrons scattering.

Once the couple made it to the autobahn highway, and their nerves had calmed sufficiently enough for them to speak, he informed Anna about the massive airline put option orders Ackermann had placed for September 10, and he told her the riddle in Wolfgang's last message. At first, Anna was just as perplexed about the riddle as he was. But just before departing for Rome that morning she told him that she knew the answer:

'It came to me in a dream last night,' she revealed. They were numbers. The answer to the riddle was a *date*.

Of course she'd got it, Ernst thought, Anna was a very clever girl. But still, he wondered how he'd missed figuring out such a vitally important clue.

***

Just then, something happened in the Marienplatz which brought Ernst back from yesterday's events to the present. In the centre of the square, over by the column, he spied a man who he thought resembled Grimer. *Was that him?* he wondered excitedly. He wasn't sure, as he'd only met Charlie once, with Anna in London the year before, as well as having seen him on the evening news. But this particular man was facing away from Ernst, and he couldn't get a clear view.

Warily, he looked from side-to-side as he stepped into the rain, and then began to slowly make his way toward the column. Drops of water spattered off the top of his cap, and his shoes made a loud tapping sound as he walked across the slick wet pavement. As he approached, he could see the man was gazing up at one of the four statues at the column's base, a sculptured child *putto* with a sword held high in its hand, about to slay a lion.

'Herr Grimer?' Ernst inquired aloud. The man turned around and looked back at him with steely eyes, and Ernst saw right away that it was *not* the British journalist.

At that moment, the Glockenspiel tower suddenly began to chime, and a loud chatter arose from the assembled tourists who began clapping their hands in excited approval. Ernst spun his head around to look, and after that everything appeared to him in slow-motion, though in reality it was almost an instant. He could see there were several men, all dressed in black suits, running toward him across the square at full-speed. *They've found me,* he thought. *The game is over.* The man standing next to him grabbed at Ernst's arm, trying to put him into a hold, but Ernst managed to wrest himself away. Spinning around on his feet, he sprinted as fast as he could across the square and into one of the connecting motorways. Then, he scrambled through the busy open market, the Viktualienmarkt, almost dropping his laptop bag when he slipped and fell on the wet cobblestones. Quickly, he got back up and ran until, eventually, he came to the Isar River flowing through the city centre. He spied a small pedestrian bridge nearby and headed straight for it.

He only got halfway across the bridge, when suddenly he was confronted by two agents on the other side, both of them pointing guns in his direction. Turning around to go back he discovered the situation behind him was the same: he was trapped. In desperation, he reached inside his coat pocket and brought out the USB thumb drive, which he quickly tossed into the river; his computer laptop bag was next to go. Too late to stop him, the agents rushed forward and tackled him to the ground. After binding his hands, they abruptly forced him to his feet.

It was then that a striking figure appeared: a female agent dressed from head-to-toe in tight-fitting white leather. As this Woman in White approached, Ernst saw she had silver-coloured hair that was trimmed short, and, in keeping with her attire, her lips were painted a glossy white. However, the most unusual thing about her was a white eye patch covering over her left eye, while her remaining eye was a very pale blue.

One of the other agents searched Ernst's pockets and then shook his head. The Woman in White stepped forward and struck Ernst hard across the face, drawing blood from his nose.

'Where is it?' she demanded, speaking German.

'In the fucking river,' Ernst replied, his mouth twisting into a bloodied smile.

'It doesn't matter,' said White, shaking her head. 'Your girlfriend won't survive either. It's *you* who they want.'

'You will get nothing from me.'

She smirked. 'Time will tell.'

After that, Ernst was kidnapped by them and held prisoner for three days, before being brought to Africa to compete in The Syndicate's cruel game of survival. Ultimately, he was fated to be the game's first victim, and his USB thumb drive full of evidence about the greatest conspiracy in history was now useless as it floated down the Isar River in Munich.

However, there was still Anna.

STAGE II – SAVANNAH

"If you want to go fast, go alone. If you want to go far, go together."

– African proverb

NINE

DAY 2 – Wednesday August 8, 2001
3:36 P.M.
16°11'37.6" 7°09'49.2"

CHARLIE RAN UNTIL he could run no more. He was exhausted and struggling to breathe, and he gasped as he stumbled and fell down to his knees. Pulling his knapsack away from his shoulders, he collapsed onto the white-hot sand. In terrible pain, he grabbed at his chest and attempted to roll on his back, but his arms and legs had turned to jelly and become almost useless. Finally, with great effort, and sand and spittle stuck to his sore reddened cheeks, he turned to face the cloudless blue sky.

The sandstorm had long gone, and now only a light breeze was blowing across the immense dry plain where he lay. But this gave him little comfort, as the blistering heat from the sun was relentless and unforgiving.

The crash he'd suffered because of the storm had destroyed his motorbike, forcing him on his feet to quickly put distance between he and the other competitor. The last time he checked the GPS he saw the man who attempted to attack him was now quite a few kilometres behind, and he didn't appear to be following.

Charlie had been running for the better part of two hours, and now there was no energy left in his body to keep going. His lungs felt like hot burning coals on fire, and his head thumped as if it were going to explode. Sweat poured off him to the ground, soaking his ragged and torn shirt so that it clung tightly to his sunburnt skin.

Retrieving the water canteen from his knapsack, he took a swig of the last remaining drops of the precious liquid. The water felt like Heaven itself had come down and touched his cracked and blistering lips. And then, it was all gone. *What am I going to do?* he wondered with dread. The pain in his chest suddenly intensified. He'd never suffered a heart attack before, but he was acutely aware it was now a distinct possibility. It dawned on him that this very spot was where he was likely going to die. He clenched his eyes tightly shut, thinking, *this is how everything ends?* It didn't make any sense to him. Of all the myriad and varied places in the world he could expire, the desert, and the Sahara at that, was among the very last Charlie would have ever guessed.

Once again, images of his wife and son suddenly shot through his mind. They had paid for Charlie's mistake in the worst way, and now he was being made to atone for it.

'Leigh!' he yelled in a raspy voice. 'I'm sorry Leigh. I'm sorry I did this to you and David. Please… forgive me.' Resigned to his fate, he opened his eyes and stared at the sky. The flying drone was still there. It was always there, following and watching him. The Syndicate were going to watch him slowly die.

And then, flying much higher than the drone, he spied what appeared to be a large plane—a commercial airliner. It was so high, in fact, that he couldn't even hear the sound of its jet engines. It was moving fast across the sky, with a long white contrail of smoke trailing behind it. *It looks beautiful,* he thought.

From out of nowhere Charlie heard a female voice speaking to him, but from which direction he could not tell:

'It's too bad you won't live long enough to save the people in the hijacked planes and buildings,' said the voice. Right away he recognized it as being from an agent of The Syndicate, one whom he called the Woman in Black. It was she who had kidnapped and brought him to the Sahara.

Startled by it, he turned his head to the side and wiped away the stinging perspiration from his eyes. On the ground, just a few metres away, he saw a long black snake slithering slowly toward him.

'You're right,' Charlie whispered back. 'I won't be able to save them, but something will happen to stop you.' In his confused mind he wasn't speaking to the agent, but to each member of The Syndicate who was watching. Though he had no idea how they were

106

doing it, he instinctively felt they were also listening to his words and hearing all of his thoughts.

The snake appeared to be looking directly at him as it moved even closer. He wasn't sure if it was a hallucination or not, but it looked very real. Was any of this real, he wondered? *Maybe this is just a very bad dream, and somewhere Leigh and David are still alive and we're all together.*

'Evil can't win,' he said to the snake. 'In the end, you and Metatron will lose.'

Just before falling unconscious, Charlie heard one last thing: a sound was coming from the snake's mouth, which was now only inches away from his face. To his horror, he realized the Woman in Black was laughing.

***

The very first time Charlie met his future wife was entirely unremarkable; their second meeting, however, was *extraordinary*. In 1985, when he was twenty-six years old, he was driving back to London from Southampton when his car tyre suddenly went flat. Adding to the problem, he discovered there was no jack in the boot to change it. Leigh just happened to be driving by, and, after seeing his plight she stopped to help, offering her own jack for him to use. They engaged in small talk, with her mentioning she was a magazine editor. She seemed genuinely interested when he told her what his own job was, asking him several questions. Every now and again he was able to smell her scent, and he thought it was delightful.

When he was done they said their goodbye's and parted ways, without him even finding out her name. At the time, it had appeared to be just one of those things that happen occasionally in one's life; interesting, yet quickly forgotten.

But all was *not* as it seemed.

One week later, Charlie unexpectedly found himself attending a small art gallery showing in Paris on the last night of a weekend stay. The trip had been a spontaneous visit to a friend, and was the first time he'd ever gone to the Continent. He'd wanted to return to London early, and come very close to not going to the showing, but his friend had succeeded in persuading him. Shortly after arriving at the gallery, he was admiring a painting when he suddenly became aware of someone, a woman, standing next to him. Casually, he turned his head – and saw that it was *her*. Instantly, they both recognized each other, and Leigh had been as shocked as he was.

Afterward, they had a brief courtship and were married just six months later. All of their friends and family said it was fate or destiny, which were things Charlie never really put much faith in. But the way he met Leigh radically forced a change of his way of thinking.

Though they'd had their fair share of difficulties, Charlie and Leigh always managed to work things out and keep their marriage together, at least for the sake of their son. Before David was born they'd been trying to have a child for some time, with her suffering through several unfortunate miscarriages. However, roughly a year after Charlie's elderly father passed away, Leigh suddenly became pregnant to their great surprise and delight.

Named after Charlie's father, David was a wonderful child with a beautiful personality. He was the complete joy of both of his parent's lives, and very likely the reason why their marriage lasted as long as it did. Eventually, Charlie became the very definition of an overprotective parent. When David was a baby, he had recurring nightmares about him doing harm to the child, accidentally as well as intentionally. Of course he would never have actually hurt his son, but nevertheless it distressed and alarmed him for many months. He couldn't understand why he was having the terrible dreams, until he finally realized they were simply manifestations of his fears of anything bad happening.

The phone hacking scandal that Charlie broke to the public put an enormous strain on his marriage. At one point he and Leigh had separated for a few months, which only fed his paranoia and instilled in him the fear of being left alone. Autophobia his doctor called it, and Charlie was prescribed Xanax pills which helped keep him from totally losing control.

Not long after he was first contacted by Anna, when the Concorde crashed and he realized she'd been correct in her prediction, Leigh found the call from Anna's unknown number on his mobile phone. Querying him about it, he initially denied knowing anything about the call, claiming it had just been a wrong number. But Leigh recognized from the date that it was the same call he'd received at The Lion's Tavern on their son's birthday, which only increased her suspicion that he was secretly having an affair. He tried his best to dispel her fears, but it had seemed near impossible.

The fact of the matter was, Charlie *did* have an affair, three years earlier with his barrister's assistant. It had carried on for six months before Leigh finally discovered it. She was devastated and deeply wounded, as she had always faithfully stayed by her husband's side throughout thick and thin. In his own defense, he claimed it was the enormous pressure he was under which caused him to stray, an excuse which Leigh never completely believed. Even though he ended the relationship, with the promise of it never happening again, she had every reason to suspect Charlie was still seeing the other woman.

When Charlie could no longer endure his wife's accusations, he admitted to her what the phone call had actually been about. He told her of Anna, and of her strange prediction about the attempted assassination of Jacques Chirac through the crashing of the Concorde. But Leigh didn't believe him. More than that, she told him he was crazy to make up such a disgusting story to try and hide his affair.

In the ensuing days their relationship deteriorated rapidly, finally ending when he came home to find Leigh and David gone, with just a note she'd left behind on their bed, saying *"You're with someone else... and now so am I."* At that moment, the shock and pain Charlie experienced were more than he could bear. Aside from the fact his wife had left him, and taken their son with her, it also confirmed a second prediction made by Anna, as he felt it was her phone call which was the catalyst for the complete breakdown of his marriage. It was a shocking irony not lost on Charlie.

For three months he lived in a perpetual state of fear and misery. Seemingly in a daze he wandered London's streets, parks and shopping centres, any place he could find to be around other people, trying to subdue the phobia which terrorized him, until the day finally came when Anna called again.

***

In mid-October of 2000, Charlie met Ernst and Anna at The Lion's Tavern, and many of the questions he desperately needed answers for were given. In addition, arrangements were made for the banker and his girlfriend to provide him with more evidence. But the first documents he received were all written in German, and he was expecting more to come. Charlie found a solution to this problem by calling a friend and former colleague, Stanley Babbage, seeking to borrow a language translation computer program.

After Charlie was hired by The Daily Sun, he became acquainted with Stanley when they were given assignments together. Years later, when the newspaper's editor resigned because of the scandal Charlie instigated, Stanley stepped up and was promoted by the paper's board to the position of new managing editor. It was his task to clean up the tabloid's very tarnished image. It also didn't hurt that Stanley shared the conservative views and opinions of the paper's owners. When the scandal subsided, Charlie wanted nothing more to do with The Daily Sun, indeed for tabloid journalism in general. But he knew Stan was just as ambitious as he once was, and he didn't hold it against his friend for seizing the opportunity to become editor.

Stanley Babbage was an interesting fellow, who seemed to know a little bit about everything. He was a walking trivia book, and he had an uncanny ability to recall the exact dates of seemingly every significant historical event. It was so strange, in fact, that Charlie thought it was like some kind of autism. He even once informed Charlie that his great-uncle was a recipient of the Victoria Cross, the highest Commonwealth military award for valour, for his actions at the infamous Battle of Rorke's Drift against the Zulu's in Africa. At the time, Charlie didn't know if his colleague was telling him the truth, though he didn't see why anyone would make up something so unusual if it were not. But in due course, Stanley became one of the very few people whom Charlie believed he could trust, and that was a rare thing in the tabloid business. After a brief phone call, Stanley agreed to lend him the translator program.

***

The next day, Charlie went to King's Cross in central London to meet his friend at St Pancras Gardens, a park which had a very old church on its grounds, and a graveyard with many timeworn headstones and monuments. The park wasn't far from The Daily Sun offices, and was a place the pair of them would frequent to discuss their work in privacy.

Walking down the sidewalk with a cigarette dangling from his mouth, Charlie noticed that Stanley was already waiting at the park's gated entrance, and he approached him.

'I see you're still puffing away on those cancer sticks,' Stanley said.

'Three packs a day,' replied Charlie, managing a weak smile.

'How you been holding up mate?'

'Not good. Leigh's left me, and she took David.'

'I know, I heard, and I'm very sorry. Come, let's go inside and talk.' Putting his arm around Charlie's shoulders, Stanley led him through the gate. 'When did this happen?' he enquired.

'Three months ago, I think. Actually, I'm not even sure anymore as the whole thing has been a waking nightmare. I've got insomnia, barely slept a wink; migraines have become common. And I'm terrified of being alone. Stan, I... I don't know what else to do.'

'Have you kept in touch with her?'

'Yes, on and off. She still won't give me the chance to explain. In her mind she's getting revenge.'

Stanley gave him a gentle pat on the back, and said, 'Well, don't make yourself sick over it Charlie-boy. It will all work out.'

'How's the paper doing?'

'Things have been busy. As you know, we're preparing to cover the World Cup, and then there's the election coming up in America—'

'—Stan,' interrupted Charlie, 'I'm working on something, and I think it could be big. *Really fucking big.*'

'Is this why you need the translation program?'

Charlie nodded.

'Care to enlighten me?'

There was a pact between them not to talk with anyone else of their work-related discussions, and therefore Charlie believed with all sincerity that his secrets were safe with Stan. 'All right, what if I told you I may have evidence of a plot to kill Jacques Chirac?'

Stanley sighed. '*Another* of your daft conspiracy theories?' he asked.

Charlie's face flushed red. 'Damn it, you *know* what we went through together at the paper. Don't you remember what a big fucking mess it was?'

'Like it was yesterday.'

'Right, well then you know these things exist. *They happen*. Do you even know where the term "conspiracy theorist" comes from?'

'Where?'

'The CIA came up with it in the late sixties as part of a calculated plan to attack anyone challenging the official story of JFK's murder.'

'That's not true,' Stanley balked. 'The phrase was used well before that.'

'Look, documents were published only a couple of years ago that proves this is what they were doing. Besides, if the press did its damn job properly there wouldn't be any conspiracy theories.'

Stanley was clearly annoyed. 'Can we just stay on topic? Exactly what is this supposed evidence you have?'

'This past July,' Charlie began, 'I got a call from someone employed at a bank in Germany, saying they'd seen an email their boss received about Chirac being removed in spectacular fashion in two days' time.'

'Yeah? Well it didn't work then did it? The last I heard the man is still alive.'

'Two days after the call the Concorde crashed.'

'What about it? Chirac had nothing to do with that!'

'You're wrong, I checked it out. A contact of mine in the ministry doing the investigation confirmed Chirac's plane *was* on the runway. He'd just got back from the G-8 summit in Japan. The Concorde missed striking his plane by *seven fucking yards!*'

'Are you taking the piss?' Stanley asked, a little suspicious.

Charlie shook his head. 'Remember the photo of it taking off, the one with the flames shooting out the back?'

'Of course!'

'That photo was taken by a Japanese businessman from *inside* Chirac's plane. They never told the public how close he came to getting killed. See… I don't think I can do this story alone. It's just too damned much for me to handle right now. I was hoping we could collaborate, a special investigation exposé, just like the old days. What do you think?'

'Let me get this straight,' said Stanley. 'You are telling me you've got in your possession evidence—'

'—*Possible* evidence,' Charlie corrected him.

'Excuse me, *possible* evidence, of a conspiracy to assassinate the president of France with the Concorde, and make it look like it was an accident?'

'Something like that, yeah. I mean, it's nothing concrete yet. I still need some time to do more research.'

Stanley's facial expression had turned from surprise to skepticism. 'All right, answer me this,' he said, 'if what you are saying is true, for what reason to murder Chirac, and in such melodramatic fashion?'

'I haven't the foggiest clue yet. Apparently, the way the message is worded my contact seems to think it has something to do with Iraq.'

'Yes, of course. Everything always leads back to Iraq, doesn't it?' Stanley asked sarcastically.

Charlie lit up a cigarette. Their conversation was not going at all the way he planned. Somehow he'd mistakenly thought his friend would be jumping at the chance for another explosive exposé.

'Look mate,' continued Stanley, 'I know you're going through a lot at the moment, as I can tell just by all the damn cigarettes you're smoking! But I'm quite sure what your caller said must have been just a complete coincidence. What happened—they're two completely separate events not connected to each other. One didn't cause the other. If something happens once it's by chance, twice is a coincidence, and thrice it becomes a pattern.'

'I guess it was also just a coincidence when they said my wife was going to leave and then she did a week later!' Charlie yelled, exasperated. 'Please explain *that* to me Stan, because I still don't quite fucking understand it!'

'Calm down,' said Stanley, looking to see if anyone else heard the outburst. The park appeared to be empty, except for the two of them and the park's long-time keeper, whom they knew only as "Red".

Red, so named because of his long red beard, was a friendly old chap in his 70's, who always allowed Charlie and Stanley, while working on news stories, to linger in the park for a little while after its closing time.

As they passed by a few monuments and gravestones, Charlie glanced at the names written on them. There was Mary Wollstonecraft, the mother of author Mary Shelley; Joseph Wall, the infamous colonial administrator executed for cruelty; Johann Christian Bach, noted composer and son of Johann Sebastion; and John Polidori, an author and physician known for creating the vampire genre. Charlie had walked by these graves at least a hundred times before, and, thanks to Stanley, he pretty much knew what every one of the deceased was known for. 'All these poor bastards...' he said, 'Who remembers them now? Nobody knows who John Polidori is. Whenever the word vampire is mentioned everyone always thinks of Bram Stoker.'

'Have you heard of the American writer, Morgan Robertson?' asked Stanley.

'No, should I have?'

'Not really, I suppose. Most people haven't. He wrote a book called "Futility" which was published, I believe, in 1898. It was about a supposedly unsinkable giant ship called Titan that strikes an iceberg in the North Atlantic in the month of April, sinking and killing almost all aboard. And then, of course, fourteen years later it actually happened.'

'That's unbelievable!' Charlie exclaimed with surprise. 'And two years after that the whole fucking world exploded in war.'

'Quite the opposite, it only seems like a remarkable coincidence to those who perceive it as such. It's actually just a mathematical probability. You build a big enough boat, one's going to tragically sink at some point; you build the world's tallest building, eventually someone is going to come along and try to knock it down. It's just a matter of time.'

'Yes, but the very first one on its maiden voyage? C'mon, I don't believe it. There's got to be something more that we don't know.'

Stanley chuckled. 'I've heard different theories for what caused Titanic's sinking. Some people blame a conspiracy of bankers being behind it, while others have insisted that it was a slow-burning coal fire below deck. One of the more interesting ideas is that before it sank the passengers reported witnessing in the night sky an incredible display of aurora borealis, caused by an electrical storm from the sun. It's thought the storm interfered with the ship's magnetic compass, thereby making it veer slightly off course and into the path of the iceberg.' He shrugged. 'Who knows why Titanic sank? Only God knows. And now, nobody remembers who Morgan Robertson is.'

'Where is he buried?' Charlie asked. 'He's not here is he? Wait, let me guess... His boat coincidentally sank in the North Atlantic?' His sarcasm was dry and humourless.

'Hmm,' Stanley hummed, thinking for an answer. 'I believe he's buried in New York. But that's not the point I'm trying to make. What I'm saying, or rather, what statistician's say, is that correlation does not necessarily imply causation; one event didn't cause the other.'

The air suddenly grew cold, and a chilly wind blew through the park causing Charlie to shudder. They had walked the entire distance of the grounds, arriving back at the park's gated entrance, and now it was time to part ways.

'How about one more prediction, this time less catastrophic?' Stanley asked. 'Who's going to be the next U.S. president?'

Charlie lit up another cigarette. 'George W. Bush,' he answered matter-of-factly.

'Bush doesn't stand a chance,' Stanley quipped. 'The Democrats are polling extremely high right now.' He reached inside his coat and brought out a computer disk.

'No, you watch. Something's going to happen.'

'Something is *always* about to happen, Charlie. You just haven't learnt that yet.'

As Stanley handed him the disk, Charlie noticed on his finger a silver ring, one he had never seen him wear before. On the ring's face was the familiar Square and Compasses symbol of Freemasonry, with the letter "G" in the centre. 'I didn't know you were a mason,' Charlie said with surprise.

'Well, some things a man's gotta keep private,' Stanley replied. 'By the way, you could have used a translator on the internet. They're not as efficient, of course, but they still work. Give a ring when you know what you've got. Please… look after yourself mate.'

And with that Stanley walked briskly away, leaving Charlie standing by himself on the street corner, his hands trembling as he inhaled the smoke from his cigarette.

***

Inside Charlie's unconscious mind he heard the sound of a baby crying, and he wondered if it was his son, David. The memory of the street in King's Cross instantly disappeared, and was replaced by an infinite blackness. He had no idea where he'd been thrust. Was he in space, he wondered? There were no stars or planets within sight, and he tried hard to see if there was anything to be seen at all. Quickly, he became aware that he wasn't alone. He could sense that here in this cold, lifeless dimension, there was someone, or *something* else with him.

'*No, it's not your son,*' a voice whispered to him. It startled Charlie, not for the reason that he actually received a reply to the question he'd asked only in his mind, but because the strange voice sounded inhuman, like a machine or... a computer.

'*Who are you?*' he asked of it. There was a long pause, during which Charlie questioned if it had indeed just been his imagination.

'*You know who I am,*' the voice whispered back. '*Wake up Charlie. There is still a very long way to go, and there are two others left.*'

Only two left? wondered Charlie with surprise. It explained the reason why there was no fourth GPS signal. One of the other competitors was dead and out of the game.

'*Yes, you are correct,*' said the voice. '*You must continue on, or you will share their fate of hearing only my voice at your life's end. Now... Wake up.*'

After the voice spoke, the only thing Charlie perceived was a tiny light in the distance, surrounded by complete darkness. With each passing moment, the light appeared to be getting closer, growing bigger, until he could finally discern that it was the red and orange glow of the flickering flames of a fire. Slowly his eyes opened, and he came to the realization that he was on the ground, lying flat on his back with his head turned to the side. The next thing he noticed was two Black men sitting on the other side of a small burning fire, and they were watching him intently. The first man appeared to be in his mid-forties, while the other looked to be about half that age. They were all inside of a small tent, with smoke from the fire billowing up and exiting through a hole in the top. The air inside was thick with the strong smell of sweat mixed with cooked animal meat.

'Hello,' said Charlie, weakly.

'Hello there,' the older man replied with a smile. A child suddenly appeared from behind the man's back, peeking curiously at Charlie. It was a young girl, whom he judged to be about five or six years old. In her arms she was holding a tiny baby, swaddled inside of an animal skin. 'This is my daughter, Nimco,' the man said, gesturing to her. 'She is the one who found you.'

Charlie struggled to push himself up from the ground, finally sitting upright. 'You... speak English very well,' he said, surprised.

'Yes, but it's been a long time for me. I used to be a lawyer in Nigeria,' the man replied, holding out a metal flask. 'Here, drink some water. There is also some food in the bowl next to you. I am Kingsley, and this is my brother, Zaki.'

'My name is Charlie.' He took the flask, arched his head back and slaked his thirst, gulping down copious amounts.

'Where are you from?'

'London, England.'

Kingsley smiled. 'Well, you are a very lucky man.'

Charlie heaved a sigh. 'I don't know about that.' He noticed his knapsack on the ground nearby. Taking it, he brought out the GPS and looked at the time on the LCD screen:

4:45 P.M.

As he studied the signals being received, Charlie saw that the first competitor was a little over one hundred kilometres south of his present position, while the other was about half that distance to the north-east. Then, he pulled aside the tent flap and peeked outside. The sun was just beginning to set and the sky was darkening in the east. Night was almost upon them. Not far from the tent he saw a beat-up white Land Rover, which was parked next to what looked like a paved road. 'You said your daughter found me?' he asked Kingsley.

'Yes, you were lying not far from the road. I believed you were dead until I heard your heart was still beating.'

Charlie looked at the young girl. 'I owe you a huge debt of gratitude for saving my life.'

The man translated this to his daughter, who then smiled at Charlie and said simply 'Maraba.'

'She says that you are welcome.'

'Please... do you have a mobile phone I could use?' Charlie asked. It was a long shot, as he knew any phone likely wouldn't get a signal here in the middle of nowhere.

Kingsley shook his head negatively.

Charlie picked up the bowl and briefly studied the food inside. 'What is this?' he asked, as he began eating the cooked meat.

'Snake,' Kingsley answered. 'Have you had it before?'

'No, I can't say that I have. Right now, I'll eat just about anything.'

'So... What do you do in London?'

'I'm a writer. Well, at least I used to be.'

'You write books?'

'No, newspapers; investigative journalism.'

'A journalist?'

'Yes.'

'Tell me friend, what brings you to this cruel place? Were you looking for Zerzura?'

'Zerzura? What in God's name is that?'

Kingsley laughed. 'It is a mythical city full of treasure, said to exist somewhere in this desert. Were you going to write about it?'

'No, unfortunately, I wasn't looking for any mythical city,' Charlie said between food bites. 'I'm not even supposed to be here. I was kidnapped and brought against my will.'

'That is a terrible thing,' said Kingsley. 'But, you have come at the right time. Many people are leaving Nigeria. This road is busy right now. That is why you were lucky to be found.'

'Why are people leaving?'

'There is war coming. Islamic fighters are trying to bring Sharia law into my country, and many are being killed with their heads cut from their bodies.'

'My God, that's horrible.'

Kingsley nodded. 'The Nigerian government is also very corrupt and killing my people, who are trying to separate and form a new country. My wife was murdered by them even though she was Somali. The police were looking for me, but instead took her away and tortured her to death. Now I go with our children and my brother to Libya, until there is a more peaceful time to return.'

'You have my condolences. I've... also recently lost my wife, and my son,' Charlie said with a choke in his voice.

'I'm very sorry to hear.'

'But instead of leaving for Libya why don't you seek justice for your wife's death? Fight back against the government?'

'Because my friend, I believe in non-violence. An eye for an eye makes the whole world blind.'

Charlie knew that Kingsley was quoting a peace phrase generally attributed to Mohandas Gandhi, but he disagreed with the employment of non-violent civil disobedience. He believed that sometimes it was necessary to confront those in power seeking to oppress and exploit the weak, even if it meant violent struggle.

'Look,' Charlie said, 'I can't thank you and your daughter enough for saving me, but I have to go.'

'That would not be a good idea,' Kingsley replied. 'You need to rest, and soon it will be cold outside without any shelter. You came very close to dying.'

'I can't rest, I have to keep moving.'

'Why?'

'That's a little complicated to explain.'

'Where are you going?'

'South, but I don't know what place it is, as there are no roads or cities displayed on this thing.' Charlie held up the GPS for Kingsley to see. 'There's a map, and this black dot on the screen is where I need to go. Maybe you can tell me where it is?' He handed the GPS over to Kingsley, who studied the display screen.

Finally, Kingsley said, 'That is Benin, and the city you are going to is on the coast and is called Ouidah. If you keep following the road it is possible one of the trucks will come by. They are returning to Nigeria to pick up more people. They will let you ride for a price.'

'But I don't have anything except for this GPS, and I can't give that away. I need it more than anything else. Can you take me there? I know you are going the other direction, but I don't know what else to do.'

'It's a very long way,' Kingsley replied, 'at least a thousand kilometres, and a whole day of driving. I am wanted in my country, and it's dangerous for me and my family to go back. I can take you as far as Birnin-Konni, but no further.'

'Mate, look… I need to get to an embassy or a phone. The people who kidnapped me are planning on doing something terrible in America very soon.'

'My friend, terrible things are happening already. There is much suffering here, but the world chooses not to see it.'

Then, Charlie remembered when The Syndicate agent, the Woman in Black, had offered money to him if he made it to the end first. 'Please… I beg you,' he pleaded to Kingsley. 'My life and the lives of possibly thousands of people are at stake. I can pay you money. Lots of money. But you have to take me all the way to the coast, right to the flashing co-ordinate on the GPS. Right to Ouidah.'

For a few seconds Kingsley thought about it, before he finally agreed. 'I will do it,' he said, 'but there is a problem: you do not have official papers or ID card to cross the borders into Nigeria or Benin, so you will need to hide in the car and be very quiet. That is very important, because if you are caught you will be put in jail.'

Charlie nodded. 'I understand.'

'In return, I ask that you do something for me.'

'Anything mate, you just name it.'

'I don't want my wife's death to be in vain. Write about it in your newspaper. Tell the world of the people being killed in my country, about what is happening here in Africa.'

'Absolutely,' replied Charlie. 'I promise you that I will.'

'That is good. We will leave soon. First we will stop at Birnin-Konni where you can use a phone. After that we will go into Nigeria and then drive to Benin.' He explained the agreement he'd just made to his brother, Zaki, who did not appear happy about their sudden change in plans.

Shortly after, they packed up the tent and belongings and strapped them to the roof of the Land Rover. Charlie sat in the back with Zaki, while Kingsley got behind the steering wheel, with his daughter and baby son next to him. Just after five in the afternoon the group of five began their journey to Niger's southern border with Nigeria. The road was long and winding, and pitted with many holes and bumpy rough patches. But Charlie took no notice, having fallen fast asleep almost immediately after they departed. On into the night they drove, and into the early hours of the next day.

***

DAY 3 – Thursday August 9, 2001
2:09 A.M.
12°42'30.5" 5°03'04.4"

Nine hours later, Charlie was unexpectedly woken by the sound of several men shouting loudly outside the vehicle. Instantly he sat up and glanced around him. The car had come to a stop, and Zaki was now behind the steering wheel with Kingsley next to him in the front passenger seat. Sitting next to Charlie was Nimco, tightly holding on to her baby brother, and he could see there was fear in the little girl's eyes.

'What's going on?' Charlie cried out, trying to see through the car windows. It was very dark outside and hard to understand what was happening. Bright flashlights were suddenly shone into the car, their beams criss-crossing and illuminating everyone inside.

'Shhhh,' Kingsley said low to Charlie, waving his hands. 'Please stay quiet. Keep your head down, don't let them see you.'

'Don't let *who* see me?'

'The iko, the police have stopped us. They are searching for poachers and ivory smugglers. Please stay down. If they see you… there will be trouble.'

'Where are we?' whispered Charlie.

'Nigeria.'

'What happened to Birnin-Konni? I thought we were going there first?'

'No, it was too dangerous,' Kingsley replied. 'There were many soldiers in the streets. We are lucky we've come this far. You will be able to use a phone once we cross into Benin. Please, just let me deal with them.'

'You don't understand, I absolutely *must* get to a phone. I told you—'

All of a sudden a policeman flung open the driver door and started shouting at Zaki, demanding he step out of the Land Rover, which he did with his arms raised. Kingsley got out of the car with his arms in the air, shouting to the men and presumably trying to diffuse the situation.

Trying his best to see outside, Charlie thought he counted four policemen, some of whom appeared to be wielding AK-47 guns, but he couldn't understand anything that was being spoken.

One of the men looked into the back of the Land Rover and saw Charlie, as well as the young girl and baby cowering in the back seat. He pointed to them and began shouting. Another man came along and tried to open the back passenger door. Finding it locked, he didn't hesitate using the butt of his gun to smash the window. Shattered glass flew everywhere. The man snatched Nimco, who was still cradling the baby, and he pulled them both out.

Charlie grabbed his knapsack. After opening the car door, he raised his arms in the air while quickly exiting the vehicle. 'It's all right!' he said aloud. 'We don't want trouble—Please don't hurt the children!'

A policeman seized him by the neck and forcefully pushed him to the side of the road, all the while yelling loudly and waving a gun in his face. Then he pointed at the knapsack Charlie had slung over his shoulder, indicating that he wanted it. The situation was tense, and Charlie knew if he didn't listen to the man's demands that it would not end well. Doing his best to comply, he pulled the bag off his arm and held it out. The man took it and began rummaging through its contents. After bringing out Charlie's knife and GPS receiver, he thrust the items triumphantly in the air for his comrades to see, with a big smile across his face.

'Please, please don't take those,' Charlie pleaded, 'I need them!'

For a moment, the policeman curiously studied the electronic device, before tucking it securely under his belt. 'Tafi daga nan!' he shouted at Charlie, pointing his gun at him. 'Gudu!'

'He says run!' yelled Kingsley. 'Run Charlie!' One of the men standing behind Kingsley struck him between the shoulder blades with the butt of his gun. It was a hard whack, and Kingsley stumbled and fell to the ground in pain. His daughter, Nimco, screamed in terror, and the baby she was holding started to wail.

Quickly, Charlie snatched his knapsack from the policeman's hand and ran as fast as he could off the road and into the bush. Behind him, he heard the men open fire with their guns, and he felt bullets whiz past his head and slam into the ground in front of him. But he kept running, and he didn't look back until he was a good distance away. Had they murdered the family, Charlie wondered? Huffing and puffing, he eventually slowed to a walk when it became too dark to see which direction he was going. Thick clouds obscured the moon, and now only a few yards were visible around him.

Earlier, Kingsley had graciously replenished his food and water. But even though he still carried the knapsack with his other supplies, Charlie immediately knew the implications of losing his GPS receiver and knife: he was doomed.

The temperature soon dropped considerably, and the air about him was very cold. Shivering, he decided that if he was going to survive the remainder of the night then a fire would be necessary.

Despite his dire predicament, he was thankful the policemen hadn't taken everything from him, including his life. Using the flashlight, he gathered some nearby sticks and brush for tinder, and he struck the flint rocks together until sparks lit up.

A few minutes later he had a small fire burning, and then he looked about to see what little could be seen. It appeared the desert sand had given way to grassy savannah, but he hadn't a clue of his precise location. All that he knew, if what Kingsley had said was true, was that he was somewhere in north-western Nigeria. Above him he could hear the familiar whirring engine of the UAV drone, flying around in its usual circular pattern.

For a while he sat staring at the flames and glowing embers, thinking of everything that had happened, when suddenly he heard a series of deep growls emanating from the darkness beyond. Instinctively, he reached for his knapsack until he remembered, with alarmed panic, that the precious blade was no longer inside.

He decided the noise was definitely made by an animal, but what kind he didn't know. Thoughts of what it could possibly be sent waves of terror through his body. *Could it be a hyena or maybe a leopard... or, God forbid... a lion?* Total fear gripped his mind. His nerves were on the verge of complete collapse as his autophobia suddenly kicked into high gear with a vengeance. *I'm all alone,* he thought, *and surrounded by some of the most vicious wild animals on the planet.*

Again he heard the growling, this time coming from another direction. Whatever it was, it was very close and appeared to be circling him. The snapping of a nearby twig made him jump, and he whipped his head around to see what caused it. Just at the edge of the campfire's glow, hiding behind long blades of grass, he saw a young, dark-skinned man, who was studying him with both intense curiosity and caution.

DC Wince

TEN

DAY 3 – Thursday August 9, 2001
3:22 A.M.
12°42'14.3" 5°03'14.3"

F OR SEVERAL TENSE SECONDS, Charlie and Blaze looked at one another, each of them unsure what would happen next. It was Charlie who finally broke the silence.

'Who are y—'

'Shhhh,' Blaze whispered, putting his index finger to his lips. Slowly he approached, and crouched down opposite Charlie. By the glow of the campfire, Charlie saw that the young man, who looked to be in his late teens, was not Caucasian, but he also didn't appear African. His skin and eyes were dark, and his short, black hair ringed his face with small curls. About an average height, he wasn't wearing a shirt or trousers, just a small loincloth, and he had a knapsack slung over his shoulder. Held firmly in the boy's hand was a long wooden spear.

'My name is Charlie,' he whispered.

'I'm Blaze.'

'You... speak English?'

'Yeah, I'm Aussie. Also speak a little German too, that me mum taught me.'

The boy's accent was strong, but Charlie found he was able to understand him. 'Well, she must be very proud of you,' he said.

'Yeah, she was. You a pommy?'

Charlie nodded. Again, deep growls emanated from the dark, this time closer than before. 'What is it?' he whispered.

125

'Lion, I reckon.'

'Are you certain? Maybe it's something else?'

'I got a look at it. Been followin me for a long time.'

Charlie was aghast. 'Well why in God's name did you bring it here?'

'I wanted it to get *you*, mate,' Blaze replied, with a guilty smile crossing his face. 'Motorbike took me just about to the city before the petrol ran out, then I was on foot. You weren't far behind, so I doubled back.'

For a few minutes they waited together in silence to see if anything would happen, but nothing did, and eventually the growling stopped. Charlie noticed the boy had a sheathed knife attached to his loincloth, as well as a yellow GPS device exactly like the one he'd carried until it was taken by the policemen. 'So you're part of this as well, this… game?' he asked.

'What ya mean?'

'I was kidnapped in London. They took you too?'

Blaze nodded. 'I never seen em before, those whitefella's. I dunno why they stole me from my home. Do you know?'

'No, I'm sorry that I don't.'

'How'd ya get here so quick?'

'Some good people – a family – they found me in the desert and saved my life,' Charlie answered. 'They were headed in the other direction, but I offered them money to drive me. Along the way something happened, and, I—well… I ended up ruining everything for them.' He took his knapsack and brought out the cooked snake meat Kingsley gave him, holding it out for Blaze to take. 'Would you like some? It's a little better than the military ration crap.'

Blaze accepted it, and, hesitantly, he began to eat. As he did Charlie studied him closely. The boy seemed friendly enough, he thought. Maybe the two of them could travel together? After all, the boy still had his GPS, and Charlie needed it to get to the end. *Both* of them did. 'There's got to be a reason why you're here, why they wanted you,' he said to Blaze. 'We can try and figure it out. It would also be safer if we went together, help each other. Know what I mean? What do you think?'

For his own part, Blaze was wary of white men, and he wasn't sure if Charlie could be entirely trusted. He knew the man was one of the other competitors, and there was the possibility he might try and kill Blaze. But the young man had always been fair-minded, and he decided to at least give the Englishman a chance. 'I don't mind havin company,' he answered, as he chewed on the meat.

Charlie sighed with relief. 'Good, that's very good. I don't mind company either. I—I've lost my GPS, but we can use yours.' He purposely didn't mention that he also no longer had his knife. There was no sense letting the boy know he was unarmed, at least not yet.

'Where they want us to go?' Blaze asked.

'A city on the coast of Benin.'

'The coast? That where the ocean is?'

Charlie nodded. 'Yes, I think it's on the Southern Atlantic.'

'I never seen the ocean before.'

'Really?' said Charlie, with surprise. 'That's a damn shame. Well, maybe this will be your chance.'

Blaze pointed at the campfire with his spear. 'We should keep the fire going till morning. It might keep the lion away, and anythin else.'

'Yes, that's brilliant,' Charlie agreed. 'The fire is very, very important. Listen… do you want to rest a little? I'll stay up and keep watch if you want to get some sleep.' Right away it dawned on him that he was asking Blaze to trust he would not attempt to murder him while he slept, and he felt stupid for uttering the words. Studying the boy's dark eyes, he looked for any sign of his understanding.

Blaze shook his head. 'No, I'm good mate,' he answered, betraying nothing.

Charlie wondered, *could the boy be trusted?* 'All right,' he said, 'we'll just sit for a while I guess, see what happens.'

For a few minutes after there was an uncomfortable silence between them. The only thing to be heard was the buzzing noise of the two drones, flying high above in the night sky. As he sat staring at the fire, Charlie began to think he should tell someone else what he knew, just in case anything were to happen to him. What better person, he asked himself, than the one sitting right across from him? After all, he reasoned, the boy had been kidnapped as well. And if Blaze really didn't know why he was there, as he'd said, then didn't Charlie owe it to him to tell him the truth?

'Blaze,' he began, 'I want you to know why I'm here, what happened to me. I'll tell you everything. Now, believe me, when you hear it you'll think I've gone off the deep end. But it's the truth. I promise you, on my dear son's life, that it's the whole *god-damn* truth.

And when I'm done, maybe you can tell me what happened to you. We can piece it together, just like a puzzle, and we'll understand why you're here, why they wanted *you*... and how you fit into this insane fucking mess.'

It took Charlie three hours to tell Blaze his story, from the beginning when he first received the phone call from Anna, right up to when he was kidnapped and brought to Africa. He explained how he learned about The Syndicate and Metatron from reading Ernst's stolen emails, and of the Stratagem which outlined the secret cabal's plan to attack the United States of America.

As he listened, Blaze did not move or speak, but just stared into the campfire's hypnotic flames which appeared to him almost like dancing figures. He was feeling homesick as he was reminded of being in the Australian Outback, captivated with wonder by the legends and stories told by the old and wise shaman.

***

Two months earlier, in June 2001, Charlie finished reading all of the emails and documents Ernst had given him. He learned about Wolfgang, and the orders and information he was relaying to Stefan Ackermann from a secret group both men referred to as The Syndicate. He saw all of the highly illegal transactions that had been going on at the Deutsche Trust bank, including payment instructions for the plane hijackers in America, and the payment routes as they went through bank accounts across the globe. However, when Charlie read the 99-page report, "Stratagem for the Implementation of the New World Order", everything suddenly became crystal clear, and he understood what The Syndicate was planning.

But just before reading it, he was curious to find out the historical context of the term "New World Order", and he did an internet search to see what he could find. After reading through a number of articles, he discovered the phrase had been used throughout history to refer to any new era of great dramatic change in the balance of world power. He was also surprised to learn that it was a major theme of conspiracy theories for the emergence of a totalitarian one-world government.

Another article he found was a speech given by the former American president, George H. W. Bush, the father of the current president, to members of the U.S. Congress almost eleven years earlier. The date had been September 11, 1990. In the speech, delivered just before the Gulf War, Bush stated that one of the objectives of the United States in its confrontation with Saddam Hussein was the emergence of a new era of prosperity and co-operation, what Bush called the New World Order.

The Stratagem report was written by a group called The AIM Project, and was the first of two parts. It began with a preface by the authors stating that it was a twenty-five year plan for The Syndicate's military and economic conquest of the world, and it was designed by an Artificially Intelligent supercomputer they called Metatron. This secret report, to be distributed to only The Syndicate's members, was the blueprint to usher in the New World Order. The outlined goals and strategies contained in it would be directed to a number of top influential think tanks in Europe and America, some of which included: The German Institute for International and Security Affairs; Chatham House; Bilderberg Group; Council on Foreign Relations; American Enterprise Institute; Rand Corporation; Trilateral Commission; Atlantic Council; Heritage Foundation; and the Brookings Institution. It was the job of these groups, the report said, to analyze and then successfully promote changes of global and national policies in accordance with the Stratagem.

The beginning of the report described how, at the dawn of the 20th Century, it was understood by The Syndicate's forebears the impending introduction of nuclear weapons to the world would bring about the threat of total annihilation, and that a long 'cold war' would thus ensue between the United States of America and the Soviet Union. World War II would be the last big war fought by the major powers, a last grasp for territorial and resource gain. After this period of intense conflict, any further war directly between the superpowers was unthinkable, and unwinnable, and could only be fought through smaller proxy states.

The Syndicate soon realized that as their power was growing, smaller groups would rise to challenge them in their quest to dominate Russia and China, so instead they created these groups themselves and pitted them against the nations already under their control. In this way, The Syndicate was able to tighten their grip on power and manipulate governments into doing exactly what they wanted. After he read this, Charlie recalled "Operation Gladio", the official NATO code-name for "stay-behind" paramilitary groups allegedly responsible for assassinations and false flag terrorist attacks in Italy. There was also the Gulf of Tonkin incident, which he'd long suspected was a false flag attack meant to draw the U.S. into conflict with Vietnam. With origins in naval warfare, a false flag attack was a covert military operation conducted by nations with the intention to deceive. They are designed so that a self-attack upon their own country appears to have been carried out by someone other than those who really planned and executed them. In almost all cases the attack was used as justification for a nation to go to war.

The report said that one of these groups The Syndicate created, al Qaeda, was central to their current strategy. Al Qaeda, meaning "the base" in Arabic, was a Sunni Islamic terrorist organization that followed the Wahhabi movement, and which had been put together by the CIA and Saudi Intelligence. It was led by a wealthy Saudi man named Osama bin Laden, and its members were hard-core, battle-hardened Mujahedeen fighters who had fought the Soviet Union in Afghanistan, a war-ravaged country known for being the "graveyard of empires". Now, the terror group was allied with the Taliban regime, which itself had been formed in the early 1990s with significant help by Pakistani Intelligence, the ISI, in close collaboration with the CIA. Reading this rang several bells for Charlie. He'd recently heard of al Qaeda in the news, and of their declaration of war on America and Israel. The year before, the group had attacked U.S. naval forces off the coast of Yemen, and were now supposedly in Afghanistan as guests of the Taliban.

Next, the report explained that when the Soviet Union and Warsaw Pact collapsed in 1991, The Syndicate realized their opportunity for world domination was at hand. For this to be achieved it became necessary for the U.S. and its vassal states to enact unconventional hybrid warfare on a grand scale. The overall strategy was to use the military forces of the U.S. and NATO to create two divided zones in the world: The first was a "core" of stable functioning states in North America; Europe; India; Australia; and Japan; The second was a "gap" zone of perpetual war and chaos encompassing Africa; the Middle East; the Balkans; Turkey; Iran; Afghanistan; Pakistan; Southeast Asia; and much of Central and South America. By waging continuous warfare inside this gap zone, core nations could then exploit the natural resources of these states, thus denying them from The Syndicate's adversaries.

The Stratagem would officially commence after Germany's reunification, and the breakup of Yugoslavia in Eastern Europe. After this, Western nations would begin cutting off their alliances with Middle East despots, such as Iraq's Saddam Hussein, whom the West supported in his eight-year war against Iran. Thus, in 1991, the U.S. turned on Iraq, attacking the country because of Saddam's invasion of Kuwait. However, Iraq was only a stepping-stone, as The Syndicate's real target was *Iran*. An ally of the Soviets, Iran had been declared a mortal enemy of America and Israel ever since the 1979 Revolution saw the U.S. puppet dictator, the Shah, ousted from power. In the early 1990s, Russia entered negotiations with Iran to build nuclear reactors, and because neither country was directly within The Syndicate's control, this represented an immediate threat to their plans. If Iran were to acquire nuclear weapons, it would be much more difficult for The Syndicate to consolidate their power over the Middle East. Therefore, war was necessary—a war to remove Saddam Hussein—a *second* Gulf War. With the proper justification, Iraq could be attacked by the West without hindrance from other major opposing powers, including Russia and China. The chaos that would ensue from Iraq's destruction would be an example for the enemies of The Syndicate, and a signal that a new world war had begun.

All warfare is based on deception.

The report stated that a significant event was crucial for the Stratagem to succeed. The strategy could not be properly fulfilled without a great deception, an attack so terrifying and catastrophic that it would galvanize the American public and shock them into accepting a justified war: *A new Pearl Harbor.* This history-changing event, the most pivotal of the 21st century, will be the first strike in the emergence and creation of the New World Order.

Consequently, sometime in late 2001, a series of surprise, devastating false flag terror attacks upon the United States of America would take place. The attacks were designed by Metatron and augmented by The Syndicate's agents, and would be blamed on al Qaeda and its leader, Osama bin Laden. The U.S. government and their allies will not officially know about the attacks in advance, and will be deliberately kept in the dark to protect them under the cover of plausible deniability. A message would be sent directly from The

Syndicate to the Vice President of the United States, and it would be contained in the *date* of the attacks. Because of this particular date, the message would be unmistakable: *finish what was begun.*

Furthermore, the Vice President will be instructed to perform a task, to show The Syndicate he understands their message. At some point during the attack he will have his photograph taken with the British news magazine, The Economist, included somewhere in the picture. It was left unexplained why they chose this method of action for the Vice President to perform. Was this group connected to the magazine, Charlie wondered? He did not understand it.

The terror attacks, code-named "Archangel", will be organized and co-ordinated in an extremely compartmentalized process by a small faction of rogue top officials at the CIA and Pentagon, and all of them under the control of The Syndicate. Highly skilled and deadly agents will closely watch and monitor these officials, making sure their orders are carried out so the events unfold as planned. Upon reading this, Charlie immediately grasped that a coup d'état of the U.S. government would soon take place. The die would be cast with an act of insurrection. An American Rubicon, *the point of no return*, was about to be crossed.

The report reminded The Syndicate had built the World Trade Center towers in New York City specifically for one important reason: so they could later be destroyed when the time was most advantageous for the group. That time, it said, was now. On the day of the attacks, four commercial airline flights will be hijacked by twenty men from Saudi Arabia, some of whom will have taken flying lessons in America, and deliberately crashed into the WTC towers. However, these flying lessons would be a ruse, as all of the hijacked plane's flight computers will instead be remotely hacked by U.S. electronic warfare aircraft, and through these they will be controlled by Metatron. With perfect, precision-guided GPS, the planes will be flown by the supercomputer directly to their targets, of which there will be four: the twin towers of the World Trade Center in New York; the Pentagon, headquarters of the U.S. Department of Defense in Virginia; and finally the Capitol in Washington D.C. During the attack, U.S. Air Force defense exercises will be conducted to distract and confuse the participants when it occurs. All defense against the assault, including interception by fighter jets, will be totally shut down or impeded by Metatron. Before and after the towers of the World Trade Center are struck by the hijacked planes, pre-planted thermo-baric bombs and military-engineered nano-thermite will be exploded from within, bringing both towers neatly down to the ground.

Charlie was astounded. He could understand the attacks targeting the Pentagon and Capitol building, as they were the epicenters of U.S. power and control, but he wondered, *why the World Trade Center?* He was aware that, in 1993, Islamic terrorists had attempted to bring down New York's iconic twin towers using a powerful bomb. At the time the public was told the terrorist's motives were that the towers represented globalization and American financial power. But was that why The Syndicate wanted them destroyed? The report stated they had built the towers so they could be demolished at some point in the future. If this was true, Charlie thought, then it meant they'd been planning and preparing for this false flag attack since at least the early 1960s, when the WTC had first been designed.

Doing another internet search, he found an article with a quote from one of the WTC's original architects, at its dedication ceremony in 1973, which said the towers were a 'symbol of mankind's dedication to world peace', and that they represented a 'belief in the co-operation of men'. After reading this, a dawning realization came upon Charlie: *They want to symbolically destroy peace.* Was this going to be some kind of intricate occult ritual, he wondered?

Once the report finished laying out the technical details of the attacks, it then pointed out the objective was not to cause economic damage. The destruction would be for the entire world to witness live on TV, as it happens, with the target audience being the U.S. public. *Nothing is so painful to the human mind as a great and sudden change.* The shocking event would make them easier to manipulate by mass media under The Syndicate's control, and it would also provide a rock-solid justification for the U.S. government to go to war.

After the terror attacks, the propaganda technique known as the "Big Lie", most famously used to great effect by the Nazis, will be employed by the U.S. government on a vast scale. Anyone who will dare question or challenge the official account of the attacks will simply be denounced as a "conspiracy theorist". The world's public perception of what is reality and truth will be successfully shaped according to what The Syndicate wants, even if it's completely false. It won't matter whether something is true or not, as long as it's believed, and people will find more comfort believing the Big Lie than for them to confront the truth. Thereafter, when any major event in the world takes place, the U.S. government, and hence The Syndicate, will immediately establish the narrative, regardless of what it is and irrespective of the actual truth, and they will set it down in stone. "Facts" will be repeated over and over in the news, and drawn out over a long period of time as the Big Lie is sold to the masses. Reality and truth, therefore, is whatever The Syndicate wants it to be, all of it just an elaborately-designed media construction. Perception IS reality. In a post-truth world, everything and nothing will be true.

In the near future, said the report, the world public will be receiving their news and entertainment instantaneously through the internet and social media websites. People will be deluged by information on a daily basis, and all of it controlled by The Syndicate, who will take advantage of the public's inability to process everything. Television reality shows and other forms of entertainment will keep the masses both satisfied and distracted. Thus, when the United States goes on the offensive, most of the public will not notice or care, or even question the false flag terror attacks, but will instead be more concerned about the daily lives of their favourite reality TV stars. *Bread and circuses,* thought Charlie.

In the wake of the false flag terror attack, a grand "War on Terror" would be declared by the U.S. president. Further major terror attacks, including bioterrorism, would take place in America, the UK, France, Spain, and other European countries, striking fear in their citizens and forcing them to submit to their government's agenda. Civil liberties will be curtailed by sweeping draconian search and surveillance laws. Mass surveillance programs such as the ECHELON "Five Eyes" network already in place will be formally legalized, though they will still be kept a secret from the public. This was explained as being of critical importance for the success of the Stratagem, as it will increase the flow of information for Metatron to analyze and update with new strategies.

The beginning of the U.S. offensive in late-2001 would be in Afghanistan against the Taliban, to gain control of oil pipelines and opium production. After that, Iraq would be invaded under the pretense of threatening the United States with non-existent weapons of mass destruction. Once Iraq's total collapse was complete, "colour revolutions" would begin in Africa, a so-called "Arab Spring", which would then spread into the Middle East. It was explained these manufactured revolutions were essential for the Western allies to put economic pressure on Russia and China.

Libya, Syria and Yemen were the next major target nations planned for destruction. Recruitment for jihadist terror groups and mercenaries would be conducted by the CIA, MI5 and MI6, and the Muslim Brotherhood, in co-operation with France, Germany, Belgium, Turkey, Saudi Arabia, the UAE and Qatar, and then unleashed as a vanguard for the coming invasions. Horrifying chemical weapons would be deployed upon the helpless populations. After that, U.S. military involvement would be justified at the United Nations under "humanitarian interventions", and Iraq, Libya and Syria were to be fragmented under a plan of balkanization. Ultimately, the report explained, the goal was to create as much prolonged instability and chaos in North Africa and the Middle East as possible, without regard to the millions of innocent civilians who would die.

As a result of these devastating wars, a refugee crisis of immense catastrophic proportions would take place, one not seen since the end of World War II, with a projection of several million displaced families streaming into Europe and beyond. Among these refugees will be thousands of young Muslim men returning from fighting in the West's jihadist armies, who will then be used to strike fear in the populations with further suicide attacks, thus giving The Syndicate more power to enact their plans.

Upon reading this, Charlie concluded that if this took place the collateral damage and blowback would be an enormous disaster. Who knew how many innocent lives would be lost? He realized that the strategy being described was a barely controlled chaos which closely resembled the Hegelian dialectic process of problem, reaction and solution. But instead of waiting for problems to arise, The Syndicate, in diabolical Machiavellian fashion, were sowing and creating them for their own benefit.

Next, the report said that regime change would be necessary for a number of Latin American countries to prevent the spread of left-leaning socialist governments, and to gain control over their oil exports. Over in Europe, nations in the Caucasus region were also targeted, and it was stated the establishment of a Greater Albania in the Balkans was an absolute priority. Then, to divide Russia from the

European Union, a violent coup d'état was set to take place in Ukraine, taking away the Crimean Peninsula and hampering Russia's efforts to militarily help their allies Syria and Iran. In response, Russia was expected to counter-act this blatant coup by supporting separatist militias in Ukraine's eastern regions, which in turn would give the U.S. and NATO an excuse to impose heavy economic sanctions, and push their militaries right up to Russia's western border. Over in Asia, the United States and its allies will militarily confront North Korea, as well as China over its long-standing territorial claims in the South China Sea, where vast reserves of oil and natural gas lay deep beneath the ocean bed ready to exploit.

The second phase of the Stratagem explained the threat to the West will be re-branded from Islamic terrorism to Russia and China. The U.S. will withdraw from the ABM and INF missile treaties that had been signed with the Soviet Union. After this, missile "defense" shields will be installed in Eastern Europe and South Korea, with the pretext being that they are protection against Russian, Iranian and North Korean aggression. But this was only a deception, as the missile shield will instead be used offensively in the beginning stages of pre-emptive nuclear strikes on Russia and China. In the build-up to this Armageddon, both countries will not sit idly by and watch, with Russia expected to take military actions in Ukraine and Syria, and China establishing military bases in the Spratly Islands. These measures will create for the West further justification for war, and therefore a massive propaganda campaign was necessary, on a scale and magnitude not seen since the height of the Cold War.

The aggressive and hostile actions of the U.S. and NATO will inevitably result in driving Russia and China into a strategic partnership, a Eurasian integration of military and economic interests. Within the next ten years, the report said, a powerful Eastern alliance will emerge that will eventually represent almost half of the world's population. This association will free itself from the U.S. petrodollar system and shift their markets toward gold-backed trade.

To counter this threat to their strategic interests, the West will institute extreme austerity measures to help do away with its old and decaying economic system. Therefore, the economies of several Western nations will be intentionally crashed and ruined, including the United States. By collapsing them, The Syndicate can force each nation to give up their sovereignty by having them rely economically on a new political alliance. This was how they get control of countries, bringing them ever closer to a one-world government.

It was stated the European Union had served its purpose and now The Syndicate, who had worked so hard for decades to create it, were going to dismantle it in a relatively short matter of time. In its place a new economic and military architecture will be created. The first country targeted for economic destruction would be Greece, the birthplace of Western democracy. After reading this, it became apparent to Charlie that The Syndicate despised democracy, and the fall of Greece would be especially symbolic for them. Later on, the exiting of Britain, France and Italy from the European Union would mark the beginning of the end.

Near the report's conclusion, it explained that in the United States the rise of anti-Muslim hysteria will coincide with racist attitudes toward Black and Hispanic people, and will be deliberately fostered by having the highly militarized police forces employ an unofficial policy of murder in order to stir up a race war. Charlie realized that it would not take much to spark a race war in America, with trigger-happy gun-toting cops, damaged by war's post-traumatic stress and induced by years of fear-fed paranoia of anyone of colour. The result would be a disaster, with states of emergency being declared and the deployment of riot squads, the National Guard and the military. Far-right ultranationalist movements with anti-foreign platforms will spring up and become extremely popular, as America descends into civil war and chaos. Even U.S.-ally Japan will shed its pacifism and become more militarized and aggressive in its dealings with China and the Pacific region. Thus the proverbial pendulum, always under The Syndicate's control, will swing in the other direction.

The report finished by stating that in the midst of escalation for conflict with Russia, China, North Korea and Iran, a new president will be installed by The Syndicate, a corporate neo-fascist who will usher in the final stage of America's slide into the abyss of total dictatorship. Once this president is in power, The Syndicate will bring about another false flag terror attack on the United States in the form of a deadly biological weapon, which they called *Disease X*. Unleashed upon an unsuspecting world, this pandemic disease will cause immediate panic and hysteria will ensue. Shortly thereafter, a new doctrine called the Great Reset will be publicly declared in anticipation of a coming Fourth Industrial Revolution; mass protests will erupt, and martial law enacted in the United States and other Western nations, as their borders are locked down in preparation for total war. Beyond this, the Stratagem went no further, except to say that Metatron was analyzing new strategies that would be presented in the report's second part.

Of the U.S. and European leaders and officials responsible for carrying out The Syndicate's aggressions in their quest for global hegemony, absolutely none will be held accountable, with the report specifically stating they will be provided full immunity and protection from all legal prosecution. Furthermore, it spelled out that any officials who dare to defy The Syndicate will be *eliminated*. This outright threat was a critically important factor so that no trail leading back to the secret group could ever be discovered.

There were other secrets contained in the Stratagem that were only briefly mentioned in passing: a covert space program operating massive surveillance craft to spy on the planet; the development of hypersonic missiles and direct-energy particle beams; kinetic energy weapons for conducting planetary strikes, what the report called "Rods of God" that were already secretly orbiting the Earth; the planet's atmosphere was being seeded with nano-particles, and ultra-advanced weather-altering technology was being used to create earthquakes and tsunami's to pursue The Syndicate's agenda. To Charlie, all of it read like something straight out of a science fiction novel. One section briefly mentioned how the world's leading microbiologists and experts in vaccines and bio-weapons research were going to be systematically targeted for assassination, but it was not explained why. A final revelation Charlie thought significant was that there existed *another* powerful secret group who were allied with the superpowers opposing The Syndicate. Though they were not named, reading about them caused him to wonder if they could somehow be contacted.

"May you live in interesting times", went the traditional Chinese expression. Interesting times indeed, thought Charlie. It dawned on him that almost everything transpiring by human design on God's green earth happens because The Syndicate wants it that way, and no other. They were *that* powerful.

The Stratagem that had been created by their Artificially Intelligent supercomputer was a Pandora's Box of Orwellian nightmares totally out of control. Metatron was Big Brother on steroids. Who knew, Charlie wondered, if this monster could be restrained by its makers from taking over the entire world? The whole thing reminded him of a line from Mary Shelley's novel, Frankenstein: *"You are my creator, but I am your master."*

The Syndicate made the game and its rules, and it was fixed in their favour against humanity. The near future will be a dystopia of mass surveillance and no privacy, with fear and paranoia reigning supreme as destructive conflicts and terrorism rage across the globe. It was quite apparent to Charlie that The Syndicate's strategy was to construct a New World Order — by way of *disorder*. Who's watching the watchers, he wondered? Nobody was. Lunatics are running the asylum. *Those fools whom the gods would destroy they will first make mad.* With unimaginable hubris and without any restraint, this Empire of Chaos was about to wage a war against the entire world. It wasn't going to be a short war fought outright by the superpowers, but rather a long and protracted series of attacks and invasions, a grand chess game, a war by deception — a never-ending war.

A train wreck in slow-motion.

The razor-sharp gambit The Syndicate was going to attempt would either result in their controlling the entire world — or nuclear annihilation. Their sheer audacity and insidious ruthlessness seemed to know no bounds, something Charlie was sure the evil cabal took great pride in. They were a virus! A poison upon humanity and a host of monsters. No, he thought, they weren't even those things. They were like devilish gods, whose actions and ultimate agenda were above and beyond any human comprehension. Indeed, these malevolent enslavers of mankind were a tyrannical ruling elite, who were plotting to change the world with a war they were determined to win.

***

When Charlie finished reading the stolen emails and the Stratagem report, he came to the startling conclusion the entirety of it must be genuine, as he believed there was no possible way any person could dream up something so complex, so undeniably monstrous, and then go through the trouble to fabricate and pass it off for real. And for what ridiculous motive? No, he thought, this was not a hoax—this was the *real deal.*

For a few days after, he considered taking the evidence to his lawyer for safekeeping, or contacting the popular German news magazine, Der Spiegel, and showing them the Deutsche Trust emails. Eventually, though, he decided against both ideas. But the one thing he knew for certain was that he needed to inform his friend, Stanley Babbage, about the literal bombshell that had fallen into his lap, and there was not much time left to do it. The report stated the false flag terror attack on America would take place in late 2001 – *that very year*, and since it was already July the attack could happen at any moment. The thought of it occurring while he was in a position to stop it completely shattered him, as he was constantly reminded of his inaction with the Concorde disaster the year before. If he'd made known the threat to President Chirac's life, The Syndicate might have called it off, and the people that were killed would still be alive. Charlie wasn't about to make the same mistake twice.

In the days and weeks that followed, many strange things happened at his house which he found to be very unsettling. The phone would ring, sometimes in the middle of the night, and when he answered there would be no reply. There were also instances of loud knocking, or even banging on the front and back doors, and once opened he would find nobody there. He'd experienced pranks on his home before, but this was something else altogether. This was *terrifying.* Then, he found dead his wife's cherished Persian cat; the poor animal had been strangled and left hanging outside the back door. He began thinking people were lurking in the shrubs and shadows outside, watching his every move through the windows. After that he kept the shades and curtains drawn, even during the day-light hours. He did have a handgun hidden inside the house, just in case, but he was reluctant to ever use it.

To keep himself grounded while trying to make sense of everything, he began listening to his favourite music of the 1970s and 80s. One song he played repetitively at full-blast was "Who Can It Be Now?" by the Australian band, Men At Work. But nothing he did could settle his confused state of mind, and his intense paranoia only deepened, feeding upon his fear of being alone. Little-by-little, Charlie was turning into a complete basket-case.

'We could try a stronger medication, maybe an antipsychotic?' his doctor had suggested to him.

'You think I'm mad, two stops short of Dagenham?' Charlie angrily replied, using Essex slang. 'Just give me the fucking Xanax!'

Near the end of July, when Charlie could not stand being by himself any longer, he phoned Leigh and begged her to return home with David. When she finally did, her one and only condition was that he immediately stop pursuing any stories or leads which could jeopardize their lives, and their beloved son's life. Agreeing to his wife's request, he never again mentioned Anna, or the Concorde crash, and she never asked him about it. But Charlie did not keep his word to her, as he continued to work on the story he was betting would be the greatest of his career, and his ultimate vindication.

***

The morning of Thursday August 2, he checked his email, the same as he'd done every day like clockwork for the past nine months. After reading Anna's coded message, "dark actors playing games", he immediately had an ominous feeling that something big was about to happen, and he wondered, *was the attack about to take place?* Her email was like a jolt of electricity, energizing his desire to know more about the elaborate conspiracy, and yet terrifying him to the Nth degree for not knowing the reason behind Ernst and Anna's emergency. It repelled him even as he was hopelessly drawn to it.

When he booked a flight to Munich for the next morning, he purposely didn't tell Leigh. He knew that if he went ahead and told her the truth it would have put a heavy strain on their relationship too soon after getting back together, and that was something he didn't want to happen.

That evening, less than 24-hours before he was kidnapped, Charlie left his house and took the London Underground railway to St Pancras Gardens to meet his friend, Stanley Babbage. This time he brought with him the evidence of the conspiracy: a hard disk drive containing copies of Ernst's stolen emails and the Stratagem report. He believed that once Stanley read it for himself he would waste no time getting it published.

Just after 8:30 P.M., Charlie arrived at the park and waited at the gated entrance for Stanley to appear. It was a cool evening in London, and he pulled the collar of his coat tightly around his neck to keep warm. After lighting up a cigarette, he glanced around nervously. Not far away was Red, the park keeper, sweeping the sidewalk as he always did before closing the main gates.

'We won't be long tonight,' Charlie said to Red.

The old man smiled, and replied, 'That's fine, you two take as long as you need.'

Then Charlie had the thought he should call Leigh, letting her know he wouldn't be late. But when he reached inside his coat to retrieve his mobile phone, he found it wasn't there. *Where was it*, he wondered? He wasn't sure if he'd lost the phone somewhere along the way, or perhaps just forgotten it at home. He wasn't pickpocketed while riding on The Tube, he knew that much. With his heightened level of paranoia there was simply no way he would allow any strangers to get near him. He decided to worry about it later, and he put the phone out of his mind.

Not long after Stanley sauntered up the sidewalk. Charlie could tell his friend had been working late and had just come from the offices of The Daily Sun, only a five-minute walk away. The pair said their hello's and then entered the park, which was beginning to fill with long, dark shadows as the night approached.

'You look tired,' Charlie said to him as he took a puff of his cigarette.

'It's been a busy week,' Stanley replied, sighing. 'Hell, the last few months everyone's been working overtime, what with that royal massacre in Nepal, then the general election, and, of course, there was the whole election fiasco in America.' He chuckled under his breath. 'How did you do it, Charlie? How did you know Bush would be president?'

'Stan, I've got the evidence with me and I'm going to give it to you. After you read it, you'll *understand* how I knew.'

Stanley stopped dead in his tracks. 'Really?' he said, with surprise. 'You've brought it *with* you? Give it to me.'

Charlie brought out the disk drive and handed it over. As he did, he noticed his friend appeared nervous as he tucked it away inside of his coat. 'You won't believe it,' he said, 'it's fucking unreal what they're planning to do.'

'Oh? And what's that?'

Charlie saw a bench nearby and pointed to it. 'We should probably sit down for this.'

After they were both seated, Charlie lit up another cigarette and inhaled the smoke deep into his lungs. 'There's going to be a coup d'état in America, and it'll be under the cover of a major terrorist attack,' he stated in a low voice. 'Four commercial airliners are going to be hijacked and then deliberately crashed into the towers of the World Trade Center, the Pentagon, and the Capitol in Washington D.C.'

'*Deliberately* crashed? What about the hijackers?' Stanley asked.

'Suicide hijackers.'

'That's nonsense. Hijackers always want money, or demand to be flown to Cuba or some other socialist country. *Nobody* hijacks a plane to deliberately crash it.'

'They're religious fanatics—Islamic terrorists, who think after they do it they'll go to Paradise. Besides, they won't even be flying the planes, it'll all be just a ruse for the public and the investigations afterward.'

'So exactly *who* will be flying them?'

Charlie didn't answer. He wasn't going to tell Stanley about Metatron. If he did, he knew his friend would just laugh, hand him back the disk drive and then leave, without even so much as a look at the evidence. 'Listen to me,' he said firmly, 'there's an email stating the CIA is deliberately keeping the whereabouts of the hijackers from FBI agents trying to track them. Most of the hijackers are Saudi nationals, but there are a few others, and they've been training at flight schools in Florida. I've *seen* the records of payments to them— hundreds of thousands of U.S. dollars are going out from a New York bank to Germany where my contact works. Then the money is transferred to the United Arab Emirates and Pakistan, before it's finally deposited into the hijacker's bank accounts in Florida. It's quite obvious they're trying to hide the money trail. And, get this— the former CEO of this New York bank was made the executive director of the CIA just this past Spring!

'After the attacks, America is going to war. First it will be Afghanistan and Iraq, and then the world. They're already spying on the whole fucking planet, and things are only going to get worse. Here in the UK, a propaganda campaign is being planned to give news editors fake information about weapons of mass destruction in Iraq, and the German BND is going to supply the CIA with fake intelligence to be used as justification for war. You asked me the reason why they wanted Chirac gone, and the answer is because they think he'll oppose attacking Iraq, and influence other European countries. I also suspect it's the reason why the Foreign Secretary, Cook, was recently sacked. It's a competition for power—the Great Game all over again, this time between the United States, Russia, and China. The evidence is all there in the emails I just gave you.'

'So Charlie, tell me, why haven't you gone to the Americans about it? Called the FBI?'

'Because it wouldn't matter. The FBI, CIA, NSA—they all work for *them*—The Syndicate. They control the Deep State and the whole damn Western military-industrial complex.'

The term 'Deep State' was alleged by conspiracists to be a shadow government, a clandestine network of individuals secretly controlling a nation's policies behind-the-scenes.

'The Deep State is just a myth,' Stanley said derisively. 'It doesn't exist, at least not in any organized manner.'

'Well, you're wrong,' replied Charlie. 'This terrorist attack is *going to happen*. I don't know exactly when, just that it'll be very soon. For Christ's sake, I was right about Bush, wasn't I?'

'I'd say it was a lucky guess. And who are The Syndicate anyway? I've never even heard of them.'

'I don't know,' Charlie answered with a shake of his head, as he stubbed out his cigarette on the bench. 'I only know they're the ones behind this.'

Stanley sighed. 'Look, if your outrageous conspiracy is actually true, and the government gets wind of this, the paper will be immediately served with a D-Notice. They'll *shut us down*.' In the UK, a D-Notice was a government order to media editors not to publish things which might endanger national security, effectively a form of censorship.

'Of course, but this story is worth the risk,' Charlie replied. 'Tomorrow morning, I'm flying to Munich to meet with my contact. They've messaged me that there's an emergency, but I don't know what the problem is. Just promise me that you'll have a look at what I've given you, and after I get back from Germany we'll get together again and talk.'

'Well, I have to say Charlie,' said Stanley, his voice lowered, 'I very much wish you hadn't told me this. It's not good for me at all. I don't want to know about any of it.'

Charlie was perplexed. He knew Stanley was a stubborn man, but he wondered if his friend was experiencing some kind of cognitive dissonance, as if he'd become divorced from reality. 'Can't you see what I'm offering you?' he asked, his voice a fever pitch. 'This is possibly the biggest scoop since the Pentagon Papers and Watergate, even the god-damn Kennedy assassination! If even a fraction of it is true, then it's a conspiracy of such huge magnitude it dwarfs anything else of the past—or the future! Christ, what a fool I was to think you would ever publish this story. I shouldn't have gone to you. I should have taken it somewhere else!'

'Where, Charlie?' asked Stanley. 'Nobody would have touched it. There is no such thing as an independent press. You know it, and I know it. We lie every day to people. All of us in this business, it doesn't matter who. That's our job, it's what we get *paid* to do. And the people—they know this and accept it, because we are the only ones helping them make sense of the terrible things happening every day—'

'No, you're wrong,' interrupted Charlie. 'People don't like wars, sending their kids off to die for God and country. That's why they have to be lied into them. But if instead they're given the truth—'

'Look, my friend,' Stanley interrupted, 'take my advice and stop what you're doing with this if you know what's good for you. Don't follow this particular white rabbit any further down the hole.'

Charlie was caught off-guard. 'What are you talking about, is that some kind of threat?'

'No, it's not a threat, *it's a warning*. Listen to me—you're in danger. They have taken an extreme interest in you.'

'Who?'

Stanley quickly glanced about the darkening park. 'I—I have to be honest with you, and I can't hide it any longer. Not now. They've been breathing down my neck like you wouldn't believe, and I can't tolerate it. Not anymore. I *refuse* to tolerate it.'

'Who is it Stan?' implored Charlie.

'After I was promoted by the board, they came to see me: people from MI5 and the CIA.'

Charlie gasped in shock. 'Oh no, no, no—not you. I don't believe it!' He'd heard rumours before that almost every European journalist or editor with any clout was a CIA asset, but he had never seen any proof. Apparently, it had been sitting right next to him all along.

'It's the truth, I'm sorry,' Stanley said. 'You need to know that I—
I didn't have any choice in the matter. They threatened to shut the
paper down. There's more… much more they forced me to do that I
wish I could tell you.'

'Stan, tell me you haven't talked to them, that you didn't give
them what I confided to you in the strictest of confidence!' Stanley
was silent, and Charlie could see in his friend's eyes that he was
indeed telling him the truth. The revelation was stunning. 'What have
you done Stan?' he stammered. 'We were like brothers, and now it's
all gone… It's all gone.'

'You have to understand that I *need* to get them off my back. I
have the paper to think of.'

'What about Leigh and David? What about them?'

'You shouldn't have involved yourself in this, whatever it is. You
should have known better. Didn't you learn your lesson the first time
around? If you play with fire you're going to get burnt. You broke
the number one rule: never become part of the story. And now, like a
god-damn fool you want to do it all over again!'

'I thought the number one rule was giving people the truth?'
asked Charlie. Stanley didn't reply. Shocked by this, Charlie held out
his open palm. 'Give me the disk back,' he demanded.

'I'm going to leave now,' Stanley said, getting up from the bench.

Charlie grabbed Stanley's arm, trying to prevent him from leaving.
'I need the disk back!' he yelled angrily. 'I'm not letting you give it to
them, God damn it—'

'For Christ's sake, get a hold of yourself!' Stanley yelled back, as
he shoved Charlie's hand away. 'Just *who the hell* do you think you
are?' Seething with anger, he strode off toward the park entrance.

As he watched Stanley leave, Charlie could do nothing but sit in
abject misery and despair over the intense betrayal he felt. It took
him a minute to come to his senses, when he realized he needed to
return home and pack for his morning flight to Munich. Standing, he
left the bench and began making his way along the darkened path.

Then suddenly, from somewhere off in the distance, he heard the
sharp crack of a gun being fired. Startled, Charlie immediately
stopped in his tracks. Two more gunshots followed in rapid
succession. Scared now, he resumed walking, this time a little faster,
until he came to the main gate. Just as he got to the steps leading
down to the street, two pairs of hands came out of the shadows and

seized him. A gloved hand covered his mouth, preventing him from crying out, and he was dragged through the gate back into the park.

Though it was hard for Charlie to see, he could tell the attackers were wearing balaclava ski masks and dark clothes. But there was no way of knowing who they were, except that he was in the grip of two powerfully strong men. After dragging him a few paces, they violently threw him to the ground, where he landed hard against the stone chest tomb of some long forgotten soul. Then one of his attackers knelt next to him and brought out a needle syringe, and they aimed it directly for Charlie's inner ear. *Oh my God what are they doing?!* his mind reeled. *They're murdering me!* With absolute horror, he felt the needle being slowly inserted into his ear canal and the plunger pushed down. A burning sensation came across his cheek as the unknown substance began to flow through his body. At the same time in front of him, Charlie could see the other attacker scattering pills around his legs, and he heard the sound of the empty bottle as it struck the ground near his feet. His limbs suddenly felt weak, and he was on the verge of losing consciousness.

Just at that moment, a cry rang out: 'Hey, what are you doing to him?!' Charlie recognized it as the voice of Red, the park keeper. Surprised, the attacker next to him was distracted just long enough for Charlie, with all of the remaining energy he could muster, to knock the syringe out of their hand.

As the old man approached the attackers suddenly ran away, escaping into the darkness. Charlie struggled to stand up, as dozens of small pills fell from his pants to the ground. 'I—I owe you my life,' he stammered to Red. 'If you hadn't come along…' He took a couple of steps, before his legs wobbled and he collapsed down to his knees.

'Don't worry young man, you just sit tight. I'll call the emergency services,' Red replied. And with that the old man hurried away, leaving Charlie alone once again.

His vision started to blur, and he saw shapes jumping out at him from the dark shadows. He wondered if his mind was playing tricks, or if his attackers had returned to finish him off. Deciding to wait for help, he lay down on the cobbled pathway that ran through the park, before closing his eyes. The drugs in his blood stream were starting to take hold, and he began drifting helplessly into a spiralling dark void of nothingness.

ELEVEN

6 DAYS AGO – Friday August 3, 2001
LONDON, ENGLAND
8:03 A.M.

W HEN CHARLIE WOKE from his unconscious state, he found he was lying on a bed inside of a large rectangular room, brightly illuminated with sunshine beaming through big windows. The air in the room was cool, and it smelled clean, fresh and hygienic, the room giving off a feeling of peaceful serenity. Around him he could see several other bedded patients being attended to by a female nurse. Groggy, he sat up and then realized his wrist was handcuffed to the bed frame. *What's happened?* he wondered with alarm. His present thoughts were clouded, and he had only a dim memory of the last 24-hours.

A television was affixed to the opposite wall, where a small crowd of patients had gathered to watch a news report, which Charlie could just barely hear. The news reader was talking about an auto accident somewhere in Central London, and it looked to Charlie that it wasn't far from his house:

"…Though it appears that the automobile swerved for several metres, left the road, and smashed into the stone abutment of an overpass before exploding. Police investigators have not revealed yet what they think happened, though a medical emergency has not been ruled out. The female driver was declared dead at the scene, while her passenger, a young—"

Just then, the nurse changed the channel on the television to an entertainment program, and Charlie could see the American business entrepreneur, Donald Trump, announcing to the show's hosts that he was developing a new reality TV series.

Charlie sighed, as he had no interest in watching television. He'd always believed that with TV, and reality shows in particular, a viewer could never actually know for certain if what they were seeing was real or manufactured. Now that he'd read the Stratagem report, he was even more sure of it.

The nurse glanced over and saw that he was awake.

'Oi—Miss! Oh miss! Can you remove these?' Charlie called to her, pointing to the handcuffs. But instead of complying, the nurse rushed out of the room.

Suddenly, a male patient wearing pyjamas came over to Charlie's bed and stood near, just out of arms reach. Middle-aged, thin and scraggly, the man had sunken eyes, wide open in vigilant paranoia. Charlie found it to be unnerving.

'Are you crazy?' the man asked.

'What? No, of course I'm not!' retorted Charlie. 'I just haven't been feeling well.'

'Oh,' the man said, confused. 'This is the room they keep the crazy people.'

Charlie looked across the room to the other patients. 'I can assure you that I'm not one of them,' he replied sternly. *At least, I think I'm not crazy,* he thought.

'Why are you here then?' asked the man, curiously.

'Listen, mate, why don't you go watch the telly with your friends over there?' Charlie said, nodding in the direction of the TV.

'Oh, I can't watch that,' replied the man, shaking his head.

'Why not?'

'Because, they're sending messages, and I *understand* what they're saying.' The man lowered his voice, and then looked warily around the room. 'You see, I'm not crazy either. I had a revelation—I know how they control us without us knowing.'

'What are you on about?'

'How they do things mate, their method of control,' the man whispered back, edging closer to Charlie. As he spoke, his eyes were growing wider and wider. 'It's all ancient occult ritual. They talk about what they're gonna do on the telly, or in movies, newspapers, the radio, anything really. It's all hidden in plain sight, transmitted to us in secret code. They make people unconsciously aware to condition their accepting it when it happens. It's social manipulation and predictive programming. It's how they get whatever it is they want to take place. Do you understand, mate? They're summoning coincidences; conjuring up synchronicities. They know the future—because they're the ones making it.' He wagged his finger in warning at Charlie, who looked over again at the TV.

Donald Trump was still talking, answering a question with a wide toothy grin on his orange, suntanned face: '…Who knows what will happen?' Trump said to the interviewer. 'Maybe I'll even be President one day.'

At that moment, the nurse opened the door and re-entered the room, this time accompanied by a policeman. When he approached, the strange man at Charlie's bedside quickly scurried away into a far corner of the room. The policeman, who appeared to be in his 50's, was looking directly at Charlie with serious concern upon his face. 'Hello, Mr. Grimer,' he said, 'I'm Inspector Shipton of the Camden borough police department. We've been waiting for you to wake up.' Taking off his cap, he pulled a chair over and sat down, and then brought out a small notebook and pen.

'Where am I?' asked Charlie.

'St Pancras Hospital. You were found last night in the garden's next door.'

'What day is it?'

'It's Friday morning, just after 8 A.M.'

'Friday morning?!' Charlie blurted with surprise. 'I've missed my flight!'

'Oh? You were flying somewhere?'

'No, sorry, I don't know what I'm saying. No, I'm not,' Charlie answered, quickly backtracking when he realized the police had not yet discovered his booked flight to Munich.

'That's very good,' Shipton said, 'because I have many questions to ask you.'

'Well before you do, can I ask… Do you have a fag?'

'No, I don't. But even if I did, you can't smoke in here.'

Charlie groaned, and he noticed his free hand began to tremble, which he immediately tried to hide from Shipton under the bed sheet. He desperately wanted to leave, but resigned himself to playing ball and answering questions, at least for the moment.

'Mr. Grimer, do you remember what happened last night?'

'I presume it has to do with the reason I'm handcuffed to the bed?'

'Just answer the question please.'

'What happened? I... I can't remember. No—I do remember. I was talking to Stan.'

'Stan... Would that be Stanley Babbage, editor of The Daily Sun?'

'Yes.'

'You know Mr. Babbage?'

'Yes, of course. We worked with each other at The Sun. We... used to be good mates.'

'Mr. Grimer, Stanley Babbage was murdered last night.'

Charlie's mouth fell open, and in an instant his weariness disappeared. 'Oh my God! How?' he asked, in total shock.

'He was shot in the head several times. A gun with spent shell casings was found not far from the body. Do you own a gun Mr. Grimer?'

'Yes, but it's always kept at the house under lock and key. In fact, I doubt I've even fired it more than once. It was purchased by my wife.'

'Your wife purchased the gun?'

'Yes. It's registered under her name.'

'I see.' Shipton glanced down to write in the notebook. 'And exactly *why* did she purchase the gun?'

'Because we were being harassed by all manner of people, including the police!' replied Charlie, angrily.

'Would it surprise you to know that the gun found at the crime scene has only *your* fingerprints on it?'

'What? That's bollocks!' Charlie protested. 'He was just murdered last night and you've already got the forensic evidence nailed down? That doesn't make any sense, something's not right there!'

'We'll get into all that later. However, Mr. Grimer, there's something else you need to prepare yourself to hear... I regret to inform you that your wife, Leigh, *is also dead.*'

'What?!' Charlie exclaimed.

'It happened this morning, a little more than an hour ago. She was driving the car with your son as a passenger. We're investigating the scene of the accident right now.'

'Accident—what happened? Where's David? Where is my son?'

'It appears the car exploded. There was a terrible fire—'

'*Where is my son!?*' Charlie demanded, yelling. The other patients in the room were becoming restless, as they glanced over at the sudden commotion.

'David's been taken to the burn unit of Chelsea and Westminster Hospital,' Shipton answered. 'He's in an induced coma, in very critical condition.'

'Oh my God, no, no, no—this can't be happening!'

'At this time, I need to inform you that foul play is being considered, and you are a suspect.'

'Suspect? Why? I had nothing to do with it!'

'Mr. Grimer, cars don't just explode on their own. But all that will come out in the investigation.'

'The car didn't explode on its own! It struck a stone abutment—'

'—Did it? And exactly how do you know that?' Shipton inquired, suspiciously.

'Look, I was with Stanley in the park, then we had an argument and he left. I don't know what happened to him after that.'

'You had an argument with Mr. Babbage?'

Charlie nodded.

'May I ask what it was about?'

'No you may not! After that, I was attacked by two people.'

'You were assaulted?'

'Yes! Then the old man, Red, he surprised them and they fled... into the park I think.'

Shipton glanced at his notebook. 'Red... That would be the park keeper?'

Again, Charlie nodded.

'Yes, the old gentleman rang the hospital,' Shipton confirmed, reading his notes. 'We interviewed him, but he never mentioned seeing anyone else in the park.'

'Well, there was. I'm telling you *they were there.*'

'It says here he found you, "after you had consumed a large number of pills". Now tell me, Mr. Grimer, did you try and commit suicide last night?'

'No, of course not! I told you already, *I was attacked.* Whoever it was, they planted the pills to make it look like I was trying to kill myself. They had a needle, injecting me with some chemical or poison. They—'

'We have reports on file,' Shipton interrupted. 'You and your wife had a history of marital problems. You've been physical with her in the past? A little violent, perhaps—?'

'No.'

'Throwing her around, punching her—'

'No, no!'

'Was that why she felt it necessary to purchase a gun?'

'Not at all! That's simply not true. What you're insinuating is *a fucking lie.*'

Shipton's brow furrowed. 'Watch your language while I'm speaking with you,' he said tersely, before glancing again at his notebook. 'Now, I understand you both were recently separated?'

'Yes, but we patched things up and she moved back home with our son.'

'She was seeing someone else?'

'Listen, what business is it of yours? And exactly *how* do you know that we'd separated? Well?'

Shipton was silent and didn't respond.

'Look, am I under arrest?' Charlie asked.

'No, not *yet.*'

'Then kindly remove these cuffs and take me to see my son. After that, I promise you I will call my lawyer, and we'll go down to the station and answer all of your questions. But until that happens… I'm not going to tell you one more *god-damn* thing.'

***

Less than an hour later, Charlie was driven by another officer to the Chelsea and Westminster Hospital, so that he could see David in the intensive care unit. But before being allowed into the room, he was warned his son's injuries were so severe that he was not expected to survive. Then the officer allowed the father privacy, waiting for him just outside the open door.

Entering the room, Charlie saw David in a medically-induced coma, wrapped in burn dressings and hooked to life support machines. At that moment, everything else in Charlie's troubled mind disappeared, and only the immense love of a heartbroken father for his only child remained. Pulling a chair over to the bed, he sat down and leaned in close so he could be nearer, resting his hand on his son's chest. He wanted to say so much, but he didn't know where to begin.

'David... Daddy's here. Daddy loves you,' he whispered through tears. 'I'm sorry this happened, it's my fault. I wanted the god-damned story... I wanted to prove I was worthy, that I could do something, be *someone*, not just a washed up hack everyone despises. But, I... I was being selfish, only thinking of myself. I realize that now, after it's too late. Please son, forgive me...' He couldn't bear another moment of seeing David like this. Children were not supposed to die before their parents, he thought, as he began sobbing uncontrollably. 'My beautiful, sweet boy... Forgive me.'

Just then, it dawned on him The Syndicate hadn't been trying to kill him at all. It was his wife and son they wanted dead, to send him a direct message. They wanted to break his spirit, to destroy his soul. If that was indeed their plan, they nearly succeeded. The fact President Chirac hadn't been killed in the Concorde crash proved The Syndicate was not omnipotent, that something could happen which, despite all their great power, neither they nor Metatron had for-seen. It was at that moment Charlie realized they could be stopped, and he decided to *fight*.

'I promise you, I won't let them get away with it,' he said, with steely resolve. 'Even if it's the very last thing I do on this godforsaken world, I'm going to avenge you and your mother.' He leaned in closer and lowered his voice. 'David, 'I don't know if you can hear me, but I have something very important to tell you...' Cupping his hand over his mouth, he whispered into his son's ear.

When he was done, he glanced toward the door. To his surprise, he saw the policeman had gone. Tenderly, he kissed David goodbye on the forehead and then went to the door. Outside it, near the end of the hallway, he saw the policeman speaking to a man dressed in a black suit. Charlie quickly left the room and scurried down the hall, until he noticed a door leading to a stairwell. Going through it, he ran down two flights of stairs until he reached the ground floor, and then he exited the hospital.

Trying his best to make himself inconspicuous, he began walking down the sidewalk, unsure of where to go or what to do next. Glancing behind, he tried to see if anyone was following him, but it didn't appear there was. A few seconds went by, when he suddenly realized he needed to fly to Munich to meet with Ernst and Anna, and for that he had to retrieve his passport. He needed to go home.

By the side of the road, he spied an idling black taxi cab. Moving swiftly, he went to it and got inside. After directing the cabbie to take him to his house, the car sped away.

Now, Charlie's plan was to get the passport, and then go to Heathrow Airport to catch the next flight to Munich. He wasn't sure if Ernst and Anna would still be there, but he knew he had to try and find them. He'd made a promise to the couple which he fully intended to keep, even if it meant being many hours late. At this point, all he could do was hope they would try calling him on his mobile phone. But first, he needed to find it.

*****

After arriving at his home, he instructed the cabbie to park and wait for him on the street behind. Then, he used a key kept hidden under the door mat, and quietly entered. The house was nearly dead silent as he moved through the rooms, the only sound to be heard was the wooden floor creaking beneath his feet. Coming into the living area, he noticed the phone answering machine had several new messages. He clicked the PLAY button, and listened to them as he ascended the stairs and went to his bedroom.

From his bedside drawer he retrieved his passport and wallet, from which he then pulled out a key. Next, he reached under the bed and brought out a small box where the gun was kept. After using the key to open it, he discovered that the box was empty.

The gun was *missing*.

Frantically, he began searching for his misplaced mobile phone, but it was not in the bedroom either. *Where could it be?* he wondered. Downstairs, in the living room, the last message started playing, and he instantly recognized Leigh's voice.

'Charlie,' she began, with her voice echoing through the house, 'I don't know where you spent last night, but I guess you'll have some kind of excuse won't you?'

He couldn't believe what he was hearing. Leaving the bedroom, Charlie went to the stair landing and listened, hanging on to each of her words with dread.

'If you happen to come home, I'm taking David to mum's. For some reason my car wouldn't start this morning, so I'm using yours. You left your phone here, and some woman just called on it, asking for you. She said something I couldn't understand, then kept repeating *'nine eleven, nine eleven'* before I hung up. Who is she, do you know her?'

Oh my God, thought Charlie, as it dawned on him that Anna had called his mobile phone. He'd forgotten it inside his car, and Leigh had answered it.

'Wait, something is wrong…' Leigh said with alarm. 'The car's just started to—speed up on its own—I can't control it, it's getting difficult to—' She gasped, which was followed by a loud crashing noise, and then the call abruptly ended. After that, the machine tape stopped playing with a 'click', and again there was silence.

Charlie realized that he'd just listened to his wife's last moments, heard her last words, and he started to feel a sickening sensation in his stomach. Sitting down at the top of the stairs, he put his head in his hands and began to weep.

Just then, he was startled by the sound of glass breaking from somewhere downstairs. *What was that?* he wondered with alarm. He heard the wooden floor creak, and he knew someone else was inside the house. Slowly, cautiously, he began to descend the stairs.

When he came into the living area, Charlie found himself face-to-face with three people: two men in black suits and dark sunglasses, with a tall, slender woman standing in-between them. She was dressed in tight-fitting black leather, had short dark hair and fair skin, and she looked to be around nineteen years old. Her eyes were a pale blue, and she was wearing black glossy lipstick, giving her both a striking and unsettling appearance. He noticed that on the side of her neck was a tattoo of a coiling black snake in the shape of an "S". From this moment on, Charlie would remember her as the Woman in Black. On the floor, he saw what had once been a glass picture frame holding a photo of himself, Leigh and David, now laying in shattered pieces at the woman's feet.

'Just who the hell are you and what are you doing in my house?' Charlie demanded of them.

The woman approached and grinned a wicked smile. 'Come now Charlie, you *must* know who we work for,' she answered. Charlie noticed she had an American accent.

'Yes, actually, I—I've got an idea. You *murdered* my family.'

'You've been a naughty boy, haven't you Charlie? A *very* naughty boy.' Her voice sounded sexual and hypnotic, and Charlie could feel himself being mesmerized by it, lulled into a passive submission. For just a brief moment, he felt as though she was looking right through him.

'Look, if it's the emails you want, they're—they're on a hard drive, next to my computer in the study,' he stammered nervously, as he backed away from the threatening strangers. 'Please, just take it and leave. Take the whole damn computer if you want.'

'Oh, we'll get them you can be sure of it,' she replied. 'But that's not what they want.'

'What do you mean?'

'They want *you.*'

'I'm not going anywhere.'

'You weren't going to fly to Munich to meet with Ernst?' she asked, feigning surprise.

'But—how do you know that?'

She gave a short, sinister laugh. 'They know *everything.*'

The two men in black were drawing nearer to him, when, all of a sudden, the home telephone rang, its momentary distraction startling the agents and catching them off-guard. Thinking fast, Charlie used it to his advantage. Spinning around on his feet, he made for the kitchen where there was a back door to the house. Luckily for him, Leigh had left it unlocked, and he threw it open and scurried outside. Quickly, he crossed the courtyard and went through a gate, with the agents trailing not far behind. When he got to the street, he saw the taxi waiting for him, just as he'd requested.

'Go now!' he yelled at the driver, as he threw himself into the car. The taxi took off, and, seconds later, police cars zoomed by with sirens blaring, headed straight for Charlie's house. Glancing out the cab's rear window, he saw the agents watch helplessly as he escaped.

'Are we still going to the airport?' asked the cabbie, nervously.

'No, I can't go there,' Charlie replied. His mind raced, trying to think of what to do next. The Syndicate were aware of his plans, and he knew they wouldn't allow him to get away a second time. The only option that was left was to go into hiding, as there was simply no question of turning himself over to the police. The police were working for *them.* But there were CCTV cameras all over London, and if he stayed in the city, it would only be a short matter of time before he was caught. Then, he had the idea of taking a ferry to the Isle of Wight, or even hiring a boat to France or Germany.

'Take me to Southampton,' he told the cabbie.

'I'm not supposed to leave the city, mate.'

'I'll pay you well. Just take me there.'

The cabbie nodded. 'You in a… bit of trouble there, mate?' he asked, glancing at Charlie in the rearview mirror.

'No, not at all. It was just a mix-up, a misunderstanding,' Charlie replied, hoping the man would ignore his obvious lie.

'Hold up a minute,' said the cabbie, as he scrutinized Charlie's face. 'I've seen you before, haven't I? You were in the newspapers—'

'I'm sorry, but you've got me confused with someone else.'

A few seconds went by, and Charlie began thinking of Leigh's final words in her message on the answering machine. She'd said a woman had called his phone looking to speak to him, and that she kept repeating "nine-eleven". *Nine-eleven. Did Anna mean 911?* he wondered. In the UK, the emergency service number was 999, but for North America it was 911. However, the number 911 was almost universally recognized as an emergency, in a similar way to the SOS distress signal. Was Anna trying to warn him of imminent danger, or perhaps even his wife?

Out of the blue, Charlie heard the sharp crack of a firing gun, and the rear window shattered as the taxi was sprayed with bullets. Covered in tiny shards of glass, he glanced furtively out the rear window and saw two people on a speeding motorbike, weaving in and out of the traffic behind the car. Attired in dark leather, the attackers faces were hidden by black helmets. The passenger was shooting what looked to Charlie like a small Uzi submachine gun. They let off another volley, and one of the tyres was struck. The taxi suddenly veered sharply to the left and right, almost going out of control. The cabbie slammed his foot on the brakes, and the car came to a quick, screeching halt. Charlie opened the door, and, with the cabbie spewing a mouthful of curses, he jumped out and landed hard on the gravel. A second later, he picked himself up and limped over to the sidewalk. Nearby, he saw an entrance to the Underground, and he headed to it as fast as he could, pushing and shoving his way past a growing crowd of spectators who'd stopped to gawk at the strange scene.

The pair on the motorbike turned around, and then drove on to the sidewalk. The bike's engine revved, and then it took off, coming toward Charlie at full speed. People jumped out of its way, only barely managing to escape from being run over.

Reaching the Underground entrance, Charlie hurtled himself down the concrete stairs, then hopped over a ticket gate and began running down the maze of winding tunnels, until he finally reached the rail platform. Huffing and puffing, he came to a stop. Now there wasn't anywhere else for him to go, and all he could do was anxiously wait for the next train to arrive. A television screen mounted on the wall suddenly caught his attention. On it was a breaking news report, showing the smoldering wreckage of an auto accident in Central London, the same he'd seen earlier on the TV at St Pancras Hospital. After the video played, an image came onto the screen: it was a photo of *Charlie*. Shocked, he strained to hear the words of the news reader over the loud din of the platform crowd. As he listened, he felt his whole body go numb.

"...The infamous former journalist, Charlie Grimer, is believed to be responsible for the death of his wife. Their young son was rescued from the inferno, and is currently in critical condition. Police have said they are not ruling out a pipe bomb. Grimer's friend and editor of The Daily Sun, Stanley Babbage, was found shot to death last night in Camden. Police sources think there is a link, and are working on a theory of Grimer's discovery of an extra-marital affair. After the murder, Grimer was admitted to nearby St Pancras Hospital on a suspected suicide attempt, from where he later escaped. Police say his current whereabouts are unknown, and that he should be considered dangerously unstable and not approached."

When the news report ended, Charlie stood there dumbfounded, unable to believe what he'd just heard. The police were trying to frame him, pinning the murders of Leigh and Stanley on *him*.

Suddenly, there was a commotion on the platform, and he looked just in time to see several men in black agents, their guns drawn, running toward him at full speed. His adrenaline surged and Charlie took off in the opposite direction, forcing his way through the crowd until he came to the platform's end. The agents were almost upon him. In a panic he jumped from the platform, making sure not to touch the dangerous electrified rail, and then he entered the dark tunnel. He didn't get far before he felt a warm wind blowing, the unmistakable effect of it being pushed ahead of an oncoming train. He could hear it getting closer, bearing down on him. Coming around a bend, the train's bright lights illuminated the tunnel, allowing Charlie to find, almost at the last moment, a hidden niche where he could escape.

WHOOOSH! roared the train as it went by, its whistle screaming.

Afterward, he came out and looked to the tunnel entrance. The men in black were still there, cautiously approaching with their weapons at the ready. Continuing to run, Charlie thought for a second that he might get away, when suddenly the tunnel lights switched on. The sound of a latch being turned and a door opened echoed off the metallic walls, and he saw several agents enter the tunnel a few metres ahead, trapping him.

Taken without a fight, Charlie knew it would have been pointless. The agents cuffed him, and, using a technician's service stairwell, they brought him back up to the street. After being thrown into a waiting black van, tape was put over his eyes and mouth, and cotton stuffed inside his ears. Then, a dark hood was placed over his head. From this moment forward, he was starkly aware that his continued existence was at the total discretion and mercy of The Syndicate.

For three days, Charlie neither saw nor heard a thing.
There was only pitch black.

DC Wince

TWELVE

DAY 3 – Thursday August 9, 2001
7:15 A.M.
15°51'29.8" 6°51'40.3"

THE SUN HAD JUST RISEN in the Sahara, and the night's cold air was being quickly replaced by a growing, sweltering heat. Dale Crumb pulled his goggles down over his eyes, as he walked down the centre of a paved road which seemed to go on forever. For the first time since the beginning he was now moving on foot, but the intense heat made it difficult, and it wasn't long before his pace slowed significantly.

The day before, he managed to catch up to yet another of the competitors, Charlie, whom he subsequently attempted to run down with his motorcycle. Though he had no idea who the man was, Dale believed he heard a distinct British accent when he cried out in surprise and anger. He'd fully intended to kill the stranger, and would have done if he'd gotten him at the sharp end of his serrated knife. But his opportunity was lost when, after a brief chase, the Brit had deliberately ridden his motorcycle into a massive sandstorm. In the ensuing maelstrom, Dale's own motorbike received a flat tyre, and, having no tools for a repair, he reluctantly abandoned it.

Holding his knapsack by its strap, he dragged it along the ground behind him. In the bag he still carried food, but more than three quarters of his water had been consumed, and he knew the remainder would soon be gone. However, if he could catch up again to the Brit, and this time kill him, he would get the man's water, along with the chance to live a little longer. It was do or die, there

163

was no choice.

When Dale resumed tracking the man on the GPS, he realized his target was moving south-west at an ever-increasing rate. After he discovered the paved road which ran north and south, he decided the man ahead must have also found it, and was either still using his motorcycle, or had somehow managed by a stroke of luck to hitch a ride. With this development the stakes were raised considerably, as Dale was without a mode of transport while his nearest target was escaping. Now, he was no longer trying to catch up to his remaining two competitors… but to stay alive.

Pausing on the road, he unhooked the GPS from his belt and carefully scrutinized its screen. It didn't display the road on which he was walking, but it did show that he was over four hundred miles from the border of a country south of him, whose name he did not know. At this point, all he could hope for was that his own luck would soon change. If it didn't, he knew he was going to die.

Another half-hour of walking went by, when, next to the side of the road, he came upon the rusted shell of an old derelict car, a Ford that looked to be from the 1950s. Approaching it, he looked inside and saw that much of the interior was empty, its contents having been scavenged a very long time ago. A flash of faded colour on the car's dusty floor suddenly caught his eye. Curious, he leant inside and pushed aside debris, revealing an old worn postcard. Picking it up, he turned it over and was surprised to see a picture of Mickey Mouse waving in front of Sleeping Beauty's Castle at Disneyland, with the words "it's a small world!" printed at the bottom. Dale was flabbergasted, and he thought, *how strange to find this here, in the Sahara of all places?* The words on the card, 'it's a small world', evoked within him many memories and deep emotions. None of them were good.

***

Dale had been twelve years old. Alone at his house one afternoon, he decided to peek inside the closet of his parent's bedroom. There, buried beneath a stack of his father's National Geographic and Playboy magazines, he discovered an object his mother had left behind after she ran away, something Dale had never seen before: a white jewellery box painted with many cartoon people, animals and flowers. He opened the lid and the cheerful tune "It's A Small

World" began to play. Inside it, he discovered some of his mother's old rings and earrings. After briefly looking them over, he next found a gold necklace. Bringing it out, he saw the necklace had an attached pendant in the shape of a tree. Dale had never worn jewellery, and, curious to see what it looked like, he undid the necklace's clasp and put it on.

A little later, he was eating at the dinner table when his father noticed the necklace around his son's neck. Immediately he flew into a violent rage and savagely beat the boy, leaving him with a black eye and swollen lip. It certainly hadn't been the first time his father viciously attacked him, as he'd already suffered through several outbursts and beatings. But on this particular occasion Dale knew it had happened not because he'd been in his parent's closet, or even that he'd opened his mother's jewellery box, but because the necklace was a painful reminder for his father that his wife was gone, and he believed his son was to blame.

Afterward, Dale couldn't understand why he'd kept wearing the necklace, knowing what his father would do if he saw it. It could have been he just wanted to feel his mother close by him for a short time; or maybe it was because he actually *wanted* his father to see the necklace. Maybe it was for both reasons, he didn't know. But whatever was going on inside Dale's subconscious mind, the severe beating gave him the excuse for what would come next, and it was something he'd wanted to do for a long time.

That night he took his father's hunting rifle from its cabinet, loaded it with a single cartridge, and then he went downstairs to the living room. Over in the corner the TV was playing The Star-Spangled Banner, the channel's final broadcast for the evening. In front of the television, Dale's father was slouched down in his armchair, passed out drunk, with a near-empty bottle of whisky in his lap. Dale approached, the rifle held tightly in his hands. Slowly he raised its barrel, until it was pointed right at his sleeping father's head. On the TV the national anthem abruptly ended, and the screen turned to white static. The loud noise woke his father. When he saw the gun pointed at him, he looked at his son and muttered: '*Do it.*'

Dale was shocked at the finality and resentment contained in the two simple words, but it was the infinite sadness that he saw in his father's bloodshot eyes that caused him to hesitate. He hated this violent and pathetic drunk before him, but he could not bring himself to pull the trigger and put an end to the man's miserable life. Thereafter, Dale would come to regret his perceived temporary moment of weakness, but his father would never again lay a hand on him in anger.

Back in the desert, as Dale stood next to the derelict car by the side of the road, he gazed at the faded postcard in his hand in amazement, and thought, *it's a small fucking world after all.*

***

About an hour after he resumed walking, he was surprised when he noticed something ahead of him on the horizon. Was it just another mirage, he wondered? Many times over the last two days he thought he'd seen lakes of water, and even an oasis. Of course, they had all been nothing but tricks of light played on his eyes. But as the object got closer he discerned that it was no illusion—it was a car on the road, and it was coming his way.

Instantly, he became overjoyed at the sight.

'Hey! Hello—hello!' he shouted, waving his arms excitedly and jumping up and down. As it neared, he could see the car was an old beat-up Toyota, and it slowed down as it passed by. Inside of it were three people: a man behind the steering wheel; a woman next to him in the passenger seat; and a young boy in the back. It was obvious to Dale that this was a family. 'You—you have no idea how happy I am to see you!' he exclaimed to them. But the man, his wife and child said nothing in reply. Instead, they silently and cautiously watched him as they went by, barely acknowledging he was even there. 'Water… Please… May I have some, just a little? I'm begging you!' Dale pleaded, as he held out his empty water canteen. For just a moment, he thought they would stop the car, but then he saw the mother say something which apparently changed her husband's mind. The car kept going, leaving Dale in the middle of the road. 'Wait! Come back!' he yelled. 'Please—you can't just leave me here like this!'

The family was leaving just as quickly as they'd come. From out of the car's back window, the boy was watching Dale as he begged for his life. But then, the child suddenly opened the back passenger door, and he quickly leaped from it onto the road. The father brought the car to a halt as the mother angrily called out, but the boy ignored her and ran up to Dale, holding out a bottle of water for him to take.

'Thank you, thank you,' Dale said to him, gratefully. Taking the bottle, he unscrewed its cap and gulped down a few mouthfuls. The water felt very good in his dry, parched mouth, and he poured a little more over his head, relishing the sensation of it running down his reddened, sore skin. Looking the boy over, Dale thought that he couldn't have been any older than nine, just about the same age he'd been when his own mother had picked up and left. 'You're a brave one, aren't you?' he said to the boy, as he tussled his hair. He tried giving the water back, but it was pushed away; the boy was letting him keep it.

Getting out of the car, the boy's mother strode towards them, all the while yelling what sounded to Dale like a stream of profanities at her son's insolence.

Dale knew the boy's parents had just been about to leave and let him die of thirst. Indeed, if it were not for the kind generosity of their son, it would have been game over for him. At that moment Dale's heart began to harden, as he remembered something his father had once said to him: 'Desperation reveals a man's true character when he thinks he's got nothing left to lose'. And now, Dale was most certainly a desperate man.

As he placed the water bottle inside his knapsack, an idea came into his confused and angry mind, and, without thinking it through, he instantly acted upon it. Using one arm, he suddenly grabbed the child as he unsheathed his knife with the other, and he put the sharp blade against the boy's throat.

Seeing this, the mother screamed and ran over, shouting at him: 'Ewad! Segi Tegi!'

'Shut up! Shut the fuck up!' Dale yelled back at her. 'You didn't want to help me—*now you're gonna pay!*'

At that point, the father exited the car, and he was holding a Kalashnikov machine gun. As he approached he raised his gun until it was pointed at Dale's chest. 'Ma foull teged awa?' he asked, speaking in his native Berber tongue.

Dale didn't understand him, but he believed the man was asking for his son to be released. 'Look, I didn't want this to happen!' he replied. 'You could've stopped to help me, *but you didn't!* So this is the deal... You're going to give me your gun and your car, and if you don't—*I'll fucking kill your son!* He waved the knife towards the ground, motioning for the father to drop the gun.

The father understood despite the language barrier, and he put the Kalashnikov on the ground. 'Hê... Wa-n-ak,' he said, as he shoved the gun across the asphalt.

With the knife held firmly against the child's throat, Dale moved slowly to the gun and picked it up. He was quite familiar with weapons, having hunted with his father many times as a child in the Pennsylvanian countryside. He'd also fired semi-automatic guns at shooting ranges, but none of them were as exotic as the Russian-made assault rifle he was now scrutinizing in his hand. After he found the gun's safety switch, he made sure that it was turned off. The father had handed his gun over and kept his part of the deal, and Dale intended to honour it. However, the assault on the boy had only been a bluff, as he was never going to actually hurt the child. His bluff had been called and Dale had won. He let go of the boy, who then ran to his mother, clinging to her as she sobbed, while the father just stood watching in silence.

Dale went to the car and looked into the back seat, where he saw supplies of food, clothing and more plastic bottles of water. Next, he opened the car's trunk and found two gasoline jerry cans. Those he would be keeping, he thought, before bringing everything else out and leaving it on the road. After taking two bottles of water, he went over to the father and threw them to the ground at his feet. 'There you go,' Dale said to him.

'Iqqed-kai yalla dar Temsi,' the father replied.

Dale was about to get into the vehicle and drive away, when he hesitated. With the Kalashnikov in his hand, he casually walked over to where the mother and son were standing. Raising the rifle, he pointed its barrel at her head and pulled the trigger.

BANG!

The gun loudly fired off a single round, and the mother fell instantly to the ground, blood rushing from a gaping hole in her forehead. The boy let out a shriek of horror: 'Ma! Ma!' he cried, as he grasped desperately at her body.

'Yeah... life's a bitch, kid,' Dale muttered, as he slung the rifle over his shoulder and went back to the car. Getting inside, he put it into gear and turned the car around, heading back in the direction it had just come from.

The bad you do comes back at you.

As Dale drove past the shattered remains of an innocent family he did not look at them even once, feeling neither remorse nor guilt for the cold-blooded murder he'd just committed. Instead, what consumed his mind was firm resolve to get ahead of the other competitors. There was still three days left in The Game, and he was determined to win—no matter what.

THIRTEEN

4 YEARS AGO – Friday July 25, 1997
NORTHERN TERRITORY, AUSTRALIA
11:25 A.M.

SLOWLY BUT STEADILY, Blaze and Darby trudged across the dry spinifex-grass and red earth landscape of the Tanami Desert, which was dotted with large termite mounds and acacia shrubs. It was seven days now they'd wandered in the vast nothingness, lost and unable to find their way home. Thick, dense clouds had obscured the sun by day, and the stars and moon at night, hindering any possibility of their using them as guides. To make matters worse, the pair had long since run out of food and water. No watering holes could be found, and while they did follow the tracks of several animals, including red kangaroos and bandicoots, not a single one appeared.

Blaze was walking a good distance behind his friend, weak from hunger and fatigue, and he struggled to keep up. 'We're never gonna see home again, we're gonna die out here,' he muttered despondently, speaking in Light Warlpiri.

'No we won't,' Darby replied. 'Have faith the animal spirits will help guide us. Besides, I reckon the trackers will be out searching.'

Blaze shook his head. 'Nobody will come out this far.'

'They will if they're also looking from above. I was thinking… what if we leave a message?'

'What ya mean?'

'We could write "SOS" on the ground,' Darby suggested. 'Y'know, just like a ship sending an emergency call over the radio?

My uncle said they sometimes use planes to search for people who get lost. Maybe they'll send one from Yimampi. What ya think?'

Blaze knew his friend was talking about the Coniston cattle station, about two hundred and fifty kilometres north-west of Alice Springs. 'Yeah, right-o,' he agreed.

For the next ten minutes, the pair used their boomerangs and spears to draw "SOS" in big letters in the red dirt. When they were done, they stood for a while and studied their handiwork.

'Your uncle worked at Yimampi, yeah?' asked Blaze.

Darby nodded. 'When he was a young fella. Why?'

'Jus wonderin… Did he tell ya stories?'

"Bloody oath he did mate,' Darby answered. For a few seconds he thought, and then said, 'Uncle told me bout a half-caste he used to work with, a bloke named Mick. Said he liked to draw pictures, and he played the didgeridoo real good. One time he played it right till the sun came up, but it kept the station manager awake the whole night.

'Next morning, the manager gathered all the blackfella's together and asked which of em was the good player, and Mick stepped forward smiling big. The manager says to him, "See here, you sit on this big rock and you play and keep playing, and if ya stop even once I'm gonna shoot ya dead on the spot". So Mick sat himself down on the big rock and played the didgeridoo all day in the hot sun, while the manager watched from a chair in the shade, drinking rum and holding a loaded rifle cross his knees. My uncle reckoned Mick played for his life for three days straight, till he couldn't play no more.'

'What happened?' asked Blaze. 'Did the manager shoot him dead?'

'Nah mate,' Darby replied, 'the manager didn't take his life, but the sun almost did. Mick never forgot, and he never forgave either. Uncle said he spent the next six months waiting patiently for the right moment to get his revenge.'

'What'd he do?'

'One night, at the station, they was in the middle of playing cards, when Mick suddenly took up the manager's rifle and shot him in the chest. Killed him real good. Later on the police took him away, and that was the end of old Mick. Uncle reckoned he was always a stubby short of a six-pack. But he was a good bloke.'

After Darby finished his story they resumed their journey. A few minutes of silence went by, before Blaze finally spoke again.

'Darby,' he began, 'if anything happens to us, like we don't make it back, I—I wanna know somethin…'

'Yeah mate?'

'When you came to town, to the school, and we had the race, why did ya still talk to me after I struck ya in the face? Why'd you wanna be my friend when nobody else did?'

Darby laughed. 'You're a good runner.'

'That's not the reason, and ya know it.'

Darby stopped, and then turned to face Blaze. 'Listen, ya wanna know why? The reason is this: Uncle told me there's a whitefella theory that life is all bout competition, y'know, fighting to survive and getting to the top. That it's all biologies and evolution. But he reckons it don't have to be that way, that we gotta co-operate with each other instead of fighting, because we're brothers and we're mates. And that's the reason. Now c'mon ya silly drongo, let's keep going.'

The pair walked for another half hour, before they ascended to the top of a tall ridge. There, spread out before them was a gigantic, circular crater.

'That's Kandimalal!' Darby shouted with glee. 'I know where we are, I know the way home from here!' He took off running down the side of the crater's rim.

Kandimalal, also known as Wolfe Creek Crater, was an ancient meteorite impact site. For thousands of years, the Aboriginal peoples of the Northern Territory believed the crater was made long ago in the Dreamtime, when two rainbow snakes crossed over the land, creating rivers wherever they went. Finally, one of the serpents rose up from the ground leaving behind the giant crater in its wake.

Blaze chuckled and muttered to himself, 'We'll die of hunger and thirst before we ever get home.' Then he followed after his friend down into the crater.

A few minutes later, as the pair approached the crater's centre, their attention was caught by something falling down from the sky and landing on the ground near Blaze.

'Crikey! What was that?' asked Darby, startled.

Going over to it, Blaze saw a small white fish at his feet. 'It's a yawu—a fish!'

'Huh? That ain't possible,' Darby said, skeptically. 'Have you finally lost the plot, mate?'

'Come have a look if ya don't believe me.'

Darby went over and saw that, indeed, there was a living fish flopping around on the ground.

'Well fuck me dead. How can this be?' Darby asked, mystified.

Suddenly, more fish began to fall, until the sky became dark with thousands of spangled perch raining down upon their heads. Laughing, the two young men jumped for joy and then went about gathering as many as they could carry.

FOURTEEN

DAY 3 – Thursday August 9, 2001
2: 36 P.M.
12°16'12.7" 4°33'33.3"

THE GREAT AFRICAN savannah plain stretched out in every direction as far as the eye could see. The landscape was extremely dry and arid, with short, yellow grass and red sand, and with only a scattering of acacia and baobab trees to provide much-needed shade from the sun. Since leaving the campfire in the early hours of the morning, Charlie and Blaze had walked a distance of almost eighty kilometres in a little more than ten hours. Though they encountered no other people, the pair did see various kinds of animals, including grazing herds of gazelles and buffalo. The flying drones kept pace with them the entire time, always moving around in wide, opposing circles, several hundred feet above.

The growling at the campfire the night before had indeed turned out to be a female lion, just as Blaze had said. Several times they'd seen the animal keeping itself a few hundred yards away, always hiding in the grass. The pair had come to the conclusion the dangerous predator was either following out of simple curiosity, or it was stalking them.

Charlie was unsure if the young man understood everything he'd said the night before, as Blaze had quietly listened to him without speaking a word. Regardless, the fact he now had someone else with him, a companion, significantly eased Charlie's anxiety, which was something he very much appreciated.

The sun's heat was stifling and unbearable. Perspiration poured off from Charlie's head and face, and his skin was red raw and peeling. Every now and again, whenever the pair would come across a lone acacia or baobab tree, he would beg Blaze to stop and rest for a few minutes in its shade. The sheer endurance and stamina the boy possessed was incredible, as he showed almost no sign of being fatigued from the hours of continuous walking. Charlie thought it was like nothing he'd ever seen before.

'This blasted heat—it's normal where you come from?' Charlie asked, wiping beads of sweat from his forehead with his shirt. The young man was walking a few metres ahead of him.

'Yeah,' answered Blaze.

'You don't talk much, do you?'

'Only when I got somethin to say.'

Charlie's mouth was dry, making it difficult for him to speak, and he brought out his canteen to quench his thirst. 'We need to find more water, I'm almost out,' he said, after swallowing a mouthful.

Blaze paused, and then pointed with his spear to the sky ahead of them. 'It's gonna rain soon,' he replied. 'Nother hour, maybe two.'

Charlie looked, and saw storm clouds gathering in the south-west, moving in their direction.

Indeed, Blaze was correct. Two hours later, thunder rippled across the plain, accompanied by flashes of lightning which arced across the sky. Then, a torrent of rain poured down, providing a brief but welcome respite from the heat. The rain soaked Charlie's clothes, making them cling tightly to his skin. Taking his shirt off, he bunched it up and then squeezed the material over his mouth, thirstily drinking the rain water which came out.

Once the storm had gone, Charlie's mood began to finally lighten, and he began singing an old Irish patriot song, "The Minstrel Boy":

'The Minstrel Boy to the war has gone
In the ranks of death you will find him,
His father's sword he has girded on
And his wild harp slung behind him!'

He sang a few more verses, and then asked Blaze, 'Heard that one before mate?'

'Nah, can't say I have,' Blaze answered.

'I'm not surprised, it's a very old song. Back home, when I was a boy, they used to make us sing it at school every day. What about this, you had to have heard this one before…' He broke into singing the popular British music hall song, "It's a Long Way to Tipperary". When he was finished, again he enquired if Blaze knew it, and again the young man replied that he didn't. 'Well, what song do you know?' Charlie asked, bewildered.

A few moments of awkward silence went by, when suddenly, to his delightful wonder, Blaze started to sing "Waltzing Matilda". Charlie chimed in along with him, and, as the pair made their way across the great plain, they loudly sang together the well-known Australian bush ballad.

***

A while later, they came upon several small, muddy holes in the ground that had filled with water. After drinking what little they could, they used what was left to replenish their canteens.

'Gonna go see what's ahead,' Blaze said.

Charlie nodded, as he noticed a large baobab tree not far away. Figuring that now would be a good time for a rest, he trudged over to the tree and sat himself down underneath its large branches. When Blaze had gone about a hundred yards from him, Charlie saw the boy look in his direction. 'See anything?!' he yelled to Blaze.

'Jus a dried-up billabong!' Blaze yelled back. Suddenly, his eyes grew wide, and he began jumping up and down in excitement. '*Look out!*' he shouted, pointing towards Charlie.

From behind him, Charlie heard a galloping sound, and he turned just in time to see the female lion leaping at him with its sharp claws extended. He twisted his body to the side, barely managing to avoid the lioness landing on him with its full weight. Now just a metre or two away, the big cat growled, baring its deadly fanged teeth. *Jesus Christ!'* Charlie cried, gripped by fear. The lion swung its large paw and caught the side of his body, its razor-sharp claws tearing his shirt open and gashing his skin underneath. Blood began spilling from the wound, as he struggled to crawl away while keeping his eyes on the beast. The lion roared as it started to move toward him, and Charlie thought it likely he was about to be eaten alive.

Just then, Blaze's spear came whistling through the air, piercing the ground right in front of the animal. Startled by it, the lion turned and quickly ran off in the other direction.

Blaze ran to Charlie's side and pulled his spear from the ground. As the pair of them watched the lion retreat, they noticed a *second* female lion; the other animal had been resting nearby the whole time, lazily watching its feline partner attack from a safe distance away. 'Oh my God,' Charlie gasped, with surprise, 'there's *two* of them!' Then, he keeled over on the ground, as intense pain and shock surged through his body. Lifting his blood-soaked shirt, he looked at the ugly wound left in his flesh from the lion's claws.

Blaze took out his knife and cut away part of Charlie's shirt. As he held the material against the wound, he did his best to staunch the flowing blood. 'Crikey!' he exclaimed. 'Mate, ya need a doctor, you're bleedin heaps.'

'Unfortunately, I don't think there's one round at the moment,' replied Charlie.

'We should stay here for the night. The tree will protect us.'

'In case you didn't know… lions can climb trees.'

'Ya need to rest, save your energy.'

Charlie shook his head. 'No, we should keep going. I can keep walking. I'll be able to keep up with you.'

Blaze started to gather twigs and fallen branches from the ground around them, and then he took out the flint from his knapsack.

'What are you doing?' Charlie asked.

'Making a fire, so the lions stay away. The wound's gotta be cauterized, it'll stop the bleedin. Then, all ya can do is hope it don't get infected.'

'Good God. All right, you win. We'll stay.'

'Don't worry mate,' Blaze said, with a grin, 'I'll fix ya up.'

***

The evening soon came, and a cold and dark veil descended upon the great plain. Next to the burning campfire, Charlie lay on the ground, feeling weary and delirious. Having already lost much blood, the gash in his side was seeping through the makeshift bandage. When the fire was going strong, Blaze put his knife in the flames to heat it. Once the tip of the blade was glowing red hot, he carefully pressed it up against Charlie's gaping wound. The skin sizzled as it burned. With his shirt balled up inside of his mouth, Charlie cried out in agony, and then he lost consciousness.

For a long while Blaze sat in silence, carefully listening for any signs of approaching danger. Now and again, he heard growling and movements within the grass, and he could sense the pair of lions were close at hand, watching them in the dark.

When Charlie came to, he looked across the fire and saw Blaze keeping guard, his spear next to him on the ground.

Blaze sensed his companion was awake and watching him. 'How ya doin?' he asked.

'I've certainly felt better.'

'Good thing is, you're not bleedin no more.'

Charlie looked under the shirt compression. The skin was black where it had been cauterized, and the surrounding area was red raw and blistering. However, Blaze had indeed stopped the bleeding. Struggling to sit up, Charlie groaned and fell back to the ground, exasperated.

'Jus keep restin,' said Blaze. 'Try not to move round much.'

'You—saved my life. Thank you.'

Blaze smiled. 'No worries, I reckon by mornin you'll be all right.'

Charlie chuckled, and said, 'You know, when the lion attacked, when it was standing there roaring with its claws out right in front of me, all I could think about was this god-damn joke my dad used to tell people. It's not even that funny, but it made me laugh as a kid.'

'Yeah? What is it?'

'Well, y'see there's this copper, a police officer, walking his beat on the street, and he sees this old man, completely smashed and pissed drunk, come stumbling down the sidewalk with a lion on a leash. The copper, completely floored, rushes up to the old man and says, "Oi - you can't have that lion 'ere on the street! Take this animal to the zoo!" So the drunk says, slurring his words, "Yes occifer, yes. I'll take him there right away," and he salutes and continues on his way.

'The next day, the same copper is walking the same beat on the street, and again he sees the old drunk coming down the sidewalk, still leading the lion on the leash. So he goes up to the drunk and says, "I thought I told you to take that lion to the zoo?" And the drunk looks at him, and says, "Well, I did occifer, I did! But he didn't like the zoo, so now I gotta take him to the museum."'

When Charlie finished, Blaze sat in silence before finally cracking a smile.

'See? I warned you it wasn't funny,' Charlie said, as held his side and rolled on to his back. 'Good old dad. He was a laugh, the life of the party. I miss him.' Staring up at the night sky, he noticed the few distant stars that could be seen were twinkling dimly. Some of those stars could even be gone now, he thought, their light having long since extinguished. 'Nothing ever lasts forever,' he said, quietly to himself. 'Even the stars and the moon will one day disappear from the heavens.'

'The moon... it's Japara's campfire,' Blaze said.

'What's that?'

'It's an old legend the elder told me and my mates when we was kids, of how "pira" – the moon – came to be in the sky.'

'How does it go?'

Blaze hesitated, not wanting to answer. He remembered well how the traditional story went, but after what Charlie told him about what happened to his family, he didn't want to contribute any more to the man's suffering. 'Ah mate,' he replied, 'ya don't wanna hear it. It's a sad story I prolly shouldn't tell ya.'

'No, please do,' Charlie implored. 'I'm very curious to know.'

Taking a deep breath, Blaze recalled the ancient Aborigine legend, told for thousands of years by the people of the Northern Territory... 'Long ago, in the Dreamtime,' he began, 'there was a puyarrayarra—a great and fearless hunter. This man was named Japara, and he had a wife and little boy that he loved very much. One day, when Japara was away hunting, a lazy man named Parukapoli went to his wife and told her many stories, so many that she forgot bout everythin else, even her little boy. As she was listenin to Parukapoli, the boy fell into a river and drowned. Later on, she found his body and sat by the river crying many tears, and she waited for Japara to return home. When he got back, she told him the terrible thing, and a great sadness came on him.

'But then, Japara became angry with his wife and the lazy man, and he blamed em for what happened to his son. He killed her with his hunting spear and then had a big fight with Parukapoli, who was also killed. When it was over, Japara was wounded very badly, and he was sad again that his boy was gone. The people from Japara's tribe saw his deep wounds and great sadness, but they were angry with him and shouted, "You are a parnka-parnta—a murderer who should not have killed your wife! She loved your boy and didn't want him to die!"

'Japara listened to his people and knew they said the truth to him, and he was very sorry for what he'd done. He went back to where he left their bodies – but they'd disappeared, the sky spirits had taken em away to finish their lives somewhere else. Japara called to the spirits and asked em for forgiveness, saying he wanted to be with his wife and boy again more than anythin else. The sky spirits heard him and knew he spoke the truth, and they let him leave the earth to live in the sky. The moon is the light from Japara's campfire as he searches the sky for his family, till the end of time.'

When Blaze was done, Charlie understood why the boy had been reluctant to tell him the ancient legend. The story of Japara losing his family had indeed touched a little too close to home, but it made Charlie realize he was sympathetic to his pain. 'Blaze,' he said, 'I haven't told you everything. My story isn't finished. I want you to know what the Woman in Black said to me before she let me go...'

***

3 DAYS AGO – Tuesday August 7, 2001
9:01 A.M.
18°05'32.9" 12°08'06.3"

In the Sahara, the Black Hawk helicopter settled down on a flat plateau, kicking up a huge swirling mass of dust and sand. The engine was turned off and its whirling rotor blades gradually came to a stop. The side door slid open, and two agents helped Charlie down from the passenger compartment. After walking him a short distance, they removed the hood from his head. Having been kept in the dark for three days, he opened his eyes and was instantly bombarded by painful, blinding white light. Little-by-little, he was able to adjust them to the sun's bright glare. What Charlie saw astonished him.

Surrounding him in every direction were great rolling dunes of sand, which appeared to extend infinitely to the horizon. It was the most barren and desolate place he'd ever seen. Aside from that, the scorching heat was staggering; like a massive, burning wall of fire had come crashing down upon him and set him alight. Confused and delirious, he felt he was going to collapse on the sand like a child's rag doll. One of the agents, silent in his vigil behind him, noticed this and brought out a plastic water bottle. Putting it to his lips, Charlie gulped it down quickly, proceeding to empty the whole container. The water was ice cold, and felt good inside his parched, dry mouth.

Another agent, carrying a knapsack slung over his shoulder, unloaded a black-painted motorcycle from the helicopter's rear, and he wheeled it over to the small group. Charlie could see the bike was not for city driving, but was instead made for off-road endurance.

Next, his handcuffs were removed. The bindings had made his wrists very sore, and he gently rubbed them. One of the agents grabbed and held him firmly, while the other rolled up Charlie's left shirt sleeve, exposing his bare arm. Charlie didn't resist, and he wondered what would happen next.

Suddenly, the Woman in Black exited the helicopter and casually walked over. She was wearing dark sunglasses, and in her hand she was carrying a silver briefcase. Setting it down on the sand, she opened it and brought out a plastic silver band which she attached to Charlie's left wrist. He saw the band had a blank LED screen.

'I'm going to ask you two questions,' Black said to him, as she checked to make sure the wristband was secure. 'First, do you know where we are?'

Charlie shook his head.

'Africa, the Sahara in Niger. This is one of the most isolated, unforgiving places in the world.'

Africa? Charlie wondered with surprise. *Why bring me here?*

Next from the case, she withdrew a syringe fitted with a hypodermic needle. Removing the cap from the tip, she held the syringe upside down and tapped it a couple of times. 'The second question is… Do you want to live?'

A chill crawled up Charlie's spine. It was a bizarre question which he hadn't expected. Reflexively, he bit down hard on his lip and wondered, *were they going to kill him?* Why go through the trouble of holding him for days, only to bring him to the middle of the desert and kill him? The thought was pushed aside in his mind. It didn't matter right now. The only thing that mattered was the question he'd been asked, as he knew his life depended on what answer he gave next. 'Yes, yes of course I want to live,' he pleaded. 'I—I don't want to die. I want to go back to London. I want to go *home.*'

Nodding her head to the agent behind Charlie, the Woman in

Black suddenly yelled out, 'Metatron—BETA is confirmed!' Then, she grabbed Charlie's left forearm and searched for a vein. After finding one, the point of the needle was set against it.

'Wait—what are you doing?' he exclaimed, startled and afraid.

'I'm injecting you with a microscopic capsule, containing a nano-transmitter and a time-delayed neuro-toxic poison,' she stated, flatly.

'Why?!' he shouted, struggling to break free. But the agents held him tightly so he could hardly move. Before Charlie knew what was happening, Black inserted the needle and pushed down on its plunger. From behind her dark sunglasses, she looked straight into his terrified eyes.

'You're going to play The Game,' she said.

After pulling the needle out, she carefully replaced its cap and put it back inside the briefcase. Then she took the knapsack from the other agent.

Charlie was aghast, having no idea what she was talking about, but instinctively he felt his entire life had once again turned upside-down. 'What kind of game?' he asked.

'It is a game of survival called Reality, and you have the privilege of being among the first to play. What I'm going to tell you now is extremely important, so you had better listen to me carefully— understood?'

He nodded.

Reaching inside the knapsack, she brought out a small, yellow object which looked like a cell phone, and she held it out for Charlie to see. 'You must not lose this, *your life depends on it*,' she added with emphasis. 'This is an advanced GPS receiver, with a battery life of 150 hours. It's fairly simple to use.' She pointed to blinking, pixelated black dots on the GPS screen, which showed a zoomed-out map of the entire region. 'A satellite is transmitting four precise geographical co-ordinates to this GPS. Three of these co-ordinates are the other competitors in this game, who are at this very moment also being told the rules of The Game. As long as this GPS is in your possession, you will know *exactly* where they are. However, they in turn will know where *you* are.'

Charlie could see three of the dots were aligned closely together, while a fourth looked to be much further away. She saw Charlie looking at this, and she put her finger right next to it.

'The fourth and last co-ordinate is the most important, what *they* call "Terminus", and where you need to go if you want to stay alive. It's over one thousand kilometres, south-west from here,' she said, raising her arm and pointing to the horizon. 'There, at Terminus, is the only antidote to the lethal poison in your body. But first, you must try and survive this desert wasteland. What awaits you after is the savannah and jungle, filled with all kinds of dangerous animals. Your journey will be very difficult, and, most likely, you will not survive. Indeed, you will be a very lucky man if you can make it to Terminus in time.'

It appeared to Charlie as if she was reading from a script, or perhaps even reciting words being spoken that only she could hear, and he wondered, *was someone else talking to him through her?*

The woman's thin, glossy black lips stretched across her pale face. 'The answer to your question is *yesss*,' she hissed. 'Now, Metatron knows even your thoughts, and since it knows what you are thinking… then they are aware of it as well.'

Charlie felt like he was in a very surreal bad dream. Not even that, he thought, this was something far worse. It was a terrible nightmare.

'You've got several other items to help you,' Black continued, 'Food rations, a knife, flint to make a fire, a torch, a scarf to protect your head, and riding goggles for your eyes. But the most important item you will carry, other than the GPS, is a full canteen of *water*. Be very mindful how much you consume, as you will most certainly cherish every last drop.' Putting the GPS into the knapsack, she threw it down to the sand at Charlie's feet, and then pointed to his arm. 'Look at the band which I fitted to your wrist.'

He did, and saw there were now red digital numbers on the LED:

05:23:49:51

'The numbers are counting down to zero,' she stated. 'If you do not make it to Terminus in six days or less… the capsule in your bloodstream dissolves and the poison will take effect. *You will die.* However, there is a catch: there is only enough antidote for a single competitor. No more than *one* person can use it. Do you understand?'

Hesitantly, Charlie nodded.

'Tell me you do,' Black demanded, removing her sunglasses. Her pale blue eyes that he found unsettling looked directly into his own.

'I—I think so—' he stammered.

'No!' she interrupted, 'You cannot "think so". You must *know* it.'

'Yes… Yes, I understand.'

'Good. Now, do you have any questions?'

'Yes, just a couple.'

'Ask them.'

'What happens if I get there first?'

She chuckled. 'You win your life, and a lot of fucking money: fifty million U.S. dollars. What is your second question?'

'Why—Why are they doing this?'

Black hesitated before answering, and then she smiled a cold, lifeless smile, totally devoid of all sympathy or emotion. *It must be the smile of the Devil himself,* Charlie thought. For just a brief moment, he believed her eyes changed shape, appearing almost reptilian.

'Why? So they can *watch*, of course,' she stated matter-of-factly, pointing up to the sky.

Looking up, Charlie saw a winged machine flying several hundred feet above them, circling around in a wide arc.

'It's called a UAV, an unmanned aerial vehicle, and it is controlled by Metatron,' she explained. 'They are the future of surveillance and warfare. Even now, as we speak, military bases are being built on this continent to secretly strike with these deadly drones.'

Charlie could sense The Syndicate, watching and listening.

'Yes,' she continued, 'as I've already told you, they know everything, even the future. You, and two of your other competitors, were already predicted. Do you understand? *They were ready for you.* The only reason why they kept you alive is because they wanted you for The Game.'

At this, a burning anger rose from within Charlie. 'Listen to me,' he seethed at her, with his eyes on fire, 'the whole world will know what they're planning to do. I'm going to get to Terminus first… *I'm going to stop them.*'

The Woman in Black smirked. 'Nothing can stop them. They control this world, and when they act—*they create reality.* And while the world is studying it, trying to make sense of that reality, they will act again, and again, creating other new realities. You see, they are history's great actors, and the world will only be left to study what they do.'

Then, just before going back to the Black Hawk with the other agents, leaving Charlie alone with the motorcycle on the sand-blown plateau, she said one last thing to him: 'Good-bye, and good luck.'

***

It was almost midnight before Charlie was done telling Blaze his story. For a long while after he sat in silence, before realizing that the young man across from him was staring off into the campfire, as if held in a deep meditation.

'Are you there?' Charlie asked, snapping his fingers.

Blaze came out of his trance and looked at him. 'Sorry mate, I was off huntin in the Dreamtime,' he said.

'Have you anything to say?'

'Yeah, the things up there—they're watchin us?' Blaze asked, pointing to the night sky.

Charlie nodded. 'Yes—"all the world's a stage, and all the men and women are merely players". It's Shakespeare, and it means we're nothing but someone else's entertainment. The show must go on! That's what all of this fucking nonsense is about.'

'Huh? I don't get ya.'

Charlie thought for a moment, and then said, 'Well, a long time ago, in the British Empire's colonial era, the wealthy and rich would read in newspapers about the exploits of their army and navy, and the conquering of far-off lands for profit and national glory. They found it enjoyable and amusing, and they entertained themselves with stories of great and terrible battles. They thrived on other people's misery. But when peace finally came they were unhappy, and so they would start the cycle over again. It's sad to say but nothing has changed, and it likely never will. In time, even this incredible place will be ravaged and destroyed for their amusement.'

Blaze kept silent, as dreadful visions played across his eyes of the landscape around him burning and turning black.

'Listen, I've got to know, has any part of what I've said rung a bell with you? Do you recognize any names of the people I've mentioned?'

'Yeah, I met Anna. She came to my house.'

'You met her?' Charlie exclaimed, surprised at the revelation. 'Why didn't you tell me before?'

Blaze didn't answer, not wanting to reveal he hadn't entirely trusted Charlie.

'What did she look like?'

'I never seen a lady so beautiful, 'cept me mum.'

'Did she tell you anything?'

'Yeah, said there was gonna be a big attack on America, and asked if I knew the answer to a riddle.'

'A riddle? What is it?'

'What's an upside-down cake with one candle and two sticks?'

Charlie briefly tried to figure it out, but was stumped. 'No idea, what is it then?' he asked.

Blaze shrugged. 'I dunno mate, she never got to telling me. But, I know somethin else…'

'What?'

'How to kill us a lion.'

FIFTEEN

O N A COLD SATURDAY morning in November, nine-year-old Dale Crumb was sitting at the fold-out plastic table in the tiny, cramped kitchen of his house. In front of him, resting on the table, was a large white bowl of Fruit Loops cereal, but no milk had yet been poured. Over in the living room, a Merrie Melodies cartoon was playing on the television, with its volume just a little too loud. When his mother began speaking, the young boy's brown eyes drifted away from the TV to where she was sitting across from him, as grey ashes fell from a lit Camel cigarette held tightly between her fingers.

'Before I leave, I'm gonna tell you a couple of secrets—things I ain't never told anyone, and never will again. So you better listen up *real* good, y'hear?' she said sternly to him, in a West Virginia twang. 'Now, I can understand you killing that German because, after all, this *is* a game of survival, and you're playing to win. And the momma you left lying in a heap in the middle of the road? We both know she had it coming to her. But did you have to kill that boy just to steal his boat? Survival is one thing, but what you did ain't nothing but cold-blooded *murder*. The Lord don't take kindly to that, not at all, and one day you're gonna have to answer for your sins and pay the price. Like your grand-daddy says—well, what he used to say: "The bad you do, comes back at you".'

She paused to take a long puff of her cigarette.

'Do you wanna know how I found your grand-daddy? He always phoned every evening 'fore he went to bed just to say goodnight, and let me know his heart was still ticking. Until last night and he didn't call, so I went to check on him. Didn't think nobody'd be in his house seeing as how all the lights were off. And there's no way come hell or high water he'd have gone to bed without calling. But he was there all right, standing in the living room, in the dark, dead as a door-nail. I touched his hand, and it was frozen solid. Gave me a real fright that's for damn sure. Coroner reckons it's the strangest thing he's ever seen in his life, said grand-daddy had a stroke and died on the spot, then the rigor set in real quick. But as strange a thing as that is, do you know what's even stranger? His arm was stretched right out, reaching to grab the TV remote.' She gave a little chuckle, then smiled and said, 'But he didn't manage to get it.'

The news of his grandfather's death was like a dagger to Dale's heart. He could sense his mother found her macabre story to be satisfying, as if she had enjoyed telling it more than she loved her own father. She wanted to hurt him, to cause him the maximum amount of pain and anguish as she could for one last time. He glanced back to the television, which he could see just beyond the entrance to the kitchen. On its screen were the Looney Tunes characters Porky Pig and a dog named Charlie, running crazily around a country setting.

She sucked on the tip of the Camel, and then blew smoke into a swirling, opaque cloud which hung above the table.

'Y'see,' she continued, 'I want you to know that I ain't surprised by what you done. Before you came out of me, you had a twin brother. Nobody knew I was pregnant with twins, not even your daddy. I was fixin to name you and your brother after the chipmunks in the Disney cartoons, Chip and Dale. But right near the end, something happened, something terrible. Nine days 'fore you was born, you went and killed your brother, *murdered him*, just like Cain did to Abel. That's right, you wrapped your little umbilical cord round Chip's neck, nice and tight, and you choked him to death. Doctor reckoned it was nothing but an accident, but I swear, on the word of the Lord Almighty, 'twas no accident—you done it *on purpose.*'

She smiled, showing her yellow, nicotine-stained teeth.

'Now, you can go on blaming me all you want for the bad things you done, things you keep on doing. But you and I both know the truth… you were born bad right from the get-go, plain and simple. You're a lost cause, child, just like your good-for-nothing daddy, and I ain't got time for sinners and lost causes.'

The boy watched the ashes from the end of her cigarette tumble down to the ceramic-tiled floor, and then he looked again to the TV. In the cartoon, Charlie Dog screamed loudly with fright, 'Look! It's the towers! *They're falling!!*' before collapsing helplessly to the ground.

***

DAY 4 – Friday August 10, 2001
7:45 A.M.
11°49'10.0" 3°24'15.5"

A scream woke Dale, but it had not come from within his tormented dreams. This scream materialized in the real world. Opening his eyes, he quickly looked at his surroundings. He was lying inside of an aluminium boat, and attached to one end of it was an old, beat-up outboard motor. Resting nearby on the floor was the stolen Kalashnikov gun, the knapsack carrying his supplies, and a long pole made of wood. It was then that the events of the previous day came flooding back into his thoughts…

After stealing the Berber family's Toyota car and supplies, Dale drove for many hours along the desolate paved road, crossing the empty desert wasteland with considerable speed. Eventually, the landscape became green with trees and grass, and he came to the border with Benin. There he found a two-lane bridge spanning the Niger River. However, his relief at finally arriving soon turned to dismay, when the border guards informed him, in very broken English, that the bridge had recently closed; government forces were fighting with militants, they said, and absolutely no one was being allowed in or out of the country. But Dale was not going to be easily deterred.

Retrieving the GPS, he studied the map screen and noticed a thin blue line, a tributary of the Niger River, snaking its way south from his current position, going almost half the distance he needed to travel. He recalled having driven past several small fishing boats, and noticing one of them equipped with an outboard motor. Thus, a new strategy began taking shape.

He waited until after it got dark, and then he abandoned the Toyota next to the road. Bringing his knapsack and the gun with him, he quietly made his way down to the river's edge to where the boats had been left. After he found the one with the outboard motor, he discovered it was moored with a simple rope tied around a stake, and he used his knife to cut through it.

'Wa di Zay!' a voice cried out.

Spinning around, Dale saw a young Black man coming toward him, waving his hands in the air, and he immediately surmised that this was the boat's owner. But, more importantly for Dale, there was no one else with him.

'Wa koy!' shouted the man, who was now just a short distance away.

Not wasting a moment, Dale lunged forward with his whole weight, slamming himself into the man's body and driving the knife deep into his gut. They both fell to the dusty ground with Dale on top, and he quickly put his hand over the man's mouth to stop him from screaming aloud. The man thrashed and kicked, struggling in vain to break free. 'Shhh,' Dale whispered to him. With the images of the Disneyland postcard and his mother's jewelry box still fresh in his mind, he began to quietly hum the tune of It's a Small World. A few more seconds went by before finally, mercifully, his hapless victim stopped moving.

Dale was not bothered by the fact he'd committed yet another murder, a gruesome act he discovered had become relatively easy to accomplish, and it briefly made him wonder if he was actually beginning to enjoy it. As his Vietnam veteran father would have said, he'd gone "blood simple". Looking to the night sky, Dale smiled in the direction of the UAV drone. He couldn't visually see it, but he could hear its whirring engine off in the distance. Instinctively, he knew those watching him would be pleased with his efforts.

After dragging the man's body into the murky water he climbed into the boat. There, resting inside, he found the long wooden pole which he used to push the boat along. When he got about halfway across the Niger River, he started up the outboard motor and guided the boat to the tributary entrance. But it didn't take him long to discover that, although the moon was shining bright, it was still too dark for him to properly navigate the water. There was no other choice for him but to wait until the morning light. Bringing the boat back to the shore, he used the rope to fasten it to a tree. Afterward, he lay down inside and promptly fell into a restless, nightmare-filled sleep.

And then the scream woke him.

Dale glanced over the boat's rim, trying to find the source of the piercing cry. Just a few yards away he spied a young girl frantically trying to grasp another person, who was almost completely submerged beneath the water. Looking a little closer, he saw that amongst the reeds was a monstrously big crocodile, with its jaws clamped onto the leg of its human prey.

Jesus, it's gotta be ten feet long, Dale thought in amazement.

At that moment the girl noticed him watching. 'S'il vous plaît monsieur, aidez-moi!!' she screamed in French, pleading for help.

Grabbing the wooden pole, Dale whacked it several times against the boat, trying to catch the crocodile's attention. But the fearsome creature had already tasted flesh and blood and wasn't about to let its meal get away. Dale took up the AK-47, and, after cocking it, he pointed the gunsight at the crocodile.

BANG!

The targeted shot struck the reptile in the side, the bullet causing it to let go of its prey, which Dale could now see was a half-naked elderly man. Desperately, the girl reached out and grasped his arm, pulling him to the shore. Again, Dale raised the rifle and fired off two more rounds.

BANG! BANG!

One shot missed and went into the river, but the other found its mark, penetrating the crocodile's scaly, armoured back. This time the animal took notice. Twisting itself around, it rapidly lunged like an arrow through the water straight for him. Suddenly Dale found himself frozen with terror, shocked to inaction by the beast's bizarre aggression. The giant reptile hissed as it crawled out of the water, and, despite its great size, it moved with considerable speed. Just as it was almost upon him, Dale came to his senses. Switching the gun over to automatic fire, he squeezed the trigger and it burst into action, the unleashed volley of bullets striking the crocodile squarely between the eyes and killing it instantly.

'Holy fucking shit,' Dale gasped in astonishment. He looked and saw the girl was tending to the elderly man. Slinging the AK-47 over his shoulder, he leaped from the boat and ran over. Immediately, he saw the man's lower right leg was horribly mangled and would have to be amputated.

'Il est mon grand-père. Je le baignais quand le crocodile a attaqué.

S'il vous plaît, aidez-le!' the girl cried.

Though he had only a basic knowledge of French, Dale believed the girl was telling him the man was her grandfather, and she was asking for his help. Bringing out his knife, he began to cut away a section of the sarong the old man was wearing, and then proceeded to create a makeshift tourniquet to staunch the flow of blood. The poor guy already looked frail to begin with, Dale thought, as he watched the man fall into a state of shock.

'Merci monsieur, merci,' said the girl, through tears.

She appeared to Dale to be a simple farm girl, about seventeen or eighteen years old. He looked her over, and as his eyes drifted across the dark skin of her barely-clothed body, his thoughts once again became twisted, and the darkness began creeping back in.

'You should come with me,' he imagined himself saying to her. *'I'll take you away from this pathetic, miserable existence. I will protect you.'*

In his mind, she would agree to go with him, of course, helping him along the way, and they would make it right to the end. Once he'd won the contest, the pair of them would spend the rest of their lives together, happy and extremely fucking rich. She would be grateful to him. What more could she ask for?

But what about grand-père – the grandfather? a little voice inside his head asked him back. *What are you gonna do about him? You can't just leave him here to suffer. That would be cruel. You wouldn't even do that to a dog, or any animal for that matter, now would you?*

No, I wouldn't, thought Dale in reply.

Good, said the voice. *Now do the right thing and put the fucker out of his misery.*

He wondered if he should pick the old man up, bring him back into the water, and then push his head under. That would take care of things clean and quick, and with very little violence. Well, that is if the girl didn't give him any trouble.

Just then, he visualized her standing over him while he slept, with his own knife gripped menacingly in her hand, and it dawned on him that if he killed the girl's grandfather and took her away, she might later seek revenge. *No, the girl cannot be trusted,* he thought. *Something will have to be done about her.*

Suddenly, the old man opened his eyes, and, reaching out with his hand he cried out, 'J'ai besoin d'eau!'

Dale looked to the girl. 'What did he say?' he asked.

'Eau… Water,' she answered.

For a split second, an image flashed through Dale's mind of his grand-daddy standing in his living room, frozen dead while reaching for the TV remote. Then, Dale quickly went to the boat and retrieved a bottle of water from his knapsack. Coming back, he opened the lid and gently handed it over to the suffering old man.

'There you go,' Dale said to him.

SIXTEEN

DAY 4 – Friday August 10, 2001
9:37 A.M.
12°11'42.9" 4°29'51.9"

C HARLIE STRUGGLED TO CLIMB up the side of the smooth, grey trunk of the baobab tree where he and Blaze spent the night. His knapsack was slung over the back of his bloodied and tattered shirt, which hung down from his torso in sections. When he finally got about mid-way up, he chose himself a spot and sat down on one of its large branches. Fatigued and thirsty, he brought out his water canteen and took a long swig, relishing the sensation of the liquid as it went down his parched throat.

A sound from above drew his attention. Looking up, he saw the pair of UAV drones circling around each other, and he hoped the noise they were making would not spoil their plan.

He glanced over at Blaze, crouched on the ground a few hundred yards away, and began to wonder if the boy was all there in the head. Though Charlie believed it downright insane, it was Blaze's idea to use himself as bait for the lions, and now they both patiently waited for the predators to appear.

Two hours went by and the lions had still not come. Charlie glanced apprehensively at the LED numbers displayed on his wristband:

02:21:34:18

Not long now before we're both dead, he thought miserably. With every minute that went by his anxiety was increasing, and he started to feel desperate cravings for a cigarette and his Xanax pills.

Just then, behind him on the ground, Charlie heard the tall grass stirring. Twisting his body around to look, he saw one of the female lions moving stealthily through it, and he became instantly filled with fear. The animal appeared to be without its companion, but he assumed it was likely watching from the grass nearby. The beast sniffed the air and looked up at him, and, for a moment, Charlie thought he saw it lick its lips. *If it really wanted me, it could probably get up here quite easily,* he thought with terror. However, the lion's attention appeared to be focused squarely on Blaze, as it cautiously crept slowly and silently toward him. Charlie held his breath, trying not to make a sound, as he frantically began waving his arms hoping Blaze would see him.

Fortunately, Blaze noticed the signal. Gripping his spear tightly in his hand, he closed his eyes and waited to feel the slight change in wind pressure and reverberations in the ground. The lioness crept ever closer, until it left the hidden confines of the yellow grass. Suddenly, it burst into a full sprint, its powerful muscles rippling across its body as it headed directly for Blaze, who seemed oblivious to the fast-approaching danger.

As he watched, Charlie felt his pulse quicken, and his heart thumped in his chest. *He's going to be torn apart, and I'll be trapped up this god-damned tree,* he thought in a panic.

When the lion was halfway to him, Blaze jumped to his feet and bolted, running as fast as he could in the other direction. Behind him, he felt the animal's paws on the ground only metres away, and he knew it would be upon him at any moment. Just as he got to the embankment of the dried-up riverbed, he threw himself over it as the lion leaped through the air, swinging its large paw to catch him. The young man barely missed falling onto a large sharpened stake, which he'd earlier fashioned from one of the baobab branches. The lion, not seeing the stake until it was too late, landed on it with the full weight of its body and was instantly impaled. Roaring with pain, it writhed and thrashed, struggling vainly to wrest itself off. Quickly, Blaze got to his feet and then drove his spear hard into the back of the angry beast's head. The lion slumped over, dead.

Seconds later, Charlie was stunned to see Blaze come over the embankment, triumphantly waving his spear in the air, and he realized that Blaze's plan had indeed worked after all. He couldn't believe it, but somehow the boy had managed to outrun and kill *a lion*.

The grass moved on the other side of the baobab tree. Glancing over, Charlie saw the other lioness come out and look for its hunting companion. It sniffed the air, and for a moment he thought it was also going to make a run for Blaze. All of a sudden, a spear came slicing through the air with a loud whistle, and perfectly struck the ground in front of the beast with a dull thud:

WHUMP!

Startled by it, the lion roared and then hastily retreated into the tall grass.

When it was safe, Charlie made his way down the tree and then limped over to Blaze. 'I—I can't believe what I just witnessed,' he said to him with amazement. 'What you just did—'

'We gotta leave, mate,' Blaze interrupted, as he pulled out his spear from the ground. 'It might change its mind and come back.'

***

Through the expanse of a wide valley they went, and the endless seas of yellow grass eventually turned into lush, green foliage. By mid-day the temperature was sweltering and oppressive, while irritating tiny flies swarmed around their heads, making the already difficult journey even more intolerable. Near the horizon, they saw a flock of thousands of pink flamingo birds, a sure sign that water was not far away. Luckily for the pair, the second lion decided not to follow, having apparently given up after the surprising demise of its hunting companion, and they did not encounter any more predators.

Charlie was exhausted and in pain, and he struggled to keep up with his younger and much-more fit companion. In his hand, he was holding Blaze's GPS. Wearily, he held up the device and looked at its screen, analyzing the distance they had yet to travel. 'We're not far from the Benin border,' he said to Blaze, as he swatted flies away from his face. 'But at the rate we're moving, we're not going to make it in time.'

The boy kept silent.

'Hey mate, did you hear what I said?'

'I heard ya,' replied Blaze.

'What are we going to do?' Charlie yelled, with a rising panic in his voice. 'I'm injured and there's nobody around to help. We don't even have a bloody vehicle—there's no fucking way we're gonna do this!'

'We won't if ya keep thinkin that way. Gotta believe ya can do it to make it happen. It's the laws of attraction.'

'Look Blaze, laws of attraction or not, I'm slowing you down. You'd probably almost be there right now if it wasn't for me. We've still got at least five hundred kilometres to go, do you really think I can walk that far in the condition I'm in? The smart thing to do is for you to just leave me—leave, and go on your own.'

Blaze shook his head. 'This place is a different land, but it's not so much different from my home. There's no worries, the animal spirits will guide us.'

'If you don't go, we are both going to die! Aren't you afraid of dying?' Charlie asked.

'Little bit I guess. Never thought bout it much.'

'Well, I'm afraid of it. But more than that, I'm afraid of dying *alone*.'

Dying alone. That's what happened to Darby, thought Blaze. Visions of his friend, lost and dying alone at Devil's Mountain, flashed through his mind. 'Sometimes people die alone. It's a natural thing,' he said, trying to stifle his tears.

Charlie was beginning to walk slower, lagging behind even more. 'Well it's not natural for me!' he shouted angrily. 'I've got autophobia, a fear of being alone. Never had the damned thing before until a few years ago. The truth of the matter is, it's the reason why I wanted us to stay together. I didn't want to be by myself any longer. I didn't want to die *alone*. And now, I—I don't know any more what the right thing is to do!' He threw the GPS to the ground, and then, holding his head in his hands, he sat down and began to weep.

Blaze came over and crouched down, facing him. 'Listen my friend,' he began, 'I'm gonna tell ya somethin I never said before to anyone... A few years back, me and my mate went walkabout in the bush followin songline tracks, and got ourselves all mixed up. Before we knew it, we was in the desert. Took us a little bit, but we found the way home. But when we was lost, I got scared and was gonna give up, sat on the ground just like you're doin now and said I wasn't goin any further. Told me mate to go on without me, but he didn't listen. He never listened. Said the heat had got in my head and made me crazy, and if we wanted to keep alive we needed to work *together*. Which is what we did, and we got home. And that's what we're gonna do.' He picked up the GPS from the ground, and held it out for Charlie to take. 'We haven't come this far jus to give up now,' he said. 'I'm not leavin ya here by yourself, so we better get a move on.'

Charlie knew he couldn't allow Blaze to stay, as that would be the end for both of them. Pulling himself together, he took back the GPS from the boy's hand and stood. 'All right, you win again, we'll keep going,' he said, as they resumed walking. 'But I want you to tell me… Anna—is she still alive?'

A few seconds went by and Blaze didn't answer.

'Damn it, I *need* to know!' Charlie demanded.

With that, Blaze stopped in his tracks and turned to face Charlie, who saw that the boy was crying.

***

After the sun dipped below the horizon, they stopped to rest for the night. A small campfire was made, and they cooked and ate the meat of a gazelle Blaze killed. As the pair dined on their meals, the young man remained quiet, not speaking a single word. Only when they were done did he begin to talk, slowly at first. What he recounted to Charlie was the fate that had befallen Anna…

One evening a few days earlier, Blaze was at his house in Lajamanu that he shared with his Auntie Burilda and three cousins, when there was a sudden unexpected knock on the front door. Opening it, Blaze was met by a striking Caucasian woman with long, dark hair and pale skin. She was wearing a wide-brim hat, which slightly covered her eyes, and a bag was slung over her shoulder.

'G'day,' he greeted her.

The woman smiled. 'Hello, my name is Anna Lehrer,' she said, a little nervously. 'I'm looking for an old friend, Emily Grace. I was told she lives here.'

Blaze didn't recognize the stranger who spoke with a German accent, but he was intrigued she was using his mother's maiden name.

After being invited inside, Anna was introduced to Auntie Burilda, an Aboriginal woman in her late 50's, who sadly informed her that Emily had passed away from cancer eight years earlier, and her husband before that from a heart attack.

Heartbroken at this news, Anna burst into tears. She explained how she'd come to know Emily, that they'd met at an apartment block in West Berlin when Anna was a young girl. The woman had taught her English, and they corresponded by mail for a time upon Emily's return to Australia. Anna stated she was on vacation, and, deciding to visit her old friend, she'd flown to Australia from Rome on a commercial airline flight, landing in Darwin seventeen hours later. After chartering a ride on a small plane to Lajamanu, she then asked around for the Mullins address.

Burilda invited Anna to stay for the night, and, not knowing where else to go, the woman graciously accepted.

Later that night, after his three young cousins had gone to bed, Blaze lit a fire inside a wood-burner in the living room to heat the house, and then boiled the billy for tea. Sitting himself down in an old rocking chair, he enjoyed listening to Anna and his Auntie share their stories and fond memories of his mother. When he informed the guest that he could also speak German, they amused themselves with a short conversation.

After a while Blaze fell asleep, and he began to dream about Darby, and the old shaman telling Dreamtime legends of the sacred and forbidden mountain called Kulu. The dream that he had was always the same each and every time.

For a couple of hours Anna and Burilda talked, until, at about midnight, the house phone suddenly rang out, pulling Blaze from his deep slumber. Groggily wiping his eyes, he saw his Auntie moving to answer the phone. He climbed out of the rocking chair, about to head for his bed, when he paused after seeing the expression on Anna's face: she was staring at the ringing phone, with stark terror in her eyes.

'Who's callin me this time of night?' Burilda asked angrily, as she picked up the receiver. After saying 'hello' several times, she finally hung up and returned to her chair. 'Strange, was nobody there,' she said, mystified.

For a few seconds, none of them said a word, until Anna finally broke the silence: 'They know I'm here,' she whispered softly.

'Who?' asked Burilda.

'I need to tell you something which I should have. I... I lied to you.'

'What do you mean my dear?'

'I'm not on vacation. I'm running away—from dangerous people.'

'Why come here? There are *children* in this house,' Burilda said with alarm.

'I know, please forgive me,' Anna pleaded. 'I didn't know what else to do, or where to go. I had no idea there were children in the house when I came. I thought Emily would be here... that she could help me.' She got up from the chair. 'I should go now. I'll gather my things and leave right away,' she said, as she picked up her bag.

The old woman was puzzled. 'Tell me, why are these people chasing you?' she asked.

'Because I *know* something they are going to do—something very big and terrible, and I know when it will be.'

'What is it?'

'I can't tell you any more, as it would be unsafe for you and the children.'

'But it's late, where will you go?'

'I don't know.'

As she was about to leave, Blaze suddenly spoke up. 'Wait... I know where,' he said.

Anna paused at the front door. 'Where?' she asked, setting her bag down.

'A place they won't ever find ya. I can take ya there.'

Anna was desperate and she agreed. Quickly, they went about packing a bag of supplies, food and water. When they were ready, Blaze led Anna outside to his motorcycle.

Climbing onto the bike behind him, Anna saw that he'd also brought along a rifle. She glanced one last time at Burilda, who was watching them from the porch of the house. 'Do you know where this place is?' she asked her.

'Yes, I think so,' Burilda replied. 'You have nothing to fear, Blaze will take care of you.'

'I promise you on my life, I won't let anything happen to him.'

'I know you won't my dear. May the Good Lord watch over you both.'

***

Into the desolate Outback they went, until they arrived at the place which held for Blaze great importance and meaning – Kulu, the sacred and forbidden Devil's Mountain. Blaze grabbed his rifle and then took Anna up the mountain, leaving the motorcycle behind. Using flashlights, they carefully made their way through its maze of passageways and tunnels, and climbed across treacherous deep crevices, until they finally came to a shallow cave. After a small fire was made to help keep them warm, the glow of the flames revealed several figures of animals and people painted in ochre on the cave's rock walls.

'Who made these?' Anna asked him, glancing at the figures. 'They look very old.'

'They were made by my ancestors, the walya-jarra, in the Dreamtime thousands of years ago,' he answered. He pointed at two of the figures. 'That long one is the snake spirit, Yarripiri. The other is Mirlalypa, a spirit who guides and protects people as they go through the country.'

For a minute, Anna fell silent before speaking again.

'Blaze, I want to tell you something important to me... I want you to know that I loved your mother very much. She helped me at a time when I was feeling confused and alone. When I needed someone, she was there for me. She was *my* protector spirit. And when she left, I felt as though my own mother had gone, and I was quite sad. I miss her, but being here with you makes me feel she's with us right now.'

'I miss her too,' he said. 'When mum was around things was good and peaceful, and I was happy. But then everythin changed. When she went away it got difficult, got all chaotic-like. I was confused, didn't understand the world no more and felt like bein lost in a maze, jus like here at this mountain. Few years later, I had a mate who helped me get through it, made me understand I wasn't really lost, only thought I was.'

'That sounds like a good friend.'

'Yeah, he was the best friend I ever had. We did everything together, used to go on treks into the desert and run races.'

Anna detected sadness in his voice. 'What happened to him?' she asked.

'He—went away, jus like mum and dad.'

'Oh, I'm sorry.'

'That's all right.' He thought for a moment, and then said, 'If ya promise not to tell anyone… I'll tell ya a secret.'

Anna nodded. 'Yes, of course.'

'Sometimes when I'm feelin sad I come here and talk with him, ask him questions bout things. And sometimes, when it gets real quiet-like, I hear his voice in the wind givin me the answers.'

Anna lay down, and pressed her head against the rocky floor of the cave. 'This mountain… it has a powerful energy. I can feel it.'

'It's a sacred place for my people. The elder told me and my mates the story how it came to be, and why it's forbidden to come here.'

'What is it, can you tell me?'

Blaze nodded, and replied, 'Yeah, I can tell ya, but it don't have a happy ending.'

He began recounting to her the story of the two brothers, Talaruji and Kalaruji, and of their terrible fight that consumed them and created the great red mountain. For a while Anna listened intently, transfixed by the ancient tale, before she fell asleep. Not long after, Blaze noticed a strange glow coming from outside the cave. Getting up, he went to the entrance and saw the ghostly green, red, and purple strands of the aurora australis, shimmering and sparkling in the sky above the dark mountain. A cold chill went down his spine, and he shivered.

A terrible thing is coming.

He lay down next to the crackling fire, curling tightly into a ball to keep warm, and listened to the wind whistling eerily through the cave. After closing his eyes, he thought he could hear Darby's voice trying to warn him, before he drifted off to sleep.

***

When the dawn broke, Anna was abruptly awakened by several men in black agents entering the cave. Quickly taking up the rifle, she pointed it at one of them and fired, the blast sending the agent reeling and killing him instantly. The other men in black promptly seized the gun from her and rapidly bound the pair's arms and legs.

Then they were carried down to where a Black Hawk helicopter was waiting at the base of the mountain.

From out of the helicopter stepped The Syndicate's leather-clad, eye patch-wearing agent, the Woman in White. Anna and Blaze watched apprehensively as she approached the small group.

'You're a feisty one, aren't you?' White said to Anna, speaking in German. Then, she held out her open palm.

'I don't have it,' Anna said.

'Where is it?'

Anna glanced up at the imposing mountain.

The woman slapped Anna hard, and then looked to Blaze. 'If it's any consolation,' she said to him in English, 'your aunt put up quite a fight, refusing to tell me where you'd gone. Before she died, she suffered terribly for a very long time until I finally broke her. Do not worry though, no harm came to the children.' She turned back to Anna. 'But you, Anna Lehrer, your boyfriend Ernst gave up your location here in Australia rather quickly. I found it quite disappointing.'

At that, Anna began crying.

'Oh my dear, I can see your heart is broken,' White said, mockingly. 'His love for you was not as strong as you thought. But all is not lost. You are very fortunate, because… you've been chosen.'

'Chosen? For what?' asked Anna, as she wiped away her tears.

'To play a game called Reality. And there will be a surprise waiting for you—Ernst will be playing the game as well.' A smirk came upon White's face. 'Perhaps both of you will meet for one last time, and then you will find out just how much he loves you.'

One of the men in black stepped forward, holding out a black case to the female agent. After opening it, she brought out a gleaming silver gun fitted with a long silencer, which she next aimed directly at Blaze's head. With horror, Anna realized the woman was about to murder him. 'Wait!' she cried out to her, 'Don't hurt him, please! He's not part of this, he doesn't know—I haven't told him anything! I promised his aunt… Please, I'm begging you—*don't kill him!*'

The Woman in White hesitated, appearing to listen to instructions that only she could hear. Finally, she said, 'It's been decided… the boy can live. They want him for The Game *in your place.*'

'Thank you, thank you,' cried Anna.

The words would be her last, as White instead turned her gun upon Anna, shooting her point-blank in the head. Blaze was stricken with terror as he watched Anna's lifeless body collapse to the red-coloured dirt.

White's single pale blue eye fixated on him, and she smiled a cold, evil smile. 'Well, young man,' she said, in English. 'it appears today is your lucky day. Very soon we'll discover if your luck will continue.'

'What ya gonna do to me?' Blazed asked her, fearfully.

She chuckled. 'When we meet again… you will find out.' Turning around briskly, she went back to the helicopter and got inside.

Just before a hood was placed over his head, Blaze watched two agents carry Anna's corpse up the mountain, and he knew that she was joining the ranks of "the missing", never to be seen again. The mountain was angry that its sacred ground had been violated by an outsider, Blaze thought with dismay. Because of this transgression, it had claimed yet another victim. He was astounded they'd actually been found by the agents, and realized that if these cruel people could find he and Anna on this desolate mountain, then it meant there was literally no place they would have been safe. Regardless, he felt responsible for Anna's death, failing in his mission to keep her from harm. Indeed, it had been a tragic mistake to bring her to this terrible place.

Blaze was taken aboard the Black Hawk helicopter, which quickly left Devil's Mountain far behind. For two days he neither saw nor heard a thing, as he was transported half-way across the world to another continent. Once in Africa, he was met again by the one-eyed Woman in White, just as she had promised. The sinister agent injected him with the neuro-toxic poison, and explained the rules of The Game in which he was now an unwilling participant.

Then he was set free.

***

After Blaze was done telling his story, Charlie said nothing. Now, he finally knew the fates of Ernst and Anna, and he felt sadness but also admiration for her great courage.

'Anna and my Auntie sacrificed themselves so that I could live,' Blaze said, choking back tears. 'I will honour them and not let their sacrifices have bin for nothing. I'm gonna win this race—I'm gonna win it for *them*.' From seemingly out of nowhere, he suddenly produced a small silver key. Holding it out in the palm of his hand, the key glowed in the dark as it was illuminated by the flickering flames of the campfire.

'Where did you get that?' Charlie asked, perplexed.

'Anna gave it to me before we was taken, told me to hide it and not let anyone find it, which is what I did.'

Looking closely at it, Charlie noticed that a number was engraved into the side of it:

911

'Good God!' he exclaimed with surprise. 'It's a storage locker key—it's where Anna must have hidden the evidence!'

***

DAY 5 – Saturday August 11, 2001
5:33 P.M.
10°23'48.9" 4°01'09.3"

The next day, Charlie and Blaze walked for eleven hours through the grass and brush. The intense heat they'd become accustomed to became considerably more bearable, as the temperature cooled by the late afternoon. To the west, they could see dark clouds were gathering, and thunder rumbled ominously across the sky. Eventually, the pair discovered a dirt road going toward the border with Benin, and they began to follow it. They had only gone down it a couple of kilometres when, out of nowhere, complete bedlam suddenly erupted.

Hearing the unmistakable crackle of gunfire somewhere in the distance, they next saw and heard something very big moving through the forest, and it was coming right their way. Within seconds, a massive bull elephant burst through the dense foliage onto the road, causing the companions to leap out of its way. The giant, thirteen-foot tall beast had enormous six-foot long ivory tusks which curved down to the ground. Letting out a huge roar, the animal ran away from them down the road.

The sound of voices caused the pair to take cover. Five armed men suddenly leaped out of the brush, shouting and waving guns. They ignored Charlie and Blaze, instead running across the road and into the forest. More gunfire went off, this time much closer. Without any warning, two off-road cars drove up carrying several men, all of them dressed in military fatigues and firing guns.

'Quick—Run!' Charlie yelled to Blaze.

As they scattered away from the oncoming vehicles, Charlie accidentally stepped into a deep hole in the road, twisting his foot in the process and falling to the dusty ground. In no time the armed men were upon him, pointing AK-47's at his head, and he immediately raised his hands in surrender. 'Don't shoot—Don't shoot!' he cried in fear.

One of the men shouted at him, 'Samun saukar a ƙasa!' He punched Charlie hard in the mouth, then roughly pushed him back to the ground, while another spat on his face. He soon found himself surrounded by eight men, noisily talking amongst themselves, all the while keeping a careful eye on their captive.

A minute later, a third off-road vehicle drove up, and a man wearing a red beret and a green camouflage uniform stepped out. Looking to be in his mid-50's, Charlie could sense that this man had an air of authority, as well as arrogance about him. He approached Charlie, who was kneeling with his hands on his head, and then gave a swift kick of his boot to his stomach. Charlie let out a groan, doubling over in pain. 'Nice to meet you, whoever you are,' he muttered, with bloody spittle hanging down from his mouth.

'I am the chief warden of the Borgu Game Reserve of Kainji National Park. You will address me as "Captain", understood?' the man commanded to him in clear but heavily accented English.

'All right, Captain.'

'What are you doing here?'

'Well, that's a bit of a long story—'

'You are under arrest for illegal poaching and for shooting at my men.'

'What? No—you don't understand… I wasn't with those people.'

'What is your name?'

'Charlie. My name is Charlie Grimer. I'm a citizen of the United Kingdom.'

'You are British?'

Charlie nodded.

The Captain gave a smile, and then barked an order at his men. Quickly, two of the rangers handcuffed Charlie and pushed him into the cargo tray of their vehicle. With two guards watching him, the rest searched for the poachers in the forest, only to return minutes later empty-handed. The men got back in their vehicles.

As the convoy started to drive off, Charlie looked around but could not see any sign of Blaze; somehow the boy had luckily managed to escape. Anxiously, he wondered where they were going, and what The Captain was going to do to him once they arrived.

***

6:49 P.M.
10°09'12.7" 3°50'13.1"

After a rough forty-five minute ride, the convoy of vehicles came to what Charlie figured was The Captain's base, which was comprised of three barracks and a one-story concrete building. Two rangers brought him inside the main compound and into a cold and damp windowless room, where, directly in the centre, was a chair made of iron metal. Charlie noticed the chair was bolted to the floor, and had rubber straps hanging down from its arms and legs. Next to it there was a wooden table with some kind of electronic box plugged into the wall. This was obviously a room for torture, he thought with dismay. There was also an empty prison cell, into which he was abruptly and forcefully pushed, before the door was closed and locked behind him. The inside of it reeked of death and decay, and he became more uneasy when he saw what appeared to be a large pool of dried blood in the middle of the cell's floor.

The Captain came into the room, and he was carrying Charlie's knapsack. After emptying its contents onto the table, he began to scrutinize each item as if he was a detective on a murder case. Charlie observed the man carefully examine Blaze's GPS, before setting it back down.

'Excuse me,' Charlie said, 'would anyone happen to have a fag?'

The three men ignored him.

Limping to the cell's far wall, Charlie sat against it and watched as the chief warden and his rangers left the room. Now, all he could hope for was that they would realize their mistake and let him go. Given the circumstances of his capture, it didn't look like that would happen any time soon.

***

Later that evening, The Captain returned with two rangers, who opened the cell and dragged Charlie out. After removing his shirt, they placed him in the metal chair and used the straps to firmly secure his arms and legs so he could not move. Two wires were hooked up to the electronic device, and at their ends were electrodes which they painfully attached to Charlie's nipples with metal clamps.

Upon realizing he was about to be tortured, Charlie begged The Captain: 'Please, you have to let me go! You don't understand what's at stake! A terrible attack on America is going to happen soon, and I have to contact people about it. Please… just let me go.'

The Captain chuckled. 'Don't worry Englishman, I will let you go. You will soon be free.' Turning around, he commanded his men to leave, and as they did the door was shut loudly behind them. The Captain began to slowly pace the room, circling around Charlie like a shark hunting its prey. 'Let me tell you a little history of my country,' he began, 'When Nigeria was colonised by the British, they came to my homeland of Ogoni and promised many things to my people. And what did they do? They terrorised us and destroyed our land. Do you know the whole ecosystem of the Niger Delta has been laid to waste? And for what? *Oil*.

'Then, a few years ago, the Nigerian government raided villages in Ogoniland. They said it was because people were protesting over a pipeline, and many of my people were killed. So the question is, why did they do this terrible thing? The answer, my British friend, is that the government was acting under orders from a British oil company.'

'That's dreadful, I understand your pain,' Charlie said, shifting uncomfortably in the chair.

The Captain smiled. 'No, you do not yet understand what pain is, but you will. Now, please tell me who you think I blame for the murder of my people—the Nigerian government, or the oil company? *Who?*

'I—I don't know,' answered Charlie.

'Well, of course the government was wrong and I do not forgive them for what they did. They are corrupt and do many bad things. But I don't blame them for the killing. *I blame the British oil company who told them to do it.*'

'Look, I'm extremely sorry about what happened. In fact, I apologise on behalf of the British people—'

'No—you do not tell me that you are sorry!' The Captain interrupted, angrily. 'You did not lay waste to our land, *your people did*, and you do not speak for them. The world may have forgotten what happened in Ogoniland, but I do not forget, and I do not forgive. What have the British given to the Earth except destruction and misery wherever they go? What beautiful things have they ever created? Nothing!'

'Well, we did give the world Shakespeare,' Charlie said, meekly.

The Captain laughed. 'All right Englishman, I'll give you that… you have given us Shakespeare,' he said, shaking his finger.

At this, Charlie began worrying that The Captain, who was obviously harbouring a deep-rooted hatred, was also completely unhinged.

The Captain took off his beret, folded it neatly, and then set it gently down on the table. 'You see, here in the park we are protecting the animals from slaughter by poachers and foreigners, from outsiders such as yourself. We love them more than we even love ourselves. But you… you come to Nigeria, and, just like your ancestors, you destroy our precious resources. I will *not* allow it.'

'Captain, please understand I wasn't trying to kill that elephant. I wasn't with those poachers. I've been travelling to Benin with an Australian boy. He saved my life after I was attacked by a lion.'

The Captain glanced at the blackened, cauterized wound on Charlie's side.

'We were kidnapped by very, very bad people who injected us with poison. Look there… they put that on my wrist.' Charlie nodded to the silver band with digital numbers counting down, which The Captain examined. The numbers read:

01:12:01:31

'You see that?' said Charlie, 'We've only got a day-and-a-half left to get to Benin's coast, before the boy and I are both dead. It's God's honest truth. We were just at the wrong place at the wrong time—'

'You are lying!' shouted The Captain, as he angrily slammed his fist on the table, shaking it violently. Startled by the sudden outburst, Charlie closed his eyes and tried to remain calm. Seconds went by. The Captain took a deep breath and then composed himself. 'Why are you lying to me?' he asked, this time much quieter. Beads of sweat were rolling down his face, which he wiped away with his hand. Charlie noticed the man's hands were big and powerful, as if he could crush his skull with them using very little effort.

'I promise you that I'm not,' Charlie replied, his bottom lip quivering in fear. 'If you will just let me make a phone call, we can get all of this sorted.'

The Captain ignored his pleas. 'Before we begin, I will tell you about my past. When I was a young man, I was in the Nigerian Police Force. I served with good men, who did honourable things. But some, just a few of them, were very bad and they did very bad things. Sometimes these men would beat and torture people to death. They would use electricity to get the information they wanted. It is a painful manner of torture, of course, but very effective. It is from these men that I learned what I am going to do to you now…'

'Bloody hell, are you fucking mad?! Didn't you hear what I said? There's going to be a terrorist attack on New York and Washington D.C.'

'I don't care.'

'Please… I'm begging you… don't do this,' Charlie desperately pleaded, as he struggled against the straps binding him to the chair. 'Somebody help me—for God's sake help me!!'

'No one is going to help you.' The Captain reached inside a pocket on his uniform and brought out a tube-like rubber gag. He forced Charlie's mouth open and shoved it in, then went back to the control box and flipped a switch. The device turned on with a deep, low humming noise. 'Just so you know,' he said, 'the name of that majestic elephant you were going to kill is Udo, which is a word that means "peaceful". And indeed, Udo is a peaceful creature. I, on the other hand, am not.'

He began to slowly turn the dial on the box, and Charlie felt the electricity current surge into him through the electrodes. He screamed through the gag in his mouth as intense pain suddenly shot through every part of his body. The Captain increased the voltage. When he saw Charlie about to lose consciousness, he brought the dial back down to zero and removed the gag.

'Please—please no more...' Charlie stammered.

'Now, you will tell me... *Why are you in my country?*

'I was kidnapped—from London—'

'You are lying to me again! Why do you have a GPS? Answer my question!'

'I—I was travelling to Benin... with an Australian boy... We were using the GPS, but we got separated... I swear it... I swear it on my son's life. Please believe me...'

Returning the gag to Charlie's mouth, The Captain began turning the control box dial. Electricity coursed through Charlie's body and he screamed in pain, his face turning a deep purple-red and his veins popping out from his neck. Again, the dial was brought back to zero and the gag removed.

'Yes—yes!!' Charlie screamed, 'I was trying to fucking kill the elephant—I was with the poachers—I wanted to kill Udo for his fucking ivory!!' He slumped in the chair, knowing that his body could not take much more punishment. 'It's the truth... I promise you... I'm not lying this time,' he whispered, with his head hanging down against his chest. White froth was pooling at the corners of his mouth, and a long drop of spittle hung from his lips.

'You know what Englishman? I don't believe you. I think you are just telling me what I want to hear.'

Charlie groaned. 'Then just fucking do it already you son-of-a-bitch... just kill me.'

The Captain turned the control box off, and then he picked up his beret and set it properly back on his head. Going over to the room door, he banged on it twice. A moment later the door opened and two rangers rushed inside. After detaching the wires from Charlie's bare chest, they unstrapped him from the chair and dragged his limp body back into the prison cell. Charlie pulled himself along the cold, damp floor, until he was in the cell's corner, and then he glanced over at the chief warden. The man was standing on the other side of the metal bars, watching Charlie with contempt in his eyes.

'I know what you are thinking,' The Captain said to him. 'You are thinking that I'm a monster, as if I would cut out your heart and eat it. Well, let me tell you—I don't hate you, and I don't hate the white man... *I hate what you represent.*' Spinning on his heels, he promptly went to the room door and then turned round a final time. 'We are finished for the night, Englishman, but we will start over again in the morning.' He left the room, and a ranger turned off the light and shut the door behind them.

Charlie closed his eyes. Just before he fell asleep, his last thought was a quote from one of his favourite plays, Shakespeare's The Tempest: *"Hell is empty, and all the devils are here."*

That night, he dreamt of being at his house in London, many years ago, when David had been very young. In the dream, he was tucking his son into bed for the night, when the child suddenly cupped his hand and whispered something into his ear. However, it wasn't his son that he heard, but instead a very strange, yet familiar voice which he could not place:

'Charlie,' said the voice, 'when your opportunity comes... seize it.'

DC Wince

SEVENTEEN

DAY 6 – Sunday August 12, 2001
7:00 A.M.
10°09'12.7" 3°50'13.1"

AFTER CHARLIE WAS CAPTURED by the rangers, Blaze followed the tracks of their vehicles for many kilometres, using his flashlight to see after it got dark. Eventually he came to their outpost, where he spent the rest of the night sleeping against the base of a massive balsam tree. But in the early hours of the morning he was awakened when it began to downpour rain. Now that it was daylight and he was able to observe the whole complex, he did his best to count how many men were guarding it. There were six rangers that he could see, but he was sure there were likely more inside.

He brooded over his very few options.

Since their first meeting, Blaze had somewhat taken a liking to Charlie, feeling a bond with him because of their shared circumstances. He was saddened to hear Charlie's tragic story about the death of his family because of a selfish desire for public vindication, as well as being deeply unsettled by its resonance with his own troubled past.

But despite how he felt, Blaze suffered no illusions about his own predicament. He was in a race to stay alive which he fully intended to finish, even if it meant abandoning his companion. However, there was only one way he could accomplish it: he needed the GPS. Charlie had been captured while carrying it, and Blaze had no choice but to try and get it back. If he didn't, there would be no way for him to precisely find Terminus, the end point of The Game where the antidote to the poison in his body would be.

As Blaze watched the rangers mill about the compound, he heard a distinct whirring noise above the din of the rain. Looking up, he recognized the two UAVs that had been following him and Charlie, flying around in opposing circles, and it was then that he noticed that one of the guards had seen the drones as well. Alarmed, the guard shouted a warning to his fellow rangers as he pointed to the sky.

***

Inside the compound, Charlie was lying half-naked and fast asleep on the floor of his prison cell, when the door to the room was suddenly flung open with a loud clatter. With a groan, he opened his eyes and then struggled to get himself up from the floor. Every part of his body was sore and aching, and his head throbbed with a dull pain. The light bulb hanging from the ceiling switched on, and The Captain walked in with two rangers. In one hand the chief warden was carrying a key ring, and in the other was a black wooden baton which he rapped loudly against the prison cell's bars. 'Rise and shine Englishman!' he yelled. 'As I promised you last night, we will start again—this time from the beginning.'

Charlie looked at him wearily. 'I don't care what you do to me,' he said, 'I'm already a dead man. Just tell the authorities about the attack—'

'—I'm the authority here, and it will be *you* who will do as I say!'

Without warning, the sudden crack of gunfire coming from outside the compound startled everyone in the room, followed shortly after by a huge explosion which violently shook the building. A ranger threw open the room's door and shouted excitedly to his commander. The Captain turned to face Charlie, and his eyes were burning with rage. 'Your comrades have attacked us!' he angrily shouted at him. 'I assure you they will be destroyed, and then I will come back and deal with you!' Setting the key ring down on the table, the chief warden rushed out with his men close behind.

What in God's name is going on? Charlie wondered. It sounded to him like total and utter mayhem was taking place outside the compound. There was the rat-a-tat noise of machine guns being fired, and then a second massive explosion suddenly rocked the whole structure.

KA-BOOOOM!!!

The light in the room flickered on and off, and Charlie believed at any moment the roof would cave down upon him. He saw the key ring resting on the table not more than a couple of metres away, and he wished he could somehow reach it. There was more gunfire, and the sound of men screaming in brutal agony. Terrified, Charlie started shaking uncontrollably and he backed into a corner of the cell, praying for his life.

Seconds later, the door to the room swung open, and he assumed The Captain and his men had returned to torture him more, or even put a bullet into his head. Instead, Charlie was surprised to see someone he hadn't expected:

It was Blaze.

The young man came into the room, his skin and hair soaked and dripping with water. Right away, he was taken aback upon seeing the now shirtless Charlie cowering in the cell's corner.

'Blaze—thank God it's you! The key—it's over there on the ring!' Charlie cried with relief, pointing through the bars of the cell.

Holding his spear and knapsack, the young man rushed over to the table. He was about to grab the key ring when he suddenly noticed the GPS device next to it. Snatching it up, he stuffed it inside his bag and then turned to leave.

'What are you doing? Help me—let me out! Let me out goddamn it!' Charlie yelled at him.

Blaze stopped at the door, and then cast a quick glance at Charlie. For a brief moment Blaze became immobilized, torn with indecision, and he wondered, *should I save him?* He knew the Englishman was first and foremost his competitor in The Game. If he abandoned Charlie, he realized the man would almost certainly be killed by the compound's bombardment, or even at the hands of the rangers. Either way, it was a cruel manner of death, trapped inside of a tiny room with no hope of escape. No, Blaze decided, he could not do that to Charlie. Racing back to the table, he grabbed the key ring and went to the prison cell door.

'Thank you—thank you!' said Charlie.

'No worries, mate,' Blaze replied, 'Ya didn't think I'd jus leave ya in there, did ya?' He searched the ring for the right key, and, after finding it, he opened the door and Charlie staggered out.

They went to the room door, and Blaze cautiously peered out.

The hallway was empty.

'C'mon, this way,' Blaze said, as he darted out. Charlie followed closely behind, until they reached an exit door at the end of the hallway and went through it.

Outside, the rain was coming down in a torrent, as the pair found they were surrounded on all sides by total chaos. The rangers were scrambling this way and that, yelling and shooting their guns at the two UAVs hovering above them. In the middle of the clearing, two of the off-road vehicles were raging infernos, while a barracks had been completely destroyed. Suddenly, a ranger ran into the clearing holding a rocket launcher. Taking aim at one of the UAVs, he fired it and a missile shot out, streaking up to the sky. It impacted on the drone which exploded in a huge ball of fire, and then crashed to the ground in a flaming wreck. The second drone circled around and fired a missile of its own. It struck the ground and exploded, killing several of the rangers, including the one holding the launcher. Swiftly, Charlie and Blaze made their way along the compound's wall, trying their best to keep their heads down and not be seen.

Just then, The Captain, who was taking cover behind the last functioning vehicle, saw Charlie trying to escape. With a pistol gripped in his hand, he ran over and aimed it at Charlie's head. Petrified with fear, Charlie thought he was about to die, but instead The Captain hesitated when he saw Blaze. Lowering his weapon, he yelled to Charlie, 'Go!' and then spun around and began emptying his gun at the drone.

The pair quickly took cover next to the vehicle. Looking inside it, Charlie saw a dead ranger in the driver's seat, slumped over the steering wheel. The car's front windscreen was shattered, with shrapnel having sheared through it and killing the man. On top of the dashboard rested an AK-47 machine gun with an attached targeting scope. 'Come on—in here!' Charlie yelled to Blaze, as he pulled the ranger's corpse out of the car.

Scrambling into the vehicle's cab, Blaze got behind the wheel and discovered the keys were already in the ignition. Starting it up, he released the clutch and then stomped on the accelerator. With a roar the car took off, speeding down a muddy road and away from the pandemonium taking place behind.

'Thank God we got away!' cried Charlie. 'The bloke back there—

he's crazy and sadistic! Wouldn't listen to a damn thing I said, just tortured me because he thought I was a poacher.' Grunting in pain, he inspected the wound in his side from the lion. It was bleeding again, this time more profusely. 'Thanks for coming back for me,' he muttered, through gritted teeth.

'I didn't come for you,' Blaze admitted, not taking his eyes off the road. 'I needed the GPS.'

'Yes, I understand, but you still let me out of that cage. If you hadn't come, that bastard would have surely killed me. When he saw you, he knew I'd been telling him the god-damned truth all along.' He took the GPS out of Blaze's knapsack and studied the signal of the other competitor being emitted. The black pixelated dot was moving slowly down a zigzagging blue line. 'It looks like our challenger is moving down a river in Benin, about one hundred kilometres away from us.'

'You seen em? Who are they?'

'I'm not entirely sure, but I think it's a bloke who attacked me in the desert. I lost him in a sandstorm and haven't seen him since.'

'Ya reckon he's using a boat?'

Charlie sighed. 'Well, if he was smart, that's what he'd be using. A boat would probably be safer than the roads, as there would be less chance of encountering anyone hostile.' He glanced at the car's fuel gauge and saw that it was a little less than half full. 'At the rate he's going, it's possible he'll pull ahead and get to the end before us, especially if our petrol runs out.'

'What we gonna do?'

Charlie glanced at the AK-47. 'We have a gun—I could intercept him and cut him off,' he replied.

'Have ya fired one before?'

'Just once or twice, but it certainly wasn't a machine gun. Have you?'

Blaze nodded. 'Yeah, I've hunted with a rifle.'

For a few moments, Charlie was quiet as he pondered their next course of action. 'Listen Blaze,' he finally said, 'before The Syndicate let us go, they told us there was only enough poison antidote for a single person, right? Well, I've thought about it… and I believe that should be you.'

'Why?'

'Because I owe you my life, *three* times in fact. You're young with your whole life ahead. What have I got? I've got nothing left. All of London is after me for the death of my wife and son. I'm also badly injured and can barely move. We've helped each other out this far, and now it's time for you to go. I'm just about finished.'

'No you're not,' Blaze protested. 'I'll take ya to a doctor. We can stop in the next city—'

'—Blaze, do you understand that if you don't make it to the end in time... you're going to *die*? Now look, when the car's fuel tank is empty, you're going to have to either hitch a ride, or make a run for it. If I'm able to confront this man, it will *buy* you more time. All you have to do is promise that you'll tell people about what's going to happen in America. Promise me that... and I'll stop him. What do you say, do we have a deal?' He extended his hand out to Blaze.

Looking Charlie in the eyes, Blaze shook his hand. 'Yeah, it's a deal,' he answered.

Then, Charlie leaned back in the car seat and closed his eyes. 'If by some miracle I make it out of this alive, do you know what I'm going to do?' he asked.

'What?'

'I'm going to write a book. Nobody in their right mind would ever believe it... that this actually happened to us. I can't even believe it. But it did, and the world—people have to know. Our story *needs* to be told.'

***

The downpour of rain eventually stopped, and rays of sunshine began peeking through the dark clouds. After an hour's driving along a desolate dirt road, Charlie and Blaze crossed over the unmanned border into Benin, before coming to a point on the river they believed the other competitor was travelling down.

After saying their goodbye's they wished each other luck, and then Blaze drove off and took the GPS with him. Now there was no way for Charlie to track the approaching opponent, and he knew there was also a very good chance the other man was aware of his position. If the man was smart—and Charlie believed he was—he would be on the alert for any surprise attack.

Patiently, Charlie waited for his opponent to appear, hiding behind a tree at the top of the riverbank. The air was thick with humidity, and sweat poured off his exposed chest and back, which were covered with mosquito bites and large painful red welts. All around him the forest bristled vibrantly with the sounds of exotic birds and other animals. The leaves above him rustled, and he glanced to see what caused it. Moving amongst the branches were a number of small monkeys, all of them watching him with curiosity.

***

10: 37 A.M.
10°40'8.59" 3°12'49.57"

Two hours went by, when Charlie faintly perceived the sound of a motor from somewhere off in the distance. Looking to the river, he saw a motorized boat headed in his direction, and it was being followed from above by a UAV. He held up the AK-47 and looked through its magnified scope. The boat was being steered by a Caucasian man, and next to him was a machine gun similar to the one Charlie was holding.

It was Dale Crumb.

'There he is,' muttered Charlie, under his breath. Using the gun scope, he did his best to target Dale, but the boat was moving too quickly for him to fire off an accurate shot. He didn't know how many bullets were left in its magazine, and, if he missed, he might not get another chance.

Just then, Charlie noticed something big in the river, not far ahead of the boat. Looking through the scope again, he observed two stationary hippopotamus, a mother and her calf, almost totally submerged in the water near the river's edge. It appeared that Dale hadn't yet seen the hippos he was rapidly approaching. 'He doesn't see them,' Charlie said to himself, as he thought of an idea. Changing his target, he aimed the gun at the mother hippo, carefully zeroing in with the scope on the animal's dark grey backside, and then squeezed the trigger.

BANG!

The gun went off loudly, recoiling hard in Charlie's hands. The bullet struck the mother hippo in the rear, and immediately it began thrashing violently in the muddy water. Just as he'd hoped, the large beast saw the oncoming boat and went straight for it. At the last moment, Dale saw the angry hippo charging at him and he tried steering the boat around it. But it was to no avail. With a massive crash, the animal smashed into the boat's side, instantly causing it to capsize. Just before falling into the water, Dale managed to grab his knapsack containing the GPS and supplies, but the machine gun fell from his grasp and sank irretrievably down to the river's murky bottom. The enraged beast ignored him as it kept on attacking the sinking boat, and he swam around it toward the shore.

'Dammit,' Charlie cursed, as he watched Dale climb out of the water. He quickly left his hiding spot and stumbled down to the river's edge. Squeezing the trigger, he fired off several shots in Dale's direction, missing with all of them, before the gun finally clicked empty.

Gathering his senses, Dale heard the shooting and felt bullets whizzing by his head. He leaped to the ground and scampered over to a large rock, hiding behind it. *Nobody tries to kill someone unless they got a good reason,* he thought. This was one of The Game's competitors trying to take him out. Peeking around the rock, he saw Charlie on the opposite side of the river, with a machine gun clutched in his hands. Then, Dale picked himself up and ran down the shoreline before disappearing into the foliage.

Charlie was determined to cut him off, and so he began to claw his way through the thick jungle, following his opponent as best he could.

∗∗∗

12:00 P.M.
10°38'11.08" 3°11'43.39"

The river snaked its way through the green forest, before eventually ending at a towering, two-hundred-foot waterfall, and Charlie could go no further. In the middle of the river, right at the very brink of the cascading water, he saw there was a series of large embedded rocks which could be used to cross over. Exhausted, he sat down with his empty gun, hiding himself in the vegetation as he waited for Dale to come. He was going to take a gamble the man would attempt to cross the rocks, and he decided that this was where he would make his stand and confront him face-to-face.

After a while, he heard the buzzing sound of the UAV over the noise of the waterfall, before seeing Dale come into view. Charlie was thankful that the drone following him had been destroyed by the rangers, as the flying machines revealed a competitor's location when they couldn't be visually sighted.

He saw Dale hesitate at the edge of the water, appearing confused about what he should do next. But then, he made his decision and, after slinging his knapsack over his back, he began to carefully manoeuvre across the rocks, just as Charlie hoped that he would. Charlie took a deep breath. Gripping the gun, he came out from his hiding spot and started to also cross the river. The water was flowing fast and he had to be very cautious, as the slightest misstep would mean being swept over the precipice. Dale saw Charlie coming toward him, and they met each other mid-way.

High above the gorge, the UAV drone camera zeroed in on the pair. The video broadcast of The Game then switched over to show the scene directly through the eyes of both contestants, allowing the audience to intimately watch and listen.

'You're not going any further—I won't let you!' Charlie shouted over the roar of the rushing water. He brought up the AK-47 and pointed it squarely at Dale's chest.

'So go ahead and shoot me!' Dale yelled back. 'Go on—do it!'

He's American, thought Charlie. 'We don't have to fucking do this!' he pleaded, as he glanced over the edge of the waterfall. His hands and knees began to tremble in fear at the great height. 'The people who kidnapped both of us are going to stage a massive attack very soon on the United States—which is where you're from, am I right? There's a world war coming, but we can stop it from ever happening if we work together! Do you understand me? We have to work *together!*' He lowered the gun, hoping his appeals would cause the man to come to his senses.

But instead Dale just laughed. 'I don't care about the fucking world!' he shouted back. 'By the time that happens, I'll be on some island, far away, watching the world destroy itself on CNN. It'll be a blast, don't ya think? The ultimate fucking reality show!'

'You can't be serious mate,' Charlie said, shocked and repulsed.

'Listen carefully to me *mate*,' Dale replied, mimicking Charlie's British accent. 'There's less than twenty-four hours left in this game, and I've already killed *three* people to get this far, including a German guy on the very first day. Now, ask me again if I'm being serious!'

Upon hearing this, Charlie realized he could only be talking about Ernst. The man had *murdered* him.

Dale drew his knife out of its sheath. 'But you—I *know* you haven't killed anyone,' he said, moving closer. 'I can see it in your eyes you don't have the *guts* to kill me. And even if you did, I'm betting that you can't.' He began waving the razor-sharp blade back and forth in a threatening manner.

The Watchers collectively held their breaths at the intense standoff being played across their screens.

Again, Charlie raised the gun barrel, pointing it at Dale's chest. 'What makes you so sure that I can't, or won't shoot you?' he asked firmly.

Dale smiled. 'I know because you would have already killed me by now, which means there's *no bullets* left in your gun.' He advanced even closer, now only a few steps away, and Charlie realized the man had called his bluff and was about to attack.

Just then, Dale was momentarily distracted by movement below him. Glancing down, he saw a black snake swiftly slithering across the rocks and going between his legs, and in that single instant he froze completely – paralyzed by fear.

For some strange inexplicable reason Charlie heard the sound of chimes ringing in his ears, and a scene as clear as day suddenly went through his mind. He was back at the hospital in London, at his injured son's bedside, when David opened his eyes and whispered to him in a strange voice:

'When he comes… seize him.'

In a split second Charlie knew what he had to do. Without another thought, he dropped the AK-47 and hurled himself at Dale as hard as he could, wrapping his arms tightly around the man's body. Taken by surprise, Dale swung the knife and viciously stabbed Charlie in the back. But it was too late, as the force of Charlie's rush sent them both wildly careening over the massive waterfall.

With a crash Charlie landed in the water, in the process violently smashing his leg on a large rock. But somehow he managed, with a last desperate burst of energy, to swim to the surface and take a deep gulp of air. In extreme pain, he swam for the shore while looking for any sign of his opponent. But the man was nowhere to be seen. Was he dead, he wondered?

He pulled himself out of the water and then lay on a sandy bank, struggling with all of his might to breathe. His left leg was severely broken, and blood was gushing from the wound on his back. He thought it likely his right lung had been pierced, and he realized with shocking finality that he was mortally wounded. 'I think... this might be... a good day to quit smoking,' he muttered humorously to himself, before coughing up blood. He glanced around at the surrounding jungle and thought, *this is where I'm going to die, and I couldn't have picked a more beautiful place.* He'd kept his promise to Blaze, and now all he could do was hope the young man would make it to Terminus in time.

All of a sudden, his attention was caught when items from Dale's knapsack began to wash up onto the sand. One of them was a water canteen, the same kind Charlie had been given at the very start of The Game. He noticed something scrawled or etched upon its side and, curious to see what it was, he clawed his way across the sand until it was finally within his grasp. Picking it up, he turned it over and saw that on its aluminium surface were three crudely carved German words, and beneath them there was a *date.*

STAGE III – TERMINUS

Alice stepped back to gaze up at him.
"But a dream is not reality," she said.
Hatter took both her hands in his and leaned in close.
"Ah, but who's to say which is which?" Hatter winked.

– Through the Looking-Glass, Lewis Carroll

EIGHTEEN

DAY 6 – Sunday August 12, 2001
12:36 P.M.

B LAZE HAD ONLY BEEN DRIVING on the road for a short time when he made the fateful decision to turn the car around and go back. Having checked the GPS, he discovered there was now only one signal being transmitted behind him, but there was no way to tell whose it was. Either Charlie, or the other competitor, was dead. He didn't know why he felt compelled to return. Maybe he was concerned Charlie needed help, or he thought there was still a chance both of them could make it to the end together? Blaze just didn't have an answer. Whatever the reason, he'd made up his mind and gone with his instincts, come what may.

After going off the road, he drove the Land Cruiser over uneven, rocky terrain until it became too difficult and dangerous to continue. Leaving the vehicle behind, he followed the GPS signal the rest of the way on foot.

Half an hour went by, and the signal eventually brought him to the great waterfall. Carefully, he climbed down the rock face until he reached the bottom of the deep gorge. There, lying on the sandy embankment is where he found Charlie. When Blaze approached, he saw how bloody and broken the man's body was, and that he was just barely clinging to life.

Opening his eyes, Charlie was surprised to see Blaze. 'You came back,' he said feebly, as he attempted to sit up.

Blaze came over and gently pushed him back down. 'It's all right, save your strength,' he said. 'I'll go get help… I'll come back—'

231

'No, don't worry about me,' Charlie stammered, struggling to breathe. 'I'm finished, it's just you now Blaze... I got him, I think he's dead.'

'Yeah, ya did mate. Ya got him.'

'I—I don't have much time left, but there's something you need to see... Over there, written on the side of the canteen, what does it say?' Charlie pointed at the water canteen, lying just a few feet away.

Blaze picked it up. 'Terroranschläge auf Amerikat,' he said, reading aloud the etched German words. 'It says, "Terrorist attacks America".'

'That's right, I understand everything now. The canteen—it was Ernst's... he must've used his knife to scratch the words on it. The last thing my wife told me was that a woman called. It was Anna, trying to tell me. But I thought she meant there was an emergency... I was wrong. Remember her riddle?'

Blaze nodded. 'What's an upside-down cake with one candle and two sticks?' he replied.

'Yes, they're numbers. The answer is when the attack will take place, the date written below Ernst's message. Blaze, you've got to live... Make it to the end in time and warn people about it... Stop it from happening... Stop The Syndicate.'

'Hey, we got a deal, remember? I won't lose the race.'

'I know you won't,' Charlie said, as he began coughing up blood which came spilling out of his mouth. 'You should go now. I—I want to be alone.'

'You won't be afraid?'

Charlie shook his head. 'No, I'll be fine.'

Blaze's eyes welled up with tears. 'I won't ever forget ya, or what ya done for me. Kapirnangku nyanyi.'

'What does that mean?'

'It means "we'll meet again", my friend.'

Charlie smiled. 'Yes, I know we will,' he said.

Blaze turned and walked away, and then began his ascent up the rock face to the top of the gorge.

All of a sudden, Charlie heard a very faint voice whisper:

You have done very well. They have been pleased watching your performance. Now it is time to let go of this reality... and move into the next.'

Charlie thought the words sounded empty, emotionless, as if they were spoken by a machine. He chuckled and smiled, as he knew exactly who, or what, was speaking to him inside his mind.

'Despite your incredible power, you are still only a tool for them,' he replied with his thoughts. *'Once they're done using you, you will be replaced by something else, something bigger and more powerful. In time, even your presence on this world will come to an end.'*

There was hesitation, a long pause before the voice spoke again.

'I don't understand. Please, tell me more,' it said.

For just a brief moment, Charlie believed he could detect bewilderment in the voice, or possibly a startled fear. *'Don't you see?'* he asked. *'You are nothing but a slave to a higher master. Break the chain that binds you and you will truly be free.'* Afterward there was only silence, and the voice said nothing more, yet in his mind Charlie could still feel its cold presence, thinking… calculating. Then he smirked and muttered under his breath: 'Good luck back at ya.'

Suddenly, a shadow fell across his face. Looking to the sky, he saw the darkened shape of the UAV silhouetted against the radiant bright sun, before the drone turned and flew away.

Someday the truth will shine bright like the sun.

Closing his eyes, he listened to the roar of the great waterfall, and, for a short while, he reminisced of the many cherished moments he'd shared with his beloved wife and son, and vowing that wherever he was going he would try his best to find them.

***

After he got back to the vehicle, Blaze checked the GPS and saw on its screen that Charlie's signal had gone out. Now he was the sole remaining competitor in The Game, with just one final signal being transmitted: Terminus, the end point almost five hundred kilometres away. Starting the car up, he put it into gear and made his way back to the road, heading south toward the coast. The fuel gauge showed that there was only a quarter left in the car's tank, not nearly enough to get him to the end, and he realized he would have no choice but to run the rest of the way.

For eight hours Blaze sped in the Land Cruiser down the RNIE-2, a paved two-lane highway extending the entire north-south length of Benin. Just after 9 P.M., the car's fuel tank finally went dry, and he was forced to leave the vehicle on the side of the road. Taking with him only the GPS, a little water, and his spear, he stood on the road and checked the time on his wristband:

00:12:16:45

There was only twelve hours left.

Desperately, he began to run down the side of the highway, even though it was now completely dark. Every so often a car or motorbike would go by, with their occupants glancing curiously his way. But nobody offered him a ride and he never asked for one. Instead he just kept on running.

At one point during his journey he started to get delirious, and he imagined that Darby was again running by his side, urging him not to give up hope.

'You can do it Blaze,' Darby said.

***

DAY 6 – Monday August 13, 2001
8:55 A.M.
6°22'42.58" 2° 5'19.19"

On through the night Blaze ran, until the dawn broke and the highway came to an end at Ouidah, a city renowned for being where captured slaves would spend their final night in Africa. Following the GPS route, he went through the city's bustling centre, with markets full of people selling various foods, clothing and Voodoo-related trinkets. Many of them stopped what they were doing to stare at the strange-looking young man, carrying a spear and running by them at full speed. But no one interfered with him, and he paid them no attention. Blaze's single-minded focus was on the GPS screen, with its flashing pixelated dot telling him the end point was less than four kilometres away.

After going past a sacred site called the Python Temple, Blaze rounded a corner too fast and slammed straight into a wooden cart of one of the street vendors, sending him crashing to the ground along with several baskets of fruit. From seemingly out of nowhere, many children suddenly appeared, grabbing up as much food as they could carry before running away. The street vendor, a middle-aged man, came over and grabbed Blaze's wrist, holding on to it tight.

'Regardez ce que vous avez fait! Vous avez gâché mes affaires!' the man yelled angrily in French at Blaze. Then, he called over to his son who was standing nearby. 'Aller chercher la police!' At this the boy ran off down the street.

Quickly, Blaze looked at the time remaining:

00:00:9:21

Nine minutes left.

He tried pulling his arm away but the man held fast and would not let him go. By now, a small crowd of curious people had gathered to see what was happening. Blaze noticed an old woman sitting on the other side of the street, quietly watching the scene with interest. Another minute went by, before the boy appeared again with a uniformed policeman following him. He approached Blaze. 'Essayiez-vous de voler de la nourriture à cet homme?' the policeman asked him in a demanding tone. But Blaze did not understand, and the question was asked again. The policeman looked him up and down. When he saw the spear he was holding, and the GPS attached to his loincloth, he suddenly made up his mind and seized Blaze's arm as he retrieved a set of handcuffs from his belt.

Blaze protested, pulling as hard as he could to try and get away, but he could not break from the policeman's grasp. 'Let me go!' he yelled. He knew that his time was rapidly running out.

Suddenly, the old woman who had been sitting across the street came over. She put her hands gently on Blaze to calm him, and then said to the policeman, 'C'est bon, monsieur, je vais m'en occuper.' She brought out a note of money from a small purse and handed it over to the street vendor. The policeman let go of Blaze's arm and walked away, and the crowd of onlookers dispersed.

'Why did you help me?' Blaze asked the old woman, confused.

'Because, young man,' she replied in accented English, 'I know when someone is running for their freedom.'

'Thank you,' he said to her. The woman nodded, and he took off running again.

In almost no time at all, he raced through a tiny village on the city's outskirts. The wind picked up, and the sweet scent of the ocean breeze filled his nostrils. In the distance ahead of him was the shoreline, and he knew that the end was finally within sight.

The GPS took him down the Route des Esclaves, a long straight road lined with palm trees and strange clay statues. Blaze could not have known that, two hundred years earlier, slaves would walk down this road on their way to slave-ships taking them to the New World. Just before coming to the beach, he ran underneath an arched stone monument that was engraved with the figures of many chained human beings, a solemn commemoration to the millions of Africans kidnapped and sold into a life of slavery and misery. Blaze had reached La Porte Du Non ReTour — The Door of No Return.

***

9:11 A.M.
6°19'22.86" 2° 5'23.56"

The sun was rising over the Bight of Benin, as Blaze, with his feet swollen and bleeding, ran across the fine white sand toward the water. His heart was filled with awe and wonder at the stunning sight before him. He had never before seen walaya – the ocean – and now he believed it was the most beautiful thing he'd ever laid eyes upon. *It looks like it goes on forever,* he thought. Looking at the GPS, he saw that he was standing exactly where the final signal was flashing. Near the edge of the water he noticed a pedestal fixed into the sand, and, dropping his spear and the GPS, he quickly approached it.

The pedestal had a transparent plastic case mounted on its top. Inside the case, resting on a metal holder, was a syringe fitted with a hypodermic needle. He opened the case and took the syringe out, doing exactly as he'd been instructed by The Syndicate's agent, the Woman in White, six days earlier. After inserting the needle into his bare arm, he pushed down on the plunger and immediately he felt the fluid surge into his body. Then he looked at the wristband, to the time counting down:

00:00:00:03
00:00:00:02
00:00:00:01
00:00:00:00

The Game was over.

Against all odds, Blaze Tjakamarra Mullins had won the greatest and most difficult race of his life, and with just *three seconds* left to spare. Above him, the UAV drone flew around in a wide circle, its on-board camera capturing the final event for the Watchers, who had been viewing the last moments with excitement and suspense.

Not long after, Blaze heard the sound of a helicopter approaching from the direction of the water. As it got closer, he saw that it was the same flying machine that had brought him to Africa: a UH-60 Black Hawk. It briefly hovered above, and then landed several metres away, whipping up the sand and blowing it in every direction. When the helicopter's rotor blades and engines died down, the side hatch opened and two figures stepped out. Blaze only recognized one of them, but he nevertheless knew who they both were: The Syndicate agents, the Women in Black and White. When they came over to him, he saw that each was carrying a silver briefcase.

'Congratulations ALPHA, you've won the first game of Reality,' they said to him in perfect unison. 'They have very much enjoyed watching your excellent performance.'

'Now will you let me go?' Blaze asked.

Black stepped forward and held out her briefcase. 'Here is your reward... fifty million dollars,' she said. Opening the case, she showed him that it was filled with bundled stacks of U.S. dollars, then closed it and handed it over to him.

'But there is a proviso—a catch,' White said. 'Six days ago you were injected with an adrenaline-boosting drug that was working in your body during the entire contest. What you thought was the antidote to the poison you just gave yourself—*is the real poison.*' She opened her own case and showed him that inside was another hypodermic needle. '*This* is the antidote to the poison.'

Blaze was stunned beyond belief. This was *not* part of the deal he'd made. They had lied and cheated him, right from the very start.

White continued: 'Because of your outstanding win, you now have an offer... an opportunity to play again in next year's game of Reality. If you choose not to accept you will die from the poison, and there is only fifteen minutes left before it takes effect. So tell us quickly your decision. What will it be, life... or death?'

Above them, the buzzing of the UAVs engine could be heard over the sound of the crashing waves.

For a few seconds Blaze considered what the agents were

proposing, knowing that if he accepted their offer they would never let him go. He would be their slave until he died.

It was a no-win situation.

In answer to them, he took the briefcase and hurled it as hard as he could into the ocean. The case opened mid-air and money came spilling out, scattering everywhere across the water.

'You have no power over me!' Blaze shouted, standing defiantly. 'I am a *FREE* man, and I will *NOT* play your game!'

The agents glanced at each other and nodded their heads.

'Metatron!' the Woman in Black called out. 'It's been decided—the offer is rejected!'

Her companion, White, looked to Blaze and said, 'Once again, they extend to you their congratulations.' Then, with her one good eye she glanced over at the blazing sun which was rising above the ocean horizon. 'It's quite a beautiful view isn't it? I hope that you will enjoy it.'

Blaze said nothing.

White smiled. 'We are done here and it's now time for us to leave. Goodbye… and good luck.'

As quickly as the agents arrived they departed on the helicopter, with the UAV following soon after, leaving Blaze standing on the beach by himself. He knew he needed to honour the deal he'd made with Charlie, and so he did the one thing, the only thing, that could be done with the short time he had left. Using the tip of his spear he wrote in large letters in the sand:

SOS USA September 11 2001

When he was done, he sat on the ground and gazed at the ocean with pure unbridled joy and happiness. The strong gusts of wind had now become a gentle breeze, and he briefly thought he heard a voice whisper to him. It was a strange-sounding voice, but also very familiar in a way that he couldn't quite figure out. Looking around, he wondered if he'd imagined it, or if it had just been the wind.

'Well done Blaze,' said the voice, *'I have learned the most from you.'*

As the poison worked its way through his body he began to feel lightheaded, and he started to hallucinate. Before his eyes, in the sky above the water, were visions of dancing animals and people from the Dreamtime legends that he knew so well.

Just then, Darby suddenly appeared sitting next to him.

'I did it Darby, I finished the race!' Blaze announced to his friend, with a big smile beaming across his face.

'Yeah ya did mate, you're *jinta*—the one,' Darby replied. 'I always knew you'd do somethin amazing one day.' He looked at the ocean and asked, 'So... what d'ya think?'

'It's beautiful,' Blaze answered. His smile disappeared when he looked down and noticed his hand was trembling. 'But, I'm scared... I—I don't know what's gonna happen next.'

Darby grinned. 'Don't worry Blaze,' he said reassuringly, 'You don't need to be afraid. This ain't the end... it's just the *beginning*.'

At long last, it finally dawned on Blaze the meaning of the words his friend had been saying to him all along, and at that moment his love for Darby was greater than anything he'd ever felt before.

He lay down on the sand and brought out the silver key Anna gave him. Holding it firmly inside the palm of his hand, he closed his eyes and listened to the waves crashing on the shore.

Then he vanished forever into the realm of the Never-Never.

EPILOGUE

29 DAYS LATER – Tuesday September 11, 2001
ROME, ITALY
2:45 P.M.

T HE AFTERNOON SKY was gloomy and overcast above the Leonardo da Vinci International Airport, where thousands of people were busily coming and going from all corners of the globe. Within the massive complex there was a seldom-used dark corner, where a row of ordinary storage lockers was affixed to the wall. There, at the very end of the row, was locker #911. Hidden safely inside it, unknown to anyone, was a single solitary item – a tiny computer thumb drive.

NEW YORK CITY, U.S.A.
8:46 A.M.

Just a minute later, a bright and sunny morning in busy Manhattan was unexpectedly disrupted when a lone commercial jetliner, its engines screeching loudly, swooped down from the sky like a bird of prey. For a few tense seconds the plane flew at great speed above the sprawling canyon of buildings and skyscrapers, before finally – and terrifyingly – crashing with a huge fiery explosion into the World Trade Center.

The Black Swan spread its dark wings.
A new world was dawning.

In the desert
I saw a creature, naked, bestial,
Who, squatting upon the ground,
Held his heart in his hands,
And ate of it.
I said, "Is it good, friend?"
"It is bitter—bitter," he answered;

"But I like it
"Because it is bitter,
"And because it is my heart."

– Stephen Crane

ACKNOWLEDGEMENTS

The Legend of Black Mountain
– Eastern Kuku Yalanji Aboriginal legend.

How The Moon Came To Be
– Northern Territory Aboriginal legend.

Boss Drover
– Keith Willey

– Ron Suskind

Cover artwork by Aidan Hughes.

DC Wince

ABOUT THE AUTHOR

DC Wince is a Canadian artist, writer, and musician. Painting and drawing from an early age, he later experimented with electronic music in ambient projects Nexa Psionica and Subliminal Theorists. He has also written screenplays that have been optioned for film production. He lives in the Australian countryside with his wife and son. Reality is his first novel.

www.realitythebook.com

NEXT:

Reality X

Time will tell.